ICED HEART

The Immortal Reign 2

ARIEL MARIE

Cover by Pretty In Ink Creations

Edited by Emmy Ellis with Studioenp.

Paperback ISBN: 978-1-956602-22-7

Ebook ISBN: 978-1-956602-21-0

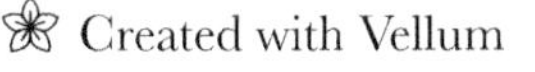
Created with Vellum

WARNING

Due to the explicit language and graphic sexual scenes, this book is intended for mature (18 years +) readers only. If things of this nature offend you, this book would not be for you. If you like a good action story with hot steamy scenes with lesbian vampires and their human mates, then you have chosen wisely…

CHAPTER ONE

"You do know you have the worst timing, right?" Lethia peered through the crack in the door. She stared at her guard and friend, Lane Hogan. This was one night Lethia had set aside for herself. She, the warden of the northeast, rarely had time for pleasure. As the middle child of the king and queen, she was a busy woman. Being a princess wasn't all fancy dresses and entertaining the elite vampires in their society.

Not that Lethia didn't enjoy the lavish lifestyle she was born into.

Her life had been spent defending her race

beside her sisters. She was the commander of her own personal army and was lethal. The rumors surrounding her and her sisters being vicious warriors were all true.

Lane had the nerve to smirk, his gaze flicking to behind her. She raised an eyebrow, waiting to see if he disapproved. His lips stretched into a grin.

"You called the madam, I see," he murmured. His dark eyes returned to her with an all-knowing look.

Maybe she had. Lately, Lethia was craving blood from the source. Madam Rice was a woman who catered to vampires. She provided men or women who wanted to experience the euphoria of a vampire's bite. They were live donors, humans who had consented to give up some of their blood and more if the price was right.

Lethia had no problems compensating a woman who wanted to get paid for her time.

Lethia was a vampire who had lived for two hundred and thirty years. Prostitution was the oldest profession, and she respected anyone who wanted to make their living selling themselves.

In this case, it was their blood and their body.

She glanced over her shoulder and took in the woman with the fiery-red hair that cascaded around her shoulders. She knelt on the floor on a large pillow, dressed in a white lace robe that didn't hide anything. It was identical to Lethia's only hers was black. Her wide eyes turned and met Lethia's. Her chest rose and fell swiftly; she was patiently waiting for Lethia to come to her.

Lethia sighed and gripped the door handle tighter. She dropped her gaze down to the box in Lane's hand. It was a virtual hologram contraption that would allow her to speak with whoever was on the other side. Apparently, her sisters wanted to have a conference.

At the most inconvenient of times.

"Do you think they will be pissed if I have you tell them I will call them tomorrow?" she asked.

"Not doing it." Lane barked a laugh and shook his head. His fangs peeked from underneath his lips. "I may be related to your sister, Velika, now, but even I don't want to be on her bad side. Hegna, we're not even going to go there."

"Remind me why I have kept you around?" She snorted. If he wasn't going to do this favor for her even though she'd saved his life, then what good was he?

"It's my personality." He snorted, too.

"Well as my personal guard, see that I am not

disturbed any more tonight." She snatched the box from him.

A small smile graced her lips as she took in his grin. There was a time when she'd thought she would never see him smile. Lane, a former human, had been captured by a rogue vampire and kept as chattel and food. His previous owner had decided they were done with him, bleeding him almost dry then tossing him out, leaving him to die. The night Lethia had found him, she had sensed his story wasn't over.

She had made him an offer. It was his to choose: death or eternal life. There had been a spark in his eye that hadn't faded yet on that fateful night.

Lane Hogan had chosen life.

She had turned him, giving him strength, power, and a new start.

As repayment he stayed by her side, training as hard as any vampire before him. She had awarded him the position of one of her personal guards.

Lane believed he owed her his life, but she didn't see it that way. She may be known as a hardened vampire warrior princess with her sisters, but she had compassion.

And that night, something had clicked between the human and her.

They had grown as close as brother and sister. Recently, he had be reunited with his sister, Quinn, who was the mate to Lethia's sister, Velika. The pair were madly in love and expecting their first child any day now. Maybe that's what her sisters wanted to talk about. The next generation of the Riskel family.

How funny fate was. Bringing two families together in more ways than one.

"Will do, Princess." He nodded before turning away.

She watched him walk down the hall until he disappeared from sight. Swiveling back to her guest, she issued a wide, fangy grin. She closed the door behind her and strode over to the sensual siren. Anticipation filled her for what was to come.

Her fangs itched to sink into the warm flesh of the woman waiting patiently. The sound of her blood rushing through her veins pulsed, almost sending Lethia into a feeding frenzy. Drinking blood warmed up and from a glass was fine, but there was nothing like sucking it straight from the source.

She had them set up in her moon room. It

was one of her favorite rooms to lounge in to enjoy the moon and beautiful night sky. Three walls were complete glass. It was decorated with all the luxuries Lethia enjoyed. Plush leather couches, carefully placed tables and chairs. It was a room in which she liked to entertain. She even had trinkets and souvenirs from her worldly travels on display.

During the day when the sun was out, as with all the windows of her castle, the steel shutters enclosed the room, blocking out the harmful rays once daylight approached.

"This shouldn't take long," she murmured. Lethia was quite irritated that this call couldn't wait. She sat the box on an ancient table she had purchased in Egypt twenty years ago. It was sturdy and the wood dark, stained with gold hieroglyphics. Matching chairs rested around it.

"There is no rush, Your Grace." The female offered a smile. Her big eyes watched Lethia as she approached her.

Lethia held out her hand for the prostitute. She assisted her up and guided them back to the table. She took a seat with the female straddling her, facing her. She could have her drink while her sisters discussed whatever was so important.

The human leaned down and nuzzled Lethia's neck. "I am to be here all night as you need me."

Lethia grinned. Madam Rice was sneaky. If she offered Lethia a deal she wouldn't be able to refuse, then she would refer more of her rich friends to the madam. Even though everyone in this territory had heard of her. Lethia would take the gift and ensure the madam was compensated.

She had an idea of rewarding her men with the madam's stable of whores. They deserved it. The madam had the best men and women a vampire could choose from. She made a mental note.

"Well then, let's see what my dear sisters want." Lethia gripped the woman's face and brought it up so she could meet her gaze. The deadly warrior in her came out. She gripped her chin firmly. "I expect anything you hear will remain in this room."

"But of course, Your Grace." The woman's eyes widened. She jerked her head in a nod. She slid closer to Lethia, closing the gap between them. "Confidentiality is part of my job."

Her full breasts brushed Lethia's. Their robes were useless. They might as well have been naked, which they would be as soon as this conversation was over.

"Good. It would be a shame for a pretty thing

like you to meet your end on my dagger." Lethia tipped her neck up, watching the pulse at the base of her neck race. She leaned in, inhaling the sweet scent of the female's skin. She threaded her fingers in the redhead's hair. She held her in place, sending her tongue on an exploratory journey. The box chirped, signaling her sisters calling. "Hologram, answer."

"Seriously, Lethia. This is how you answer?" Hegna's exasperated voice filled the air.

Lethia tilted her head to the side to take in her sisters' figures. Hegna with her infamous scowl stood with her arms folded in front of her. Velika, a smirk on her lips, strode over and leaned back against the table.

"You are the one calling me, interrupting. What do you expect me to be doing? Sitting around waiting for the moment you decide to call me?" Lethia's free hand was on a mission of its own. Maybe if she made her sisters uncomfortable they would reschedule the call. She bit back a snort.

"This is important," Hegna growled.

"All calls between us are important," Velika muttered. She glanced at both of them. "I can't stay away from my mate too long. She isn't feeling well."

"Is it the babe?" Lethia asked. Her roaming hand had opened the redhead's robe. It fluttered open, showcasing her perfect dusky areolas.

Yes, they needed to hurry the call.

"Not sure. The healer has said that Quinn is full-term and the baby should be arriving any day now." Velika stood tall, pride in her eyes.

There was a small twinge of jealousy in Lethia's chest. Out of the three of them, she was the only one who hadn't been fazed at their mother entering them into the draft. She had hoped to be matched, but it would seem fate had gifted Velika first.

Lethia wouldn't mind a mate of her own. Someone she could spend her life with. If ever that day came, Lethia vowed her mate would never leave. Even if it was a human who didn't want to be mated to a vampire, Lethia would make them. She'd keep them locked away until they couldn't help but love her. For vampires, it took only one look and one scent, and they knew. For humans, it wasn't that easy.

Velika was lucky. Quinn had come around and fallen in love with her sister.

"Well, if Velika can't talk for long, and I'm preoccupied…" She grasped the female's ample ass in her hand. She moaned, leaning her head back for Lethia. The move pushed her breasts forward, presented her neck, and she pressed her hot core to Lethia's waist. "Let's get this over with."

"Fine." Hegna pinched the bridge of her nose. "We've tracked a large pack of lycans headed to your territory, Lethia."

"Going where? You need to be more specific than that." Lethia wasn't too impressed so far on this important discussion. She gave half her attention to her sisters while the other half was on her prostitute in her hands. She slid her tongue along the slender, pale column of the redhead's neck. Her fangs, already descended, pierced her slightly. The woman's strangled moan filled the air. A small drop of crimson appeared where Lethia had nipped her. Lethia growled low, lapping up the tiny drops.

"Maine," Velika answered. It was she who had put her men in charge of tracking down the lycans. Rumors had been swirling around that their numbers were increasing. For centuries their numbers had died down, but word on the street was they had a new leader and were organizing them.

Lethia blinked.

Maine.

She was located in the small coastal town of Crystal Cove, Maine.

It had been her home for over a hundred and twenty-five years. She ruled this town and this territory. She'd be damned if lycans would come here causing trouble.

"How many is in this pack?" She tilted the blood-giver's neck back, no longer able to wait for her drink. Her vision was clouding over, and she heard the need in her deepening voice. She had waited too long since her last feeding. She still had control of herself and would try not to hurt the female.

The thirst must be satisfied.

"One hundred," Hegna answered. "We believe this alpha is with them."

Lethia closed her eyes. Yes, this was damn important. They couldn't have some new alpha lycan running loose, trying to claim lands that were now ruled by vampires.

Vampires had made their presence known, creating a chaotic society that couldn't withstand the revealing of their kind. Humans had been ignorant, assuming they were the only ones inhabiting the earth. War had broken out with the humans with vampires as the victors. Now they lived in a new world governed by the seven vampire kings. Lethia's father, King Niall Riskel, ruled the North

American continent.

"This new alpha. Does he have a name?" Lethia asked. The scent of her guest's arousal was thick. Lethia licked her lips, wanting a taste, but it would appear her sister was correct. This would need immediate attention.

"The new alpha is a female," Velika announced. She stood to her full height, her gaze landing on the redhead writhing in Lethia's arms. "Do you want me to send the intel to you tonight? Or should I wait until tomorrow?"

Lethia growled, frustrated.

"Send it and I will look it over," she bit out through clenched teeth. They already were dealing with rogue vampires, human rebels who retaliated against vampire laws, and now the lycans.

"If you need assistance, we are a phone call away." Hegna gave her a satisfied nod before she and Velika disappeared.

"Call terminated," the box announced.

Lethia was determined to have her drink. She gripped the redhead's hair tight, yanking her head back, fully exposing her neck. Her gaze zeroed in on the rapidly fluttering pulse. The female gasped, her body trembling.

Lethia struck.

Her fangs sank deep into her neck. Warm, thick copper filled her mouth. She may not be able to enjoy all the woman had to offer, but she'd make sure she was taken care of.

Lethia brought her body close to allow her to slowly drink her fill. Fingers threaded their way into Lethia's thick blonde strands. Her whimpers filled the air, Lethia sensing she was already close to climaxing off the bite alone. She slipped a hand in between them and found her core drenched. Lethia parted her slit and pressed on her swollen clit. She strummed it while she continued to drink.

The woman stiffened, her hips rocking forward to meet Lethia's fingers. Her cries rang out, breaking the silence of the room. Lethia lifted her head, releasing her neck. She licked the puncture wounds; the proteins in her saliva had a healing mechanism that would seal the small holes.

The redhead's body collapsed against Lethia; she was obviously spent. Many humans craved the bite of a vampire. Had Lethia had more time, she would have taken a few more drinks before morning.

Lethia withdrew her fingers from the wet cunt and offered them to her. The human immediately licked her fingers clean. Her pale skin now had a rosy blush to it. Her hooded eyes were filled with lust and need. The first bite always had them craving another. Lethia stood and carried her to one of the oversized couches and laid her down.

"Are you going to send me away?" she asked, looking up at Lethia. Her robe was askew, revealing her beautiful body. She widened her legs, showing off her slick pussy. Her mound was free of any hair, and her swollen nub peeked out from between her fat labia.

Lethia almost caved and put aside her duties, but she knew she couldn't. Fighting for her kind was of the utmost importance.

"Business calls, I'm afraid, but I'll make sure you are taken care of. What is your name?"

"Savanah."

Lethia strode over to an old rotary phone sitting on a small table next to the couch. She lifted the receiver, pressing it to her ear.

"How may I help you, Your Grace?" the voice asked.

"Send Lane to me." She replaced the receiver in the cradle and turned back to her guest.

She was still in a state of euphoria, almost like a high. Her hands skated along her body while her gaze tracked Lethia's movements. One of her hands dove between her thighs, reaching her core.

A knock sounded. Lethia cursed, spinning on her heel. She tightened her robe while padding over to answer the door.

Lane stood waiting.

Lethia scowled at him.

"I take it the call didn't go so well." He chuckled.

"Oh, you know my sisters," she replied, her words dripping with sarcasm. The one day she'd planned for herself was ruined. At least she'd got to briefly feel a soft woman in her arms and drink from her. "But you're in luck. Take the night off. Consider Savanah a gift."

A soft moan sounded behind her. Lane flicked his gaze over Lethia's head before settling it back on her.

"Don't mind if I do." His grin spread across his face.

She widened the door and stepped aside to allow him to enter. He followed behind her as she returned to Savanah.

"Since I have to leave, I'm gifting you to Lane for the rest of the evening," Lethia said.

Savanah's attention landed on Lane. Approval

filled her eyes. She openly rubbed her clit while meeting his gaze.

"I hope I'm pleasing to you," she said softly.

"Don't worry. You'll do." He tossed Lethia a wink.

She turned, stalking from the room, shutting the door behind her. If she couldn't enjoy a night between Savanah's pale thighs, then at least her good friend could.

Lethia took the back halls and stairs that would lead to her private quarters. She would change her clothes then head to her office to review what Velika was sending over. She would deal with the lycans.

If she couldn't fuck, then she would hunt and kill.

Both were in her nature.

CHAPTER TWO

"We are not just food. We have rights!" Reed Hull shouted. He glanced around the room amidst shouts and cheers.

Alima Morgan stood off at the back of the crowd watching the Rebels leader give a speech.

They were in an abandoned warehouse where the Rebels had gathered on the outskirts of town. They met at high noon when the amount of vampires circulating would be at its lowest. The suck-heads were unable to withstand sunlight, and humans were safer then.

Alima had joined this group years ago and was

what one would consider a foot soldier. The Rebels was a resistance movement consisting of humans who fought against vampire rules and laws. She stood to her full height, proud to belong to this great organization.

The war between vampires and humans had taken its toll on the world. Had she been old enough at the time, she would have joined in on the fighting. But the war ended years ago when she was just a young child. Now she chose another way to fight against the species who'd tried to eliminate hers.

Alima scanned the room and took in the crowd mesmerized by Reed. He had a way about him that attracted people to him. Every person in the organization was dedicated to him and would be willing to do whatever he requested in the name of mankind. Those attending the event were the locals. The Rebel organization needed funding. What they did, they couldn't do without financial support or donations. This was the point of the events that Reed hosted. They had to connect with the community, and with each rally, they gained more followers. Word had gotten around, and more people showed up with each event they hosted.

"He sure knows how to work a crowd," Terry murmured beside her.

She glanced over at the foot soldier. He had been around longer than Alima had.

"Yeah. I'm sure everyone will support him after this." She chuckled and folded her arms. No sooner than she'd spoken, people shouted out their agreement. Donation buckets went around, and any money that could spare was being dropped into them.

"This should be ending soon. Once everyone is gone, Reed is calling a meeting for us," Terry said. He patted her on her shoulder and dipped away. He walked around the edge of the crowd and went over to another Rebel. He must be spreading the word so they didn't leave once the event was over.

Alima wondered at the nature of the meeting. Knowing Reed, he'd gotten some intel on the vampires and had a mission for them. Alima lived for the thrill of defeating the suck-heads. Crystal Cove had been overturned by vampires. Apparently, the town had been inhabited by vampires for centuries and humans never knew. Alima shuddered to think that they had been living unknowingly beside the monsters.

When vampires first presented themselves, the

world had burst out into chaos. Vampires proved they were higher up the food chain.

They were masterful hunters.

Their prey—humans.

Anger and rage grew in Alima at the thought. Her family had certainly paid the price from vampires hunting. She had lost her younger sister, Joslin, to vampires. Joslin had been hunted down, her throat ripped out, and she'd been left for dead.

This was why Alima had pushed for her parents to leave the town they had lived in their entire lives and escape to a human settlement over the border in Canada. It was a beautiful, small community of just humans. It was safe. Alima had stayed behind so she could avenge her Joslin's death.

There were countless stories just like Joslin's. This was why Alima fought. So that humans would have a chance and could live in peace. With the vampires running everything, that day would never come. Humans needed to take back what was theirs.

The human governments all around the world folded, giving vampires power of the planet.

The Rebels' prime goal was to give that power back to humans.

Applause broke through Alima's thoughts. She

blinked and took in the crowd dispersing. She nodded to a few and moved to open the doors behind her that led to an alley beside the building they were in.

Once everyone had left, they locked up the building and tried to make it look as it had before the meeting. They always covered their tracks. Words was the vampires had heard about their organization. At the moment, their human group wasn't thought of as a threat to the vampires. The vampires underestimated the drive of the humans.

One day, they would take their town back and then move on. There were other Rebel groups forming all over the country. Alima looked forward to the day where she could safely bring her parents back to the town they loved. It had torn her apart to send them away. Crystal Cove was a beautiful coastal town in Maine. Some parts hadn't been affected by the war. It still held on to the old-world charm it was known for, while other areas were abandoned and looted when mankind had gone into survival mode.

The most devastating part of the war had been the loss of life. Many of the humans had been drafted into the war. If they were healthy and able-bodied, they were outfitted with a weapon and marched to fight. The numbers the humans lost worldwide was depressing, but lately, numbers were beginning to rise. Alima grimaced, not understanding why anyone would want to bring a child into this world.

But alas, it was all part of nature—procreation.

At one point in her life, she had dreamed of having a family. Finding a partner, settling down and having a baby or two. That dream was snatched the moment she had seen her sister's mangled body. Reality had set in that this world was cruel. No one cared about the loss of a human's life to a vampire except their family.

Alima took one more glance around the room and saw there was nothing else left for her to do. It was once again in shambles, appearing undisturbed. She made her way to the stairwell that led to the basement level. It was dark and eerie, but it was the perfect place for them to meet. It was hidden away from the world and was near a series of tunnels built underground.

Alima arrived, finding Reed already pacing in front of her fellow foot soldiers. His second-in-command, Nolan Culp, leaned against the wall nearest him.

Something was wrong.

Alima took in the sight of her good friend, Javari. He waved her over to where he stood near a table and chairs. A few other people came in behind her before Nolan moved to close the door.

"Is that everyone?" Reed asked.

"Of who was here, yes," Nolan replied.

She gave Javari a nod and stood next to him. He motioned for her to take a seat at the table, but she shook her head. If he was standing, so was she.

Javari and she had been friends since their school days. He was one of the few she would call a true friend. He'd seen just as much horror in the world as she had. He was someone who she could count on and was there for her when her sister was murdered. He had been a great comfort for her, having experienced his own loss. Both of his parents had died fighting in the war when he was a kid. He and his brother had practically raised themselves with the help of their father's brother.

"Stubborn," he murmured, resting a hand on her shoulder. He gave her a squeeze and let go.

She stuck her tongue out at him. At one point, a few people had thought something would come of her and Javari's relationship, but it was strictly platonic. He was a good friend and someone who she knew would always be there for her. She didn't want to lose what they had. It meant too much to her.

"There will be double the number of drafts this week. Due to the successful mating of Princess Velika with her human mate, the number of vampires entering into the draft has exploded," Reed started.

Alima stiffened. She turned to her leader, wanting to ensure she paid attention to what was going to be discussed this week. The low chatter died off as Reed became everyone's focus.

"As always, if any members are chosen for a blood sample, we will fight as we always do."

Nods went around. There was a protocol for this wretched draft. Alima shook her head, still unable to believe how their government consented to such a thing.

Vampires were in search of their "mates." Apparently, their race would die out if they could not find the one designated for them. For vampires, the only way to produce heirs was with their fated mates. Through scientific testing, it was learned that humans were compatible with vampires and could produce children.

Humans had no say about this, it was required that all humans chosen for the draft were to report to a vampire laboratory to register and submit a blood sample. It was then entered into a database where it was determined if they matched to a vampire. If a match was found, then that human was forcibly escorted to their vampiric mate.

The Rebels fought against this. It was their duty to free any human who didn't want to be matched with a vampire. There were some who did, and that was their right. Even though the Rebels may disagree with their decision, it was theirs to make. Their organization would rather put their focus and resources to those who requested help.

That was the purpose of the secret rallies. They had to get the word out that there was help. When a person was contacted about the draft, they could reach out to the Rebels. Like a well-oiled machine, the Rebels gathered the person, a few belongings, and helped them disappear, giving them a chance at a new life and a new identity.

Alima had assisted with plenty of relocations. She felt good with each one, knowing she was helping someone take their life back. Her assigned job was that of a driver. They had acquired some tough off-road SUVs that allowed them to avoid roads in some areas to get to their destination. She wasn't one of the fighters, but as with all members of the organization, she had been trained in self-defense.

"If your name is drawn, you need to contact us immediately. There is a short time frame before you are arrested and taken against your will to their so-called labs," Reed snarled.

Alima's phone call would be to Javari and his call was to her. The moment they had joined the group, their decision had been made. They would then activate the relocation protocol amongst organization members. With as much danger they were exposed to by being members, they'd both agreed to contact each other's families should something happen to the other.

"Now I understand some of you have cell-phones for emergencies for personal reasons. I just want to remind you that is a way for them to not only contact you but track you. If you are able to, I would get rid of them."

Alima had long ago disconnected from the digital world. There was no trace of her that could be found. She didn't trust any of it anymore. She'd heard tales of how the world used to be dependent on the internet and how everything was once connected to it, from communications, banking, to business. It was no wonder vampires had overtaken the world as fast as they had. Everything was uploaded in a way that put the world at their feet. Not having a cell made it harder to communicate with her family, but she had been creative in notifying them she was alive and healthy.

Even if the vampires wanted to sequester her for the draft, they had no way of contacting her or finding her. She had chosen to live off the grid in a small human compound.

"With this new knowledge, we will need everyone available all times. We are sure the relocation requests will increase," Nolan said. He braced his hands on his waist and glanced around the room. "Now what we really wanted to meet was to discuss our plans to neutralize the labs. It is imperative that we move up our timeline of attack."

"He's right," Reed said.

He walked around the small area. Members parted to allow him room to move. Alima grew excited about this. They had been meeting and strategizing on ways to take out the labs throughout the entire state. It was a high number considering there was one in each town and multiple ones in larger cities.

"This will be dangerous, and once we make our move, vampires will react. So this will have to be a joint effort with our branches around the state. We pull this off, and it will be a large blow to vampires."

"WANT to stop and get something to eat?" Javari asked.

They strode along the sidewalk in what was considered downtown Crystal Cove. They were a few blocks away from the warehouse. She took in the beautiful stone and brick buildings that housed small shops, inns, and restaurants on one side of the road that faced the river. The waterline enhanced the beauty of the once-thriving human town.

"Save your money for something more useful," she murmured. A slight breeze blew across the river. Even though the sun was high, it was still chilly. She tugged on the edges if her hoody and zipped it closed. She pulled her hood over her head to ward off the chill.

"There's something more important than eating?" Javari paused.

She took a few more steps before she stopped and spun around. He stood in front of a sandwich shop. The scent of fresh bread hit her and sent her stomach into a rumble. His dark-brown skin glistened from the sunrays. His hair, twisted into locs, hung just above his shoulders. He was fit and kept himself in shape with workouts. He'd tried to get her to join him, but it just didn't interest her. Not that she had much of a life. Javari was handsome, and she never understood why he was still single. There were plenty of women who showed him interest at the compound. That was one thing she never knew about her friend. Was he a male whore in secret or was he truly celibate?

She ambled over to stand next to him, catching their reflection in the window. Where he was tall, over six feet; she was of average height at five and a half. He was lean and muscular, she was thick with wide hips, a narrow waist, and full breasts. Last she was weighed, she was around two-forty. She sighed, taking in her fair brown skin and her dark hair she kept plaited in two braids. Maybe she should take him up on his offer to work out.

"We can go to the soup kitchen, that's free," she said.

He grimaced at her response. Alima, having lost her job a year ago, had learned to rely on the free handouts at the soup kitchen or barter for work doing odd jobs to pay for things she needed. She hadn't gotten so desperate to have to sell her body.

At least not yet.

Work was difficult to come by. Javari held a part-time job working in the mines. It was hard, back-breaking work, but it paid him a decent wage each week as long as he was not injured. Men who were hurt and unable to perform were let go and replaced immediately.

"I can afford to buy us two sandwiches," he muttered. He snatched her hand and tugged her to the door.

She tried to pull away, not wanting him to spend his hard-earned money on her. "You don't have to buy me—"

"Shut it," he snapped.

She stopped struggling and followed him inside. The aromas assaulted her as she stood beside him in front of the counter. The woman behind it eyed them. Alima knew the look. She was trying to determine if they could afford to be in there or if they were thieves.

Alima hated the feeling the woman's appraisal brought about in her. She turned away, not wanting her to see the anger in her eyes. She did understand that there were plenty of thieves who would steal what they needed—and what they just downright wanted.

"You have cash?" the woman asked. She reached up and pushed her bright-pink hair behind her ear.

"Of course I do. I wouldn't be in here if I didn't," Javari retorted. He placed a hand at the small of Alima's back and guided her forward. "What do you want?"

"It doesn't matter. Order me whatever." She glanced out the front window and took in the pedestrians going by as he placed their order. Alima winced at the amount the woman said it would cost. She would find a way to pay him back for her half.

"Come on. Let's grab a seat." He ushered her over to a table that was next to the window. He dragged out her chair and assisted her into it.

"Manners, I see. Someone will be lucky to have you," she joked, trying to break the sour mood she knew she had cast over them by not wanting to eat there.

"Hush up." He rolled his eyes and walked back over to the counter.

Alima turned back to the window and wished

this was a regular day, no vampires, no dangerous threats, no draft to worry about.

She watched the people pass by as if it were any other day. Some looked like her, a little ragged, presentable but poor, while there were a few who appeared well-off. She wondered how they had survived the war untouched.

One thing they all had in common—they could be drafted. Money, wealth—or lack of it—didn't mean crap when it came to being sent off to live with your matched vampire.

"Here we go." Javari arrived back and placed a tray with two large sandwiches, two bowls of steamy soup, and two drinks.

"Javari, this is too much," she exclaimed.

"No it's not. It's a meal that I wanted to buy with my own money to feed myself and a dear friend." His dark eyes met hers.

She softened, her shoulders slumping. Javari was too good to her.

"Just think of it as a one-time splurge," he said.

"Okay." She reached for her sandwich. She could no longer fight the scents, and her stomach was growling. She took the first bite and couldn't help the moan that escaped. The bread was warm and flaky. The tastes of the meats, the lettuce, and tomatoes exploded on her tongue. It had been a long while since she had eaten something so fresh and divine. She picked up the spoon and tasted the soup.

She was in heaven.

Javari's chuckle broke into her food-laden lust.

"What?" She blinked.

"Nothing. I'm just glad you're enjoying it." He jerked his chin toward her food.

"How could I not?" She sighed and ignored his knowing grin. He was going to take great pride in reminding her of this day and how she'd tried to resist.

He left her alone, and they ate in a comfortable silence. The little shop was nice. A few patrons came in and ordered food to go while others settled in and enjoyed their meal. Alima sat back in her seat, belly full and her meal all gone. She bit her lip, thinking maybe she should have saved some of the food for later. It would have been nice to eat it before bed.

"Thank you." She glanced over at Javari.

He leaned back, too, and shook his head.

"There is no need to thank me. If the roles were reversed, you wouldn't let me thank you."

He was right. There were times in the past

when she had treated him with cookies or baked goods she had purchased at the farmer's market. Now she didn't have a job, those little perks were gone.

"Still. It's the proper thing for me to say." She shrugged.

They stood and cleared their table, carrying the trash over to the receptacle. They exited the café and ambled down the sidewalk.

"What do you have planned today?" Javari asked.

She went to answer, but her words were drowned out by the screeching of wheels. Alima turned around and took in two large black SUVs headed their way. She stared at Javari with wide eyes.

It could only mean one thing.

One of them had been chosen for the draft and had missed the appointment.

"Run," he shouted.

They took off sprinting along the pavement. Alima's heart pounded as she tried to keep up with Javari. Her chest burned with her trying to bring in gulps of air. She wasn't going to outrun them.

"Come on." He grabbed her hand and pulled her with him.

"I'm going to slow you down. Leave me." She gasped.

They turned the corner, but they weren't going to be able to beat the speeding vehicles.

"I'm not leaving you," he growled.

They dashed across the street but were cut off by one of the trucks. The other one parked behind them, trapping them. The doors opened, and guards on the vampire payroll exited with guns drawn. They were dressed in full tactical gear, and their fierce expressions led her to believe they wouldn't hesitate to shoot them.

"Alima Morgan," one of them shouted.

Alima closed her eyes. It was her they were after. She held her hands up and peered over at Javari who had a murderous look on his face. His hands were fisted at his sides. She shook her head, already knowing what he was thinking.

"Don't," she whispered.

"They can't take you," he snarled.

The men approached with their guns aimed at them. Tears welled up in her eyes. She refused to watch her friend be shot for trying to prevent these men from taking her.

"It will only be to the lab. I'll be free to go after

that, then you will do what you know you need to do for me," she murmured.

He turned his eyes to hers and gave her a nod.

She breathed a sigh of relief. She faced the men. "I'm Alima Morgan."

CHAPTER THREE

Alima winced at the tightness of the cuffs surrounding her wrists. Her shoulders burned from her arms being restrained behind her. The truck rocked taking the corners. She held back the tears that threatened to spill. Javari's expression had been furious, but he hadn't said a word as they'd led her away.

Apparently, her name had come up where she was to report to the lab and had missed her dead-line. She wasn't sure how they were able to track her down to the café, but they had.

Once they'd taken their sample, she would rush home so Javari could activate her escape plan. She'd leave Crystal Cove and start a new life somewhere. She'd get word to her parents later, but first she had to leave.

She remained quiet. The truck turned into an alleyway. The men in the vehicle had not said a word to her after they'd charged her with evading the draft. The truck drew to a halt at the back of a building.

The lab.

Alima swallowed hard. It was just registering and submitting a blood sample. After that she would be free to go. She'd have to race home, pack her one bag, and disappear before they could determine if she matched any bloodsucker.

The men exited the SUV. Her door opened, and she was pulled out. She struggled to land on her feet, not wanting to fall to the ground. She had some dignity left and, dammit, she was going to keep it.

She'd walk into this building with her head held high.

"Watch it," she muttered. The grip on her arm was tight. She glared at the guy manhandling her. How could he turn on his own kind?

"Shut up," he said.

"Traitor to your own kind," she uttered.

"What did you say?" He swung her around, meeting her glare with a hard one of his own.

"You heard me. All of you should be ashamed of yourselves," she cried out. She couldn't help it. How could they do this? How could they knowingly lead a fellow human to their end? The draft took everything away from humans.

"Shut your trap. You know nothing," he growled.

"Move, Ducane. I'll take her." Another one pushed him away from her.

Ducane's hand fell away from her as the other guard took his spot.

"Come this way, ma'am," this one said.

They marched over to the building. The doors automatically slid back, allowing them to enter.

"Another outburst like that from you, and I'll duct tape your mouth shut."

Alima sniffed and shot him an evil glare. She prayed that one day, they would have to experience their loved one being dragged to this place. Alima looked around and took in the stark white walls. The smell of antiseptic filled her nostrils. The four men marched along with her. She smirked, wondering why it would take four of them to bring her in.

They made their way through interconnected hallways until they came to a desk with a female sitting behind it. Alima eyed her and recognized she was a vampire. Her pale skin was the first hint, but the fangs peeking from under her lip were a dead giveaway.

"What's her name?" the vampire asked. She turned to the computer in front of her and typed out a few commands.

The guard squeezed her arm.

"Alima Morgan," Alima answered. She grimaced, sensing she was going to bruise from their manhandling.

"Ah, yes. Here you go. We've been trying to reach you." Her fingers flew across the keyboard before she focused her attention back on Alima. The printer behind her flared to life. "Your name was drawn four days ago."

Alima's eyebrows shot up high. Four days? She smirked, wishing she could have hidden longer. Had she known her name was drawn, she would have left.

"That's it?" Alima couldn't help the smart-ass comments that flowed from her mouth. She was proud that it had taken them that long to find her.

"Four days is nothing. One human took us three months to find, but we brought her in." The vampire smirked.

Alima's smile disappeared, replaced by a scowl. The petite female rose from her chair and strolled over to the printer, picking up the papers that sprouted from it. She walked back over to them, a grin on her lips. Her fangs were in full view.

"Take her to room thirteen."

"Yes, ma'am." The guard tugged on her arm, directing her down the hall. Another one flanked her other side as they traveled to where the vampire had requested.

She felt like a common criminal. Not someone who wanted to make her own decisions in life.

They arrived, and he practically shoved her in. She stumbled, then righted herself.

"Sit down," he growled. He motioned to the chair next to a desk.

The room resembled a doctor's office. Alima had assumed they would look like torture chambers. Something to hold her down while they took all the blood they wanted. She shivered and nodded to her arms.

"Can these come off?" she asked.

"No." He grunted, moving toward the door.

"Well, how the hell are they going to draw blood from me?"

"Turn around," he commanded.

The other guard stood in the doorway, watching. She followed his instructions and felt him tug on her handcuffs. Within seconds her arms fell away, free. She rotated them, glad to finally be able to move them. A sharp pain radiated from her shoulder blades.

"Thanks," she muttered.

"Have a seat, don't move, and don't touch nothing," he barked. He stalked out and shut the door.

She sighed and sat. It wasn't like there was much for her to touch. The room was windowless and had all the standard things a doctor's office would have.

Her foot nervously twitched while she waited for someone to come in. How much blood would they take from her? What would they want from her? She rubbed her eyes, wishing she and Javari had been able to dodge them.

At least she had some information that someone had evaded them for months. She would definitely have to share this with Reed and the others. Her boss would definitely want to hear this tidbit. How had they done it? How had they got caught?

Alima stood and paced. Patience wasn't one of her virtues. Her mind raced with all of the things she would have to do when she left here. It was sad that she would have to leave her beloved town, but it was necessary. She could transfer to another town and work with a local Rebels' group if not start one herself. She knew all of the ins and out of the organization.

Alima swung around at the sound of the door opening. A tall male vampire walked in with a few items in his hands.

"Please, Miss Morgan. Have a seat. This won't take long," he said.

His voice was light, and there was a hint of an accent she couldn't decipher. Her gaze moved to the guard scowling at her from the doorway. The vampire lightly closed the door and motioned to the chair.

She took her seat and eyed him warily. He sat on the stool in front of the computer. He tapped out a few commands and asked her standard questions about herself. Full name, date of birth, height, weight, clothing size and more. He even took her photograph.

"What do you need to know all of that for? Isn't my blood sample the only thing you care about?" she snapped.

"Miss Morgan, how much do you know about the draft? I'm going to assume it's not much," he said. His tone was very condescending.

She glared at him but remained in her seat. There was no point in trying to attack him—he was a vampire. Even if she did, those guards would be in the room in a second to restrain her.

"I know enough. Your people take my people against their will and ship them off to a bloodsucker who will probably use them as food." Her hands curled up into fists. She refused to be one who submitted to the draft. Whether or not she was matched today, once her name was entered, she could be pulled in the future. If her vampire mate wasn't entered yet, but decided to enter in five years, they would seek her out. That was why some people chose to give up their lives; they had to disappear.

"You believe that vampires who are presented

with their mates, someone they will cherish for the rest of their lives, would be so cruel as to use their humans as food?" He arched an eyebrow at her. He shook his head. "This draft is bigger than you or I—"

"Save it. I don't want to hear it." She turned away and focused her attention on the wall across the room.

He sighed and finished typing out a few commands on the computer. He asked her more useless questions. She answered them with one-word replies.

"Now we will take your sample." He stood and donned a pair of gloves.

"Just make sure you leave enough for me to live," she muttered.

"This is what I'm taking." He held up a three blood vials. He narrowed his gaze on her after placing them down again.

He pulled the armrest up from the side of her chair and placed her arm on it. She stiffened, having never liked needles. She really didn't like the fact that a vampire was the one who was going to draw her blood. What if he saw it and wanted a taste—

"I am not going to drink your blood," he bit out.

She flicked her surprised gaze to him. How had he read her mind? She didn't think they could do that.

"It was apparent on your face," he said. "Please. I have more decency than that."

"Well, most don't," she replied dryly.

There were plenty of vampires roaming the streets hunting down humans. Some who didn't care about human life and thought of humans as only food. There were times when she'd picked up nights to help with the patrols because of her insomnia. Bad dreams of her sister's death plagued her. So on the evenings she wasn't working as a driver, she volunteered for the patrols. She'd lost track of how many human attacks she'd come across. Some they had been able to help, others had already been gone from the amount of blood loss.

He didn't reply to her but carried out his job and drew her blood. The small prick was the only pain she felt. He had her bandaged up and the vials labeled before she knew it.

"Just so you know, I don't smell any disease on you," he said.

"Excuse me?"

"Aside from testing for the match, we run health screenings on each human to ensure they are healthy."

"Why? So if not, they can be put out to pasture?" She smirked. Wouldn't it be like the vampires. Not finding a perfect human and discarding them like waste.

"No, so we can offer treatment. Vampires cherish their mates. The humans who are matched are well taken care of."

"Whatever." She rolled her eyes. Her thoughts flicked back to some of the humans she had seen walking down the street looking well-off, not as if they were starving.

Were they humans bonded to vampires?

She'd never be bold enough to ask a person why they weren't living in poverty like her and the others.

"The drawing is tonight. We need your telephone number." He sniffed, turning back to the screen.

"Does it look like I own a phone?" She motioned to her clothing. It was clean but faded and purchased secondhand. She was jobless, living in a compound, and here he thought she would own a phone.

"So that explains why you were unaware of your name being drawn."

"Not everyone is as lucky as others to have a television." She folded her arms in front of herself.

"Don't worry. If your name is drawn, they will find you."

A shiver rippled down her spine. She held back a smile.

That's what they thought.

* * *

ALIMA SCURRIED DOWN THE STREET. She glanced behind her, making sure she wasn't followed. She dipped down an alley and jogged. It was a shortcut that would take her to her living quarters. She was sure Javari was worried shitless. She was going to miss him, but there was nothing else she could do. She had to disappear if she wanted to survive. They would be able to connect later.

She continued on until she came to the building where she stayed. She walked through the front door of the old, abandoned brick structure. She ran up the stairs until she came to the room she shared with a few other women. She paused outside the door and decided to go find Javari first.

Packing her belongings wouldn't take too long. She didn't own much. Spinning on her heel, she went back down a level to find him. He shared an area with men. She arrived at their door and banged on it. She stood back and waited. The door flew open with Javari standing there.

"Alima." He strode forward and wrapped her in his arms. He pulled back and assessed her. "They didn't harm you, did they?"

"No, they were asses, but just took blood for the most part." She sighed.

He shut the door and took her hand.

"We don't have time. Let's go. Pack your bag." He towed her behind him and marched to the stairs.

Even though she didn't want to leave him, she must. She bit her lip and followed him back to her level. They arrived at her apartment. They went in and headed straight to her room. There wasn't much in there. A mattress on the floor, a crate with some of her belongings stored there. In the closet hung her meager clothing, and on the floor was a bag.

She swallowed hard, unable to believe she was going to have to use the bag.

"I've already put everything in motion. Reed was notified that you were taken to the lab."

"Okay." She blinked and flew into escape mode. She grabbed her bag and stuffed her clothes in it. She walked over to the crate and took a picture she had of her family before her sister had been taken from them. She smiled at it, tears forming. She blinked them back and gently slid it into the side pocket, not wanting to damage it. This was the only photo she had of all of them together.

Once done, she turned to find Javari staring at her.

"What is it?" Alima hefted the bag on her shoulder. Her heart raced at the thought of her new beginnings. It would be scary, and she'd be truly alone until she got to know new people. She had been used to having Javari at her side.

"I'm going to go with you," he said.

"No." She rushed across the room and took his hands in hers. "You can't. You have a good job you can't give up."

"But it doesn't mean anything if you are out there with no money or anything." He brought her close and held her.

"Once I'm settled, maybe I'll allow you to send me money." She stepped back and tilted her head to meet his gaze.

"Allow me?" His lips curved up in the corner. He shook his head and ran a hand along his jaw. "You have always been too damn stubborn for your own good."

"And you know I don't like hand-me-outs. I can take care of myself." She softened her voice and stared at her friend. "I can't have you leave everything behind. You know you can't know where I went. I'm sure if I'm chosen and they can't find me, they will interrogate any known associates. If you don't know, they can't get to me."

"But if I go with you, then I won't be here for them to question." He arched an eyebrow at her.

She shook her head fiercely. He'd said *she* was stubborn.

"I will send word that I'm okay once I get to my destination. I promise. We'll find a way for you to help me."

He studied her for a moment before apparently giving in. "Fine. But I want word immediately. I'm going to worry."

"I'll be okay. And if I'm not chosen, then all will be well. I'll definitely be safe." She offered him a smile and took his hand. She just prayed her name wasn't chosen. A part of her looked forward to seeing other parts of the country. She'd never been far from Maine. In all of her thirty-two years of life, this would be the first time she'd left the East Coast. "Let's go. We don't have time to waste."

CHAPTER FOUR

"When was the last time a lycan was spotted?" Lethia growled. She paced back and forth in her war room. Anger radiated inside her due to the knowledge that the lycans had moved in quicker than they had anticipated. She faced the room. Her gaze landed on her second-in-command, Dru Moldark. She had been at Lethia's side for decades. She had worked her way up the ranks and had become a trusted warrior under Lethia's rule.

There was no other vampire dedicated to her outside of Lane.

Dru's ice-blue eyes glowed with her own rage. She hated being caught off guard.

"Two days ago, Your Grace," Dru replied. She stood from the table and walked around toward the map of their town and the coastline of Maine. "And I'm afraid to share that it was here in Crystal Cove."

"What?" Lethia roared. She stalked to the table to see where Dru pointed. It was near the outskirts of town close to the ocean. The area was rocky and had plenty of places where lycans could build a lair.

"Why don't we take a small task force and go search the area?" Aubrey Lafayette spoke up. She was Lethia's primary advisor. She held Lethia's ear when it came to the livelihood and safety of vampires under Lethia's care.

"I like that idea. Gather twenty warriors. We will go out on a scouting mission. From what my sister reports, there could be at least a hundred lycans in the pack." Lethia leaned on the table and studied the map. She knew her own state and area she ruled like the back of her hand. Centuries she had spent here. Even with the change in times, she knew every nook and cranny a lycan could possible hide in.

"Aubrey, I want a detailed blueprint of the sewer systems. I don't doubt that they would hide down there if not in the caves." Lethia glanced up to find Aubrey's attention on her table. Her advisor didn't respond as she read whatever was more important than their current discussion. "I'm sorry, Aubrey, are we bothering you?"

Lethia narrowed her eyes on her advisor. This was very disrespectful, and she would never expect this type of behavior from Aubrey.

"I'm sorry, Your Grace." Aubrey glanced up with a small smile on her lips.

Lethia bit back a growl at the tilt of her advisor's lips. What the hell was she smiling for? Aubrey stood from her seat and walked over to stand beside Lethia.

She handed her tablet to her. "You need to see this."

Lethia took it from her, curious as to what would be more important than hunting down the lycans. They couldn't afford to have the beasts roaming the streets.

She scanned the document and paused.

Princess Lethia Riskel, second-born daughter of King Niall and Queen Mira Riskel, commander of the east, has been matched with her fated mate. Preparations for the arrival of said mate should be made hastily. She will be delivered promptly. Details will follow soon.

"Wait, does this mean—?" For once in Lethia's life, she was rendered speechless. She glanced back up and froze in place.

Aubrey's grin grew wider. She nodded, excitement lining her face.

"You have been matched," Aubrey exclaimed. She clapped her hands together.

"Congratulations, Your Grace," Dru murmured. The hardened warrior cracked a smile of her own. She rested her hand on Lethia's shoulder. "I will lead the task force. You will stay, greet your mate."

"But I want to—"

"You are going to be needed here for when your mate arrives," Aubrey said softly. She took the tablet from Lethia. "She will need you. There will be so much I'm sure she will need."

"What are you talking about?" Lethia asked. She scrubbed a hand along her face, her thoughts racing. She couldn't be in both places at one time.

"She's human. I'm sure this will be an adjustment."

Lethia closed her eyes and nodded. She remembered speaking with her sister, Velika, about when Quinn had first come to her. The poor human had been frightened and scared of their kind. There was no telling what state of mind her mate was in. Would she be a human who would want to be with a vampire? Or one of those against being with a vampire?

Something stirred inside Lethia.

Her mate had been found.

Already with this knowledge, her body was responding.

Once her mate arrived, she would never leave.

Lethia would ensure that. Whatever she had to do to convince the woman to take a chance on what fate had designed, she would see their lives would be for the better.

"I am very capable of leading men, Lethia. Stay with your mate. No one can take your place with that."

Lethia straightened and turned to Dru. She was correct. Dru had led her warriors into plenty of battles. She was a seasoned warrior and very well-respected throughout Lethia's army.

"Okay. I want to be kept in the loop on everything." Lethia turned to Dru. It was her responsibility to ensure the lycans were taken care of. She would hate to have to call in her sisters, they would never let her live it down if she couldn't handle one hundred lycans. "If the alpha is indeed there, then you are to leave immediately. We don't want them to know we are scouting them out. We wouldn't want them on the run. We'll need to contain them if we are to destroy them."

"Yes, Your Grace." Dru nodded.

This was not the time they would fight. They needed to research first. Gather as much data as possible. A new alpha who was organizing the lycans was dangerous and powerful.

"I have a feeling they are only showing us what they want us to see." Lethia switched her focus back to the map and leaned down. "If my sisters' intel is correct, there is more than one hundred. They wanted us to know they were here. I'm so sure of it."

"Don't worry, Your Grace. We'll gather as much information as we can, and I'll report back to you by tomorrow."

"See that you do."

Lethia stood to her full height and faced her second. Dru thumped her chest. She marched out of the room, and Lethia was confident she'd lead the mission as she would.

"Now, Your Grace. We need to discuss your mate. We don't have much time," Aubrey said. She glanced down at her tablet. "The other details have been sent."

Lethia took the device from her and clicked on the link in the email. It was a file and a photograph of her mate.

Her cold heart was sluggish, but it beat for this woman she stared down at. She was African American, with big eyes, almond-shaped, set against warm, golden-brown skin. Her hair, held back in two identical braids, rested on her shoulders.

Alima Morgan.

Lethia scanned the document and took in all the information that was provided for her. Height: five and a half foot. Weight: two hundred and forty pounds.

Lethia loved thick women.

She didn't mind them all, but the ones with the additional cushion on them were her favorite. She was built muscular due to her training and hefting weapons. It was always nice to slide her body against one who was soft and curvy.

Her fangs pulsed with the need to sink them into the column of Alima's neck.

"Only the finest for my mate," Lethia rasped.

She read that her mate was unemployed, having been let go from her factory job a year ago. Thanks to Quinn, her sister's mate, the royal family had been brought up to speed on the conditions some humans faced.

"But, of course, Your Grace. Shall I prepare a separate room for her at first?"

"Yes, the one next to mine."

* * *

"WHAT DO you mean you can't find her?" Lethia growled. She stalked forward to the guard and stood in his face.

Two SUVs that should have been carrying her mate had arrived moments ago. Lethia, Lane, and Aubrey stood waiting to get the first glimpse of her mate, Alima. The moon was at its highest point. The warm air grew icy-cold as she stared at the humans before her.

But the guards who'd stepped from the vehicles were empty-handed.

"This isn't the first time she has been hard to locate. When her name was pulled for the draft, I'm told it took them four days to find her just to get her sample." The guard stuttered. He took a step back from her, his eyes widened with fear.

She scented his fear along with the other humans who stood around the trucks. She should kill them all for their failure.

But that wouldn't bring her mate to her.

It *would* make her feel better.

Then she thought of what she was wearing. She would hate to get blood on her clothing. It was a bitch to get cleaned off.

Lethia had chosen an outfit that she thought would be welcoming to her new mate. She hadn't wanted to appear battle-hardened, wearing her fighting leathers as her two sister wore consistently. Her hair was pulled back on the sides and held by two gold clips while the rest of her golden tresses flowed down her back. Her willowy dress was made of the finest material, but it didn't keep her from having weapons adorning her body. Even though she appeared regal, showcasing her royal status, she was prepared for a fight.

"Lane," she snapped.

"Yes, Your Grace." He moved to her side.

She turned to him, anger bubbling inside her at the lack of incompetence of the draft guards standing before her. How hard was it to find a human?

"I want my mate found." She glared at him, resting her hands on her waist. She would go look for her mate herself. "I want my personal guards ready in ten minutes."

"Yes, Your Grace." He gave a nod and stalked toward the castle.

"We can assist you," one of the other humans offered.

"You have done enough." She swiveled a scorching glare their way. "This will be remembered. Now leave before I decide to punish you instead."

Lethia marched toward her castle. She snarled, thinking how she should be escorting her mate inside to show her where they would spend the rest of their lives together. She was proud of her home. It was rich in history, a castle a few hundred years old. She'd acquired it when she'd been appointed as the warden of her territory.

She walked through the massive double wooden doors, her butler, Sterling, standing by. He had been loyal to her and her family for centuries. He had trained under the butlers who worked for her parents.

"What would you have me to do, Your Grace?" Sterling asked, walking alongside her.

She headed toward the grand staircase. He ran her home like a well-oiled machine. There was nothing that went on in the castle that Sterling wasn't aware of. The tall, lanky man with gray hair had been a mate who was formerly a human and turned. Most of the butlers the royal family employed shared the same story. In exchange for loyalty and a lifetime of service, they would live.

"We will bring my mate home. She is to be welcomed with open arms." She paused at the base and turned to him.

"Of course, Your Grace." He bowed his head.

Lethia took the stairs two at a time. Using her vampire speed, she raced to her private quarters. The door slammed open with her swiftly going to the walk-in closet. The massive rows of clothing and shoes were ignored. She went over to the corner where she stored her fighting leathers and a few weapons she kept close to her.

She reached out a hand, touching the soft black material. She growled, snatching what she needed from the hangers. She would never have figured she would be the one who would have to go chase down her mate.

What if someone had taken her?

Was that the reason the lycans were moving in?

Word that Velika had mated a human had made worldwide news.

If the lycans had harmed one hair on her mate's head, she would rain down everything she had and hunt them down to extinction.

She threw her new clothing on then tied up her boots. She rearranged the weapons she had worn underneath her dress and outfitted her body with them and more.

She jerked around, ready to go searching for her mate. Whoever was responsible for Alima's disappearance would pay.

Lethia made her way out of her room and through the castle. She exited through the back doorway that the servants used. Lane stood by with her other personal guards, Enoch and Izora.

"Your Grace." Izora thumped her chest.

"I'm sorry to hear of the disappearance of your mate," Enoch said. He stood to his full height, thumping his chest as well.

Her three personal guards held a status above all other warriors. They were elite soldiers who were to protect her back. Not that she couldn't take care of herself, but she couldn't be too careful.

"I appreciate it. We are going to get my mate and bring her home." Lethia stood before them. She eyed each one and gave a slight bow to them, acknowledging their loyalty. Each one of them would lay down their lives for her and do anything she asked.

"I've taken the liberty of acquiring a few other warriors as backup," Lane said, motioning to the men and women standing beside a black van. He held up papers. "We have her last known living location and the location of where they arrested her."

"Let's move out, now," Lethia said.

Izora held open the back door of the dark SUV. Lethia climbed inside and settled in. Enoch got into the driver's seat while Izora took the passenger. Lane sat beside her. The truck rocked as Enoch guided it around the castle. Lethia glanced behind to see the van of her warriors following them.

She leaned back and reached for the papers Lane held.

"You are a good man, Lane," she murmured. Her vampiric vision allowed her to read the writing in the dark. She read the details of her mate's capture. She'd been found leaving a café with a human male. Jealousy reared its ugly head.

Who was the male?

What was he to her?

A lover? Her human husband?

Whatever he was to her would cease, even if Lethia had to kill him.

The rest of the report spoke of the chase, the capture. There were no details on whether or not she was injured. If so, Lethia would find the guards who'd arrested her and deal out a swift punishment of death.

But then a thought crossed her mind.

This entire time, her mate had lived in the same town she had.

How was that even possible?

"What is that smirk for?" Lane asked.

"I was just thinking how it took the draft to point out who my mate was and she has been living under my nose this entire time." She looked up from the papers.

"Well, from what I know, fate can be a bitch." He chuckled. "No stone will be left unturned until we find your mate."

"I expect nothing less." She set the papers down and watched the scenery go by. It was evening, and some of the shops in the downtown area were still open.

They arrived at the café Alima had visited with Enoch parking in front of the building.

Lethia stepped from the vehicle and stared at the café window. It was a sandwich shop that faced the waterfront and was owned by humans. She was curious as to what her mate had eaten. Could she even afford to pay for her meal?

Vampires did not need to consume food. Blood provided all of the nutrients they needed. Once she completed the mating bond with Alima, Lethia would feed no more on anyone else. Her mate would be all she needed.

A door slamming broke into her thoughts. The warriors stood by the van, awaiting orders.

"Your Grace." Izora held the door open to the shop.

Lethia strode forward and entered. She was assaulted by the scents of freshly baked bread. Gasps echoed through the establishment. There were a few patrons enjoying their meals scattered around the small café.

Lane, Enoch, and Izora filed in behind her. The scent of fear permeated the air. A male and a female human were working behind the counter but had paused, their attention locked on her and her vampires.

"Get the customers out of here," she murmured. She didn't have to check to see if her order was being followed. Lethia walked to the counter and rested her hands on it. She took in the two employees who were froze in place. "Do you know who I am?"

"Princess Lethia," the male stuttered.

The woman with bright-pink hair cowered back, leaning against the counter behind her. Her body trembled as she took in Lethia. "Please don't hurt us."

"Now why would you think I would do something like that?" she asked, arching an eyebrow.

They remained silent.

Which was to their benefit.

"Were either of you working earlier today?" Lethia asked. The sound of low voices and the door to the café shutting was behind her. Lethia kept her focus on the pair.

The male pointed to the pink-haired woman. "Frankie was."

The woman's audible swallow met Lethia's ears. She narrowed her gaze on her.

"I didn't do nothing," Frankie muttered, shaking her head.

"Who accused you of anything? I need information," Lethia snapped. Irritation filled her as she stared at Frankie who inched away from the male. Lethia zeroed her gaze on her, sending the pounding of her heart skyrocketing. "I wouldn't think of it if I were you."

Frankie didn't heed her warning. She dashed away from the counter in a feeble attempt to get away. Lethia sighed, watching Enoch land in front of her. He'd moved so fast there was no time for her to slow down.

She barreled right into his chest and fell to the floor.

"Bring her to me." Lethia turned and waited.

Enoch dragged Frankie kicking and screaming from the floor.

"Please don't kill me. I didn't do anything," Frankie cried out.

Enoch held her in front of him and stood before Lethia.

"Stay there," Lane warned the male.

Lethia closed the gap between them and stared into the human's eyes. It didn't take much for her to connect with Frankie. She fell limp against Enoch's chest. The power of compulsion came in handy at the most convenient times.

"Release her, she's not going anywhere," Lethia murmured.

Frankie stood straight, following Lethia's unspoken order. Her body relaxed, and the terror in her eyes was gone, leaving nothing but emptiness.

"Much better."

CHAPTER FIVE

Lethia wasn't going to get the information she needed from Frankie from just talking with her. The human had been downright terrified and in the midst of a panic attack. The best way was to see into her memories. Lethia moved forward, tilting Frankie's head to the side. Her gums burned and stretched as her fangs broke through, descending.

"Please don't hurt her," the male cried out.

Lethia ignored him, her fangs sinking deep into Frankie's neck. Her thick nectar flowed into Lethia's mouth. She sucked it down, drinking from her and seeking what she needed to know. Flashes of memories from the day filtered through her eyes.

She watched Frankie arrive at work, beginning her duties to open the shop. Lethia pushed harder, anxious to get a glimpse of her mate. Finally, a male and a female came into view. He scowled at something Frankie said. The two of them appeared poor and hungry. The woman with him angled herself away as if ashamed. She turned, and her eyes met Frankie's. Lethia's air escaped her. Alima was gorgeous. She turned away again, sidling near the male. Once he was done with his order, he escorted her to a table by the window. Fast forward, and he came back to get their food then returned to her.

Lethia pulled back, gasping for breath. She had not only witnessed the female's memories but had experienced her feelings. She eyed the oozing wound and licked it to seal it closed. She handed Frankie back to Enoch and moved away. She slid her tongue over her lips and stared at the table her mate had sat at while eating her meal.

Lethia released Frankie from her hold.

Her screaming ensued again.

Lethia ignored it and took a seat in the same chair Alima had been perched in. She ran her hand over the table, breathing in deeply. Multiple scents filled her. Were any of them Alima's?

"Did you see her?" Lane appeared at her side, her voice low.

Lethia jerked her head in a nod. She looked out the window and wondered when Alima had sat here, what she had seen.

"I also saw the male who was with her," she growled. She glanced up at Lane, a fierce scowl taking over her face. The male had touched her. He was too familiar with her.

"He will be dealt with," Lane promised. His eyes lightened to iridescent blue.

She knew his word was sound.

"Come," Lane said. "Her steps were documented when she left the lab. We know where she resides."

Lethia stood and followed him. She glanced over at Frankie who sat on the floor in front of the counter. She jerked away and scurried back from Lethia. She gripped her neck, her eyes wide.

"Will I turn?" she whispered.

"You aren't worthy to be a vampire," Lethia snarled, continuing behind Lane.

They left the shop and entered the truck. She had felt the disdain Frankie had projected when

Lethia's human and the male had been ordering their food. She'd made Alima feel unwelcome when they had only sought nourishment. Her mate had a right to be there. They had paid for their food. Lethia never understood the workings of humans. Before the war, they were fighting each other. It was only once vampires had presented themselves that the humans banded together to fight.

Once Alima was brought home to her, she'd never feel unwelcome ever again. Lethia would see to that.

Enoch drove them to the next location. It was about twenty minutes from downtown on the outskirts. This was a large, abandoned building that looked as if a strong wind would topple it over.

This was where her mate lived?

Lethia studied the structure. It was brick and appeared to not have electricity, or at least they weren't using it. Soft light flickered beyond some of the windows. They were using candles. A few humans lingered around the front door. They eyed the vehicle warily. She prayed this wasn't their security.

"I want the warriors to spread out, covering all entrances. There is no telling what we will encounter," Lane announced.

"Definitely." Enoch brought the vehicle to a halt and cut the engine.

Lethia exited and walked around to the back of the truck. Enoch was speaking with the driver of the van. Her vampires followed orders, leaving the vehicle and disappearing into the night around the building.

There were three levels, and Lethia was not leaving until they had searched every square inch. It had been a few hours since her mate had left the lab and the draft had been declared.

"Who are you?" one of the males demanded.

The other two stood behind him. It was then she saw the wooden stakes in their hands. None of them looked fit enough to really take on a vampire. Their weapons would be useless against Lethia and her highly trained vampires.

"We want no trouble." She strode forward with Izora and Lane flanking her.

"That's what all vampires say before they kidnap and murder our people for food," the bold male snarled.

Lethia saved that comment in the back of her mind. That would be something she'd have to look into. Rogue vampires did not abide by the rules of vampires. They had been a thorn in her and her sisters' sides for years.

She stopped a few feet from them, resting her hand on the blade at her side.

"It's the princess," one of the other males gasped.

"I don't give a shit. She's a vampire, and that's all that matters," their leader griped.

"You should give a shit," she replied haughtily. She brandished her fangs unashamedly. "I'm the one vampire you should fear."

Their audible gulps were their only response.

She took another step forward, unafraid of their wooden weapons. She only allowed them to keep them to make them feel safe. She was only here for her mate.

"Now, when I say we don't want any trouble, I mean that. You have the word of a princess and the warden of these lands. I am in search of a woman," she announced.

They stared at her for moments before the leader spoke again.

"It wouldn't be the same one the draft guards came looking for, would it?" he asked. His grip tightened on his stake.

"I'm sure it is. This woman is my mate, and I

intend to collect her. That is all I want. Nothing else," she said softly. If she won their trust, then maybe they would give her information she needed. She eyed them. They could each gain some weight. "How many humans live here?"

"You think we will tell you that so you can have your vampire buddies come here for a buffet?" he said.

"No, I'm asking because I will send enough food to feed the inhabitants of this building for a month." She wasn't below bargaining to get what she wanted. She had learned much from Quinn. People on the brink of starvation would be willing to do anything.

Even rat out a fellow human.

"Two months," he retorted.

The male to his left nudged him as if he had become too bold.

Two months of food for humans was nothing. Lethia would be willing to pay much more for her mate.

"Done. I will have the first shipment delivered tomorrow."

"Well, just like I told you, she's not here. She lived on the second level, apartment three. But you won't find her," the leader said.

"And why is that?" she asked.

Izora shifted beside her. Lethia sensed her guard was getting irritated with the humans.

"She's a Rebel, and by now they will be relocating her."

* * *

ALIMA SIGHED, leaning her head against the window. She watched the scenery fly past. It was strange sitting in the back seat. Normally it was she who would be driving someone who wanted to get away.

Now the shoe was on the other foot, and she was being carted off to start a new life. Her driver was male and hadn't said a word to her. Which was the norm. If he was caught, it was less information he would have.

She thought of Javari's face when she'd entered the vehicle. He had remained strong for her. His last hug had been tight, and she was proud she was able to keep herself from crying. He'd helped her into the small vehicle and shut the door. He had been her rock for a long time, and now she was going to start her new life alone.

Alima had sensed that one day she'd have to

leave Crystal Cove, but she had hoped it would be to go join her parents.

Instead, she was being whisked away somewhere far.

Alima tightened her hold on her bag. She kept it braced against her. It was the only thing that would be familiar for her. They were headed south, and once they reached certain point, this driver would hand her off to the next car who would pick her up. There was an organized system set in place to move humans. Once daylight came, it would be a little safer. It was always more dangerous to leave at night, but she didn't have a choice. They had a few hours until daylight came where they would be safe.

Her stomach rumbled. Javari had given her a few energy bars and a small amount of money until she could get to her new location. She had at first tried to reject the money, but he wouldn't hear of it and had become almost angry with her. She unzipped her bag and eyed the four bars and pulled one out. She hadn't eaten since they had gone for sandwiches. She tore it open and took a bite. It was dry, made of granola and some dried fruit. It wasn't a gourmet meal, but it would keep her hunger at bay for a while.

"Two hours until we reach our destination," the driver announced. They had already been on the road for a while, and she was sure they were approaching the border soon.

"Okay."

That was the extent of the conversation allowed. She took slow bites, not wanting to gulp the bar in one bite. She had to make these last. She was unsure where he was taking her and if there was anywhere she could get food. She finished off the bar and placed the wrapper in her bag. She zipped it up shut and settled back in the seat.

Her eyes fluttered closed. She needed to take advantage of this time in the car and get some shut-eye. Once she arrived at her final destination, she wasn't sure how long it would be before she was able to sleep.

The gentle rocking of the vehicle helped her drift off. Dreams filled her mind. A female's face floated in front of her with blonde hair and sharp fangs. There were images of Alima tied up and the female drinking from her. Alima struggled to awaken while fear consumed her.

The driver's curse broke Alima from her subconsciousness.

"What the hell?" he murmured.

Alima blinked until her eyes came into focus. She wasn't sure how long she'd been napping, but the strange, plaguing dreams worried her.

"What is it?" She sat forward and leaned to the side so she could see through the windshield.

The hairs on the back of her neck stood to attention.

A barricade was blocking the two-lane highway up ahead. A few men stood outside their cars, holding up their hands for the drivers to stop.

"Play it cool," he said. He coasted to a halt and rolled his window down.

A man dressed in an official royal uniform approached the vehicle. He was a member of the royal army.

She tried to keep her eyes down, not wanting to attract attention to herself, but why would members of the royal army be setting up barricades?

"State your business?" the vampire demanded.

"We are just passing through," the driver announced. He held his hands up away from the steering wheel. "We're on our way to New Hampshire. A friend of ours is deathly ill."

"Why is the female in the back seat?"

Alima kept her head down, staring at her

hands. She could feel the heat of the vampire's gaze on her.

"She gets car sick easily. You know women have weak stomachs." The driver chuckled.

Alima held back the rolling of her eyes. That was a weak excuse, but she kept her mouth shut, not wanting to blow her cover.

"Get out of the car." Apparently, the vampire wasn't believing the driver.

"I haven't done anything wrong—"

"Get out of the car on your own or I'll drag you out." The vampire's voice was cold, sending a ripple of fear through Alima.

"Fine." The door opened, and he stepped out. "What is the meaning of this?"

"None of your business. We are looking for a human." Another one came to the car and stood by her door. He was in a solid black uniform. It was the same as the draft guards.

Fear snaked its way through her. They were searching for her. She knew it without a doubt.

She bit her lip, thinking of how unlucky she was.

Her door opened.

"Get out, ma'am," the human guard said. He held out his hand to her.

She ignored it and stepped from the car, keeping her head down.

"What is your name?"

"I haven't done anything wrong," she said softly. She tightened her hands on the straps of her bag. She still kept her head angled down, but she could see the woods across the street. If she could break free and make a run for it, the trees would hide her. She could try to make a run for it, but she wasn't sure how far she'd get from the vampires.

Brightness flashed before her. She squinted as he aimed his flashlight at her.

"Hey, it's her!"

The bottom of Alima's stomach gave way.

Just her luck. They had been searching for her.

Alima took the guard by surprise and shoved him away from her. She raced toward the trees, slinging her bag on to her back. There was no way she was leaving it behind. Shouts echoed behind her.

She was almost to the trees when arms circled her and lifted her from her feet.

"Let me go!" she screamed.

She kicked and thrashed her body around, trying to get free. Her adrenaline kicked in. The person carrying her had to be vampire. He wasn't even out of breath, and he carried her like she was a child. She tried to wiggle around, sending her nails scraping along his face. She'd rather die than be taken to a vampire and become their possession.

"Stop it, you stupid bitch," he hollered. He tossed her to the ground.

The air whooshed from her.

"Are you out of your mind? She is not to be harmed," another voice said.

Two vampires stood next to her. She glanced up, unable to see their faces. She pushed off the ground and made another attempt at escaping but failed. The second vampire snatched her by her bag and pushed her down on the ground. He knelt with his knee on the back of her thigh. Her bag was ripped off her. He grabbed her wrist and slapped a pair of handcuffs on one and then the other.

She cried out, yanking on her restraints. He hefted her up from the ground and dragged her over to the waiting van.

"No. You can't do this!" she screamed.

"We can and we are." He shoved her in the back of the empty van and slammed the door shut.

Alima screamed and kicked at the door. Tears streamed down her face.

This couldn't be happening. Not to her. What

had she done in this life for this to be her fate? Why had the gods been so cruel? They'd sent the vampires to destroy their world, killed her sister, and now made her the mate of one.

Whoever it was must be powerful to be able to arrange something like this so swiftly. She rolled around the floor of the van as it pulled off. She wasn't going to go easily. She would stand up to whoever it was. They weren't going to just take her and use her. She just rather they get it over and bleed her dry.

She never wanted to be the mate of a vampire.

She let loose another scream of frustration, but no one cared. Alima looked around but couldn't see anything in the darkened area. They were transporting her like cargo. No seats, no safety belts. She slid across the floor when the van took a turn.

Alima scooted to the farthest corner away from the doors. She huddled there, awaiting her fate. She brought her knees up to her chest and rested her forehead on them. She tried to push down her fear, but it was overtaking her.

"I'm strong. I can resist," she murmured to herself. She didn't know why the word resist had come out of her mouth, but she knew she had to remain strong. She was sure the vampire was going to break her. Probably try to make her some mindless shell of herself so they could take all the blood they wanted.

This mating business was a just ruse for them to have an endless supply of blood. They'd survived this long without human mates, why all of sudden did they want them now?

Her mind wandered.

Who was the vampire?

What if it was someone who was nice?

Alima shook her head. No matter what, she would escape. She wouldn't stop trying until they killed her. She refused to be the property of some vampire. No matter what tricks they tried. A life as the property of a suck-head wasn't one for her.

Alima was jostled hard and slid onto her side. She opened her eyes, unsure of when she'd fallen asleep or how long she'd been out. She struggled to right herself back up into a sitting position. Listening, she strained to hear to what was going on outside the van. The pounding of her heart was the only thing she could hear. Frustrated, she sat back and waited.

She shifted her arms and winced. The handcuffs were cutting into her skin, and her arms tingled as if they had fallen asleep.

Voices sounded outside the van. Alima froze, waiting to see if the doors would open. Biting her lip, she scooted toward the doors. She'd take her captors by surprise and try to make run for it. Even if she didn't get far, she needed to see what was around her. It would help in her escape later to see where the road or some other landmark was.

Alima somehow got herself in a crouching position and waited.

The door opened, and she launched herself at the person. He stumbled back with a grunt. She staggered but managed to remain on her feet. She frantically scanned the area, taking in the road, her surroundings, and that the sun was rising. These men were human guards, and her luck had just increased.

Alima ran but didn't get far. Strong arms enclosed around her.

"Where the hell do you think you're going?" a deep baritone voice clipped out.

"Let me go!"

She tried to wiggle free, but his vice-like grip wasn't loosening. She threw her head back, connecting with his face. A horrifying crunch sounded from the crack to his nose. Another guard ran toward her. She brought her feet up, kicking him in the chest. The one holding her released her. She fell to her knees on the gravel.

She gritted her teeth and stood. She took off running, this time across the yard toward the small thicket of woods. She didn't know where it led, but anywhere was better than in the hands of a vampire. Curses sounded, and the pounding of footsteps behind had her trying to run faster.

Dammit! She should have listened to Javari. If she ever saw him again, she would admit he had been right and she'd start working out.

"Stop!" someone shouted.

Alima was almost to the trees when she was tackled from behind. She rolled over with her attacker and swung her bound fist with all of her might. She connected with her attacker's face. He flew back and fell off her. She scrambled to get up, but a foot to her back pushed her down.

"Stay down," the newcomer threatened.

Alima growled and pushed off the ground again. She had to get away. She would fight them off if she had to.

"I said stay down," he shouted.

"No. Let me go!" she yelled.

She rose to her knees to try to get up. Her body was hit with a strong electrical current. She screamed, unable to control her body. She trembled, a hot, searing pain carrying through her limbs. She toppled over, falling to the ground. Her body, uncontrollably jerking, writhed on the soft grass. She wheezed, trying to breathe, but the darkness reached for her, consumed her, and then there was nothing.

CHAPTER SIX

"They found her, Your Grace," Lane announced. He stood in the doorway of her office, waiting.

"Where?" Lethia put down the reports Dru had submitted. Her second-in-command had done well. She'd collected photographic proof along with a detailed write-up of their findings of the lycans. There was no sign of the alpha, but Lethia had a gut feeling the pack leader was near.

"They located her three hours from here."

"And the person or people helping her?" Lethia arched an eyebrow. She was curious now about this Rebel group. The human radical group was against vampires and the mating of humans with vampires. The local group had been identified, and Lethia had been keeping an eye on them. They had been growing in numbers. She had anticipated stepping in soon to diffuse them, but now she saw they may have been the cause of some local vampire mates going missing.

"There was one man with her. Not the one you gave a description of. We are still looking for him." Lane stood to his full height and bowed his head.

"Well, this is wonderful news." She'd hated that she'd had to return inside due to the rising sun. They had turned the search over to the human guards on her payroll. She had gone home, changed her clothes, and she should have slept. It was close to noon, and the sun was at its highest, and she should be resting, but there was no way she would be able to sleep with the knowledge that her mate was somewhere out there. A statewide hunt had commenced for her. Lethia stood and brushed her hands along her pants. "Where is she?"

She glanced down at her loose linen pants and top, wondering if she should change her clothes.

"The dungeon, my lady."

Her eyes snapped to Lane, anger filling her. She couldn't believe what she was hearing. They had placed their future princess in the dungeon? She rested her hands on her waist and glared at her guard. Lane almost looked afraid of her reaction. It had been a long while since she had seen fear in his eyes.

Especially of her.

Calming slightly, she relaxed so she could listen to him. There had to be a rational reason they would have put her mate in the dungeon.

"Why is my mate in lockup?" she asked through clenched teeth. It took everything she had to not storm from her office and kill everyone who had something to do with Alima's retrieval. She sneered, thinking of her human guards she'd had to use. They would need more training. It was either that or kill them. The ones she employed were the best, but they weren't as good as her vampire warriors. Their loyalties didn't run as deep as a vampire's.

"Because she injured four human guards, attempted escape twice, and threatened to do it again." Lane swallowed hard. He stood to attention with his hands folded behind him. "They didn't want to risk she'd escape before you'd gotten to meet her."

Lethia straightened at the knowledge that her

intended had given them hell. She grinned. It sounded as if she had spirit. It was interesting to hear that she was part of the human group, the Rebels. Lethia knew that would mean Alima would be stubborn and resistant to the idea of mating with a vampire. The Rebels were humans loyal and dedicated to their kind.

Alima would probably hate her for being a vampire and hate her for being matched to her.

But Lethia was up for the challenge of breaking her.

Velika's mate had struggled at first with the notion of mating a vampire, but her sister had won her human over. According to Velika, it had taken time.

It was a good thing Lethia was a vampire.

She had all the time in the world.

Lethia was known to fight dirty. She wasn't above stooping low to get what she wanted. Her gums burned and stretched as her fangs descended. The thought of bringing Alima to her knees, begging for her bite, sent a rush of excitement through her.

"Take me to her," Lethia demanded. She stalked to him with her head held high. She would go to her mate dressed as she was. She would take a soft approach first to test Alima out.

"Yes, Your Grace." Lane nodded and turned on his heel and led the way.

They walked through the castle, finding it buzzing with activity. Humans and vampires were employed under her. During the day, the steel window coverings were activated, blocking the sun's deadly rays from any vampires. Even though they were nocturnal creatures, they had found ways to function during daylight.

Lethia nodded to everyone she passed. Today she didn't have time for short conversations. She normally took the time to speak with those she employed. It helped with the morale of the humans. For some, it had been an adjustment to work for a vampire. For others, not so much. She had employed humans for hundreds of years.

Even when vampires were still hidden, many humans were aware and had been sworn to secrecy. Her family always paid their humans well and treated them kindly.

For thousands of years, vampire legends and stories were passed down through the generations. Some hilariously outrageous, while some were very close to the truth. But they had all been started by humans whispering about what they thought they'd seen or heard. Most legends may have even started from the humans who knew the truth about her people, but other humans expanded the tales because they didn't believe the stories, twisted them around to make great tales to tell to scare children as bedtime stories.

How could humans not believe in vampires but believe in witches?

Humans had hunted witches down until they had to join vampires and shifters in hiding. It was then they realized humans weren't ready for the coming of the supernatural beings.

But finally, vampires decided they were tired of hiding and they would rule. It was time for the world to face reality that humans were not the only beings living on this earth.

Vampires were the superior race, and now they'd make themselves known. Humans with their fragile egos wouldn't stand the thought that they were no longer at the top of the food chain.

Hence, the start of the war.

Lethia's father and the other six kings around the world had taken a stand against the armies of every nation. This was one war the humans were never meant to win. Vampires were stronger, faster, and very hard to kill.

Cities and towns were decimated. Some survived while others were still in the rebuilding stages. The relationship between humans and vampires was still estranged. Over the years, things had calmed down and settled. Many humans had fled once it was discovered that a vampire—one of the royal princesses—oversaw Crystal Cove.

But just as some humans didn't want vampires and humans cohabitating or mating, there were some vampires with the same mindset. To these vampires, humans were food and should not treated as anything else. They were set in the ways of the old, not wanting to mix the two races.

They believed vampires should only mate with other vampires.

Keep the bloodlines as pure as possible.

But that would not be the case.

Vampire numbers had been on the decline because of not being able to find their true mates.

Only with a true mate could a vampire produce a child.

There were many who believed vampires were being too impatient in waiting for fate to present their mate to them.

But it was Lethia's father who thought outside the box. King Niall had his scientist look into humans and whether they were compatible with vampires.

To their surprise, humans were a direct match, capable of procreating with vampires.

Once the war was over, the draft was initiated.

This was widely supported by the other six kings. It was for the good of vampires that they ensured their species did not die out.

Lane held the door open to the stairwell that led to the lower level. Alima moved to go through it, but he held up his hand.

"I just want to warn you that she isn't too happy about this," he murmured.

"I imagine, but she's my mate and will have to accept it," she said.

He paused, searching her eyes. He stepped away from the door.

"I hope so, Your Grace." Lane smirked, bowing his head.

Lethia descended the winding staircase. Where the castle was lush and full of the luxuries of her wealth, the lower level was different.

The deeper she went beneath the earth's surface, the lower the temperature dropped. She trailed her fingertips along the stone walls. The light from the top of the stairs slowly disappeared, leaving her in the dark.

Her vision adjusted, allowing her to see clearly.

Soft footsteps followed behind her.

Her heart's pace increased. Anticipation at finally meeting her mate face-to-face filled her. The image of Alima's picture had floated in her mind. Her warm brown skin, those big brown eyes. Lethia inhaled, trying to remain calm.

The dungeon level of her property had never been updated to the present. The latest technology would never been needed. It was still that of the old world. It was forged with the strongest magic to hold in the most powerful of beasts, vampire or others.

She arrived at the lower level and waited for Lane. He crept passed her, leading the way. They rounded the corner and walked down the hall. Her gaze landed on two guards standing before a cell.

The click of her heels along the floor reverberated, announcing her arrival.

"Your Grace," the guards echoed. They pounded their fists to their chests in respect.

She stopped in front of them with Lane. She bit back a growl at the conditions of the cell. She usually didn't give a shit about what the cells looked like, but there was one thing she knew.

They weren't meant for her mate.

Flames flickered in the sconces in the dreary aisle where they were. She didn't see anyone in the cell yet.

"Move aside and open the gate," she murmured.

"But, my lady—"

"Do as your princess said. Now." Lane's deep growl resounded beside her. He stepped forward, towering over one of the guards. His palm rested on the handle of his dagger kept sheathed to his waist.

"Yes, but of course." They bowed and swung away from the bars.

Lethia's gaze landed on a figure sitting on the floor in the corner. Her head resting on her knees. The steel door jerked, swinging open slightly.

Lethia gave Lane a nod and stepped inside. The door closed behind her. She stood staring at the woman who would belong to her. Lethia balled her hands into fists, fighting the urge to dash toward Alima and lift her from the floor.

She needed to see her face. Her eyes. Lethia

wanted to see her mate naked. She was sure she would be perfect.

It was then she got her first wish.

Alima raised her head and gazed upon Lethia.

"You are the vampire who owns me?" Alima's voice was husky and barely audible.

"According to the draft, you are my mate," Lethia responded.

Alima snickered and rested her head back against the wall.

"Like I said, you own me." She eyed Lethia and paused.

She squinted, and it was then Lethia remembered humans were unlike vampires and had poor eyesight in the dark.

"Do you know who I am?" Lethia asked quietly.

"They haven't told me shit," Alima spat. She shifted on the floor and winced. "They snatched me and dragged me here."

"I heard you put up a fight."

"Wouldn't you if someone was kidnapping you and taking you to some unknown place, to some unknown vampire where only God knows what will happen to you?" She pushed the wayward strands of hair that escaped her braids away from her face.

She scowled at Lethia. "Wouldn't you put up a fight?"

"That I would. I can respect that." Lethia folded her arms in front of her. She motioned for Alima. "Come to me."

"Fuck off."

Lethia growled at her response. She pushed down her first instinct to force Alima up. She would give her another chance. Patience. That was what Velika had said she would need if she ever matched to a human.

"I promise, I am not the one to piss off around here," Lethia murmured softly.

"And I promise you that I will escape. You can't keep me here. I have rights." Alima's voice shook with rage.

Lethia inhaled, scenting not only anger radiating from her mate, but fear, too. Lethia narrowed her gaze on the human. She was much smaller than Lethia had anticipated. She, of course, had read her mate's draft intake questionnaire repeatedly until she had it memorized, but it didn't take anything away from the person in front of her.

"Don't make me control you. I'm offering you a chance to do something here of your own free will," Lethia rasped. She could be cruel and compel her human to come to her, but Lethia wanted her to walk to her on her own, taking her in. If she were under Lethia's power, she would have no memories, and Lethia wanted Alima to always remember the first time she had seen her.

"So you are gifting me the ability to stand and walk to you?" Alima huffed. "What a welcoming gift."

"You haven't even begun to feel welcomed by me yet." Lethia snorted. She looked around at the small cell that had no windows, a mat in the other corner that she questioned the cleanliness of, and a hole in the ground for…well, Lethia didn't want to think about what it was for. "You in the dungeon was not how I imagined meeting you. Now get off the fucking floor and come to me."

Alima stared at her for a moment before she pushed off the floor. Lethia, pleased, watched the woman stand to her full height. She tilted her chin up and ambled toward Lethia. She paused a few feet from her.

Lethia could feel Lane standing behind her, watching. She wouldn't need his help. She would be able to control her mate if she decided to try anything like she had on the human guards.

Alima's eyes widened. She was apparently able to make out Lethia's features.

"Shit," she whispered.

"Is that how you greet your mate?" Lethia arched an eyebrow. A small smile came to her lips. "Do you know who I am?"

"You are Lethia Riskel, the princess." Alima's eyes fluttered closed. She shook her head. "Fuck me."

"Oh, don't worry. That will come." Lethia grinned, brandishing her fangs.

"Just kill me and get it over now." Alima's eyes flew open. She sneered at Lethia. "That's why you vampires created this wretched draft so you can have a human to feed from whenever you want."

"You humans don't listen. The draft was more than for feeding," Lethia said. She was getting tired of the misinformation that floated around. Didn't the humans understand what mating meant? A vampire mated for life. Once they sealed the bond with the other half of their soul, there was no turning back. There was no such thing as separation or divorce.

"Do it. Bite me now and drain me dry." Alima yanked on her shirt, exposing her neck.

Lethia eyed her, fighting the urge to take what

she offered. Would she drain her dry? Of course not, but it was too tempting to not take a little sip of her mate.

"Is that what you want? My fangs to sink into your neck?" Lethia stepped forward, her gaze connected with the smooth span of skin exposed. Alima's pulse pounded. Lethia heard the rushing of her mate's blood flowing through her body. It magnified as she drew closer.

Alima's body trembled, and she stared wide-eyed at Lethia.

"I want to be free!" Alima's hand shot out, catching Lethia off guard.

The punch landed in the middle of Lethia's chest. She stumbled back for a moment before righting her footing. It didn't hurt much, but it was a solid hit. Her mate flew at her, arms swinging.

Had she been a human, Alima may have connected. Might even have caused damaged.

But not to Lethia.

She was a seasoned warrior, one of the three Riskel sisters who had trained to fight since they were children. King Niall had placed a sword in all of his daughters' hands by the time they were five years old. He had known all of his children were meant for greatness.

She and her sisters had trained hard their entire lives, never getting a break, having higher expectations to meet than any other warrior around them because of their last name.

Becoming a warden had not been handed to her.

No, each of the Riskel sisters had earned their positions.

Alima would never be an equal when it came to the art of fighting.

Lethia grinned, dodging her mate's advances. She whipped around her, using her vampiric speed, encircling her.

"You will never leave me," Lethia announced.

Alima spun in her direction, but Lethia was too quick for her human eyes in this low light. The scent of Alima's fear permeated the cell. Lethia would love to train her. Help her develop better skills. As the mate to a princess, she would need to know how to protect herself.

She would be a target, and being human made her even more vulnerable.

"Stop that," Alima hollered.

"You belong to me." Lethia moved again once Alima rotated toward her voice.

She swung behind her and wrapped her arms

around her. Alima screamed, trying to break Lethia's hold on her.

Lethia leaned over, her lips brushing against Alima's ear. "Alima Morgan, you are my mate. You will submit to me."

"Never," Alima growled.

She tried to kick backward, but Lethia was able to avoid getting struck. She tightened her arms around her voluptuous woman. The sensation of her mate in her hold was increasing her arousal for Alima.

Her human continued to struggle against her. "I will never stop trying to escape. Ever."

"Then I will convince you to stay."

CHAPTER SEVEN

"Where are you taking me?" Alima demanded. She was once again handcuffed and being dragged to somewhere she didn't want to be. Her gaze landed on the princess walking ahead of her. She tried to beat down her fear of the woman, but it wasn't going anywhere.

Everyone knew of Lethia Riskel, the middle daughter of the vampire king. Of all the vampires she could have been matched with, the gods saw fit to align her with one of the most deadliest vampires around.

And Alima had struck her with her fist.

The vampire princess could have killed her immediately, but she had toyed with Alima. Lethia had been the hunter and Alima the prey in that cell.

I was better off in the cell.

Alima blinked and tried to keep up with the pace of her vampire guards flanking her.

"I said, where are you taking me?" Alima repeated.

They were walking along a maze of hallways. Alima had tried to pay attention to where they were going for her escape, but they had made one too many turns.

But that was okay.

She'd figure out sooner or later how to bust free.

A chill went down her spine remembering Lethia's words.

Alima Morgan, you are my mate. You will submit to me.

What the hell did that mean? Submit to her? Didn't the princess want to drink her blood? Alima had made the crazy offer, desperate to get swift death, asking for her to drain her dry. She grimaced at the memory.

"We are taking you to your quarters." Lethia turned, leveling her with her ice-blue eyes.

Now in the light, Alima could see how beautiful Lethia was in person. The woman had easily taken her on dressed as if she were going to a brunch with some friends. Her heels had her topping six feet in height. The vampire was toned, lithe, and womanly. Alima would have never thought the combination worked, but on Lethia it was natural.

She shivered, thinking how dangerous this woman was. She had moved around that cell like a ghost. Alima hadn't felt or seen her. It was then Alima realized her training with the Rebels hadn't prepared her for someone like Lethia.

A fluttering feeling appeared in her belly at the memory of Lethia holding her. The vampire could have ended her right then and there. Alima had assumed her skin would have been cold against hers, but it was warm, and her floral scent had confused her.

Alima blinked.

Was she attracted to the woman?

Alima's gaze moved back to her. She exuded beauty, wealth, and power.

She was also very deadly.

Especially to humans.

Alima shook her head, trying to ignore the attraction she felt. She needed to escape. This woman was going to kill her. The vampire would take what she wanted and discard Alima like yesterday's trash.

No matter what, she would resist.

Break free then go report her findings to Reed. It was protocol for any Rebel who was captured, and freed no matter how, to report everything they had learned.

"Quarters? For what?" she asked.

Did they have another prison where they kept humans? She glanced around and took in as much as she could. She was shocked at what she could see of the castle. It was a mix of old and new technologies. She had never stepped foot in it before. It overlooked the town from the hills, and she'd always thought it was beautiful.

"For you to clean yourself." Lethia eyed her clothing before turning to a small woman standing at the base of a wide staircase. "I'm sure someone like yourself would appreciate a warm bath, fresh clothing, and a hot meal."

"What's wrong with my clothing?" She already knew the answer, but she had pride, dammit. Her clothes may not be the finest, but they were clean—at least her version of clean.

Lethia chose to ignore her as their entourage arrived at the woman. She was tiny, thin, with brown hair pulled back in a low bun. Her blouse and skirt were black, highlighting her pale skin. She smiled, her fangs peeking from underneath her top lip.

"My lady." The woman bowed her head to Lethia. She lifted her eyes to her princess, a look of respect in them. "I am beyond honored for this opportunity to serve you and your mate."

She turned to Alima, bowing her head as she had done to Lethia.

"You have earned it, Zetta. You have come highly recommended." Lethia rested a hand on the smaller vampire's shoulder and turned to Alima. "This will be your servant. Zetta comes from a long line of personal servants. She will see to your needs."

Alima was taken aback by the notion of having someone serve her. She glanced at the woman whose smile widened.

"I have been highly trained in human and vampire relations, human culture current and past," Zetta announced proudly. "I will also be your guide when it comes to our coven, vampiric traditions, culture, and your role as a new member of the royal family."

Alima glanced down at her cuffed wrists. This was how they greeted and welcomed new members of their royal house?

"Come, let's go upstairs." Lethia beckoned them to follow her.

"Yes, please follow me." Zetta led the group up the stairwell.

It was then Alima took notice of the steel coverings over the windows. She tucked that tidbit of information away. It would make sense to block all sunlight from entering the castle since the vampires were unable to tolerate the sun. Her training had taught her that there weren't many ways to kill a vampire. Decapitation, bleeding them dry, and sunlight.

Do these coverings open at night once the sun is no longer a threat?

Alima would have to wait for nightfall to get her answer. If they did, then she could plot her escape.

They walked up the beautiful winding staircases, stopping two floors from where they'd started. Alima inhaled slowly, seeing she was the only one slightly winded. It didn't help that her hands were restrained in front of her.

A guard stood at each end of the hall. This must be where Lethia resided, but that wasn't what captured her attention, causing her to pause.

The decor captivated her. Alima had never seen such beauty in a home before. She'd seen pictures of homes and mansions previous to the war when humans could afford luxuries. Marble flooring, crystal chandeliers. Expensive, plush rugs lined the floors in certain areas, and tasteful artwork hung on the walls, all giving Alima the sense that she had stepped into a fairy tale.

How strange was it that when she was an innocent little girl, she had fantasized of being a princess and living in the castle that sat perched in the hills. She had been a young child who'd had a vivid imagination. She and her sister had played pretend as young children would do. They dressed up in their mother's dresses and heels.

Joslin had crafted a tiara from a brown paper bag. She had drawn the jewels on it and colored some green, signifying diamonds and emeralds.

"Your Royal Highness, I present your crown." Joslin held out the tiara. She gave a curtsey to Alima.

Their parents had allowed them to play in the yard with

the promise they wouldn't go far away from their small two-bedroom home.

"Why, it is beautiful and fit for a princess." Alima smiled.

Seven-year-old Joslin was a promising artist. She always loved to draw.

Alima bent her head and allowed Joslin to place the crown on her head. She adjusted it, finding it fit her nine-year-old head perfectly. She stood to her full height, finding Joslin kneeling before her.

"Rise, Lady Joslin," Alima commanded. "I thank you for the gift. Now I can rule these lands, and everyone will love my crown."

"So when do we move in there?" Joslin pointed to the castle off in the distance.

Alima shivered, following Joslin's finger. Even as a child, Alima knew the dangers of who lived there.

"Never. That's where the vampire princess lives." Alima suddenly didn't want to play anymore. Her gaze was locked on the castle. Her parents had always warned them about going near it and any vampires they came across.

Vampires were deadly.

"But if you moved there then you'd be a real princess and could help everyone."

Alima blinked, coming back from her memories. She had all but forgotten the days where she and Joslin had been innocent children with wild imaginations. A trail of warm tears coated her cheeks. She hadn't realized she was crying. She sniffed and raised her restrained hands to her face to wipe them away.

"What is it?" Lethia's gaze landed on her. She stepped in front of Alima, curiosity in her stare.

"Nothing." Alima bit back a grimace when she saw everyone was looking at her.

"It doesn't seem like nothing." Lethia reached up with her hand.

Alima jerked back away from her.

"Leave it alone." Alima cleared her throat and tilted her chin up. Crying wasn't what she needed right now in front of the vampires. That she would do when alone, but for now, she would be strong and see what awaited her.

Lethia studied her for a moment longer before turning on her heel. She nodded to Zetta who was waiting at the front of the group. They continued on, only this time Lethia walked beside Alima.

"I have prepared the suite that you requested and made sure it would be appropriate for your mate." Zetta stopped in front of two massive wooden doors that stood at least double her height.

They were old, engraved with symbols and words that were in some other language.

Alima wanted to reach out and touch them but kept her hands to herself.

"There shall always be a guard posted at this entrance," Lethia announced.

"Yes, my lady," the two echoed.

Alima bit her lip. Her chances of sneaking out through the doors was dwindling. There was no way she would be able to take on three vampire guards.

"So I am a prisoner." Alima snorted.

"No, you are my mate." Lethia closed the gap between them. Her ice-blue eyes grew iridescent while she stared at Alima.

"Handcuffs, guards…sounds like a prison to me," Alima retorted.

"The guards are for your safety, and as for the handcuffs, they will be for pleasure."

Alima's mouth dropped open. She stared at the vampire who turned and walked into the room ahead of her.

What did she just say?

"Go on," a gruff voice sounded.

She stumbled forward from a shove from behind. She righted her footsteps before turning to glare at the culprit. The guard had a scowl on his face, accented by a scar that ran along his eyebrow to mid-cheek. Vampires, Alima assumed, healed quickly, leaving no scars. This guard must be a turned vampire. Alima's curiosity was growing. Human guards, turned vampires, vampires serving humans—what else would she discover here?

"Touch her again and you will face me in the pits." Lethia's voice was eerily soft and chilling.

His gaze flickered to the princess, and his already pale skin lost even more color. He immediately cast his eyes to the floor.

"My apologies, Your Grace. I didn't mean anything by it." His fist pounded his left breast. "I would never intentionally harm your mate."

Alima turned around and, one look at Lethia, even she took a step back. The deadly princess' gaze was hard, revealing her killing nature. This was no longer the wealthy, vampire princess who enjoyed luxuries that Alima could never fathom.

Before them stood the warrior princess, commander of the eastern armies who fought and won battles. Alima had heard of the tales of the Riskel sisters. What human who lived on the northern continent hadn't? Their stories were legendary. Too bad the most recent battles of war were against humans.

The pits?

That didn't sound good, and Alima almost pitied the guard.

Almost.

He shouldn't have pushed her.

"My ladies. Please allow me the opportunity to show you around," Zetta said, breaking the tension.

Lethia blinked, then switched her attention to Alima. She quickly gave her the once-over as if ensuring Alima was unharmed.

"Stay at the door." She sent another chilling glare to the guards, returning her attention to Zetta. Lethia cupped Alima's elbow and guided her into the suite.

Now that she could see where she'd be staying, Alima's gaze widened. Her suite apparently had a foyer in it. She tried to keep her awe in control. Her gaze took it all in as they entered the bedroom. It was larger than her apartment she had shared back at the compound.

Hell, it was larger than her childhood home.

A big king-sized bed was the center point. There was an area with couches and a fireplace. Floor-to-ceiling windows filled the room, but they were blocked by the steel coverings. Alima felt a slight hint of disappointment at not being able to see the view.

A chandelier hung from the ceiling casting bright light in the room. It shined like clear diamonds filled it.

This was the life of luxury at its finest. There were additional doors that were closed.

"This is my room?" Alima gasped.

If this was hers, what did Lethia's look like? She swallowed hard and spun around and stared at the princess who was quietly studying her. Alima shifted her gaze to Zetta. She was safer to look at.

"Yes, ma'am. Do you like it?" Zetta paused as if holding her breath.

"It's gorgeous," Alima breathed.

Zetta beamed, waving for them to follow. Alima ambled behind her. She sensed Lethia trailing after them. Zetta revealed an unbelievable walk-in closet. There were so many clothes and shoes in it. There was no way they could be for her.

"We took the measurements that were submitted and filled this with everything you could potentially need," Zetta said from the doorway.

Alima slowly made her way into it, her mouth agape. She moved around and eyed Lethia.

"You paid for all of this?" she asked.

"Of course. The delay in finding you gave us more time. But if none of it is to your liking, we can replace it all with whatever you like." Lethia leveled her with her icy gaze.

Alima tried to not show excitement at the prospect of owning such nice clothes. The little girl in her was screaming and jumping up and down. The urge to tear her clothes off and try everything on was burning bright.

No.

You are not staying, she reminded herself. *You are going to escape and leave. You will not become a vampire's play toy.*

Plus, Alima knew this all came with a price.

"I'm sure it is all fine. I wouldn't know anything about the latest fashions." Alima gave a tight smile.

They walked toward the next door that led to the bathroom. Alima again paused in the doorway. This was too much. Why would Lethia put her in such an extravagant room?

A clawfoot tub was the centerpiece. More marbled flooring, and exposed wood beams on the ceiling that matched the woodwork in her bedroom and the foyer. A walk-in shower behind a wall of glass, magnificent tile work along the walls and the sink vanity, a separate privacy room for the toilet, all were luxuries she could not get used to.

Once they'd finished the tour around the suite, Alima's gaze landed on an additional door Zetta had not mentioned.

"Where does that lead?" Alima jerked her chin toward the mystery exit. She prayed it was to some secret stairwell that would take her to the main level of the castle.

"That is the doorway to my private quarters," Lethia answered. A devilish grin, showcasing her fangs, spread across her face. "I'm sure it will be a door you use frequently."

"I doubt that." Alima snorted.

"Don't be so quick to dismiss something you know nothing about." Lethia strolled over to her with an air of confidence.

The woman was so sure Alima would fall for her. Just because she was wealthy, powerful, a warrior, and gorgeous didn't mean Alima would allow her to use her body for blood and other things.

Looking into Lethia's eyes, Alima knew the vampire princess was wanting more than blood.

Alima tore her gaze from her and glanced down at her wrists. They were raw and bruised. The skin had broken open from how tight the cuffs were placed on her.

"Bring me the keys." Lethia snapped her fingers at the guards standing by the doorway.

Scarface brought her the key, not meeting her gaze.

Lethia closed the gap between them. "Lift your arms."

Her gaze narrowed on Alima's wrist. A low growl escaped her while she inserted the key into the restraint. The cuffs opened, slipping off her. Alima inhaled sharply at the stinging pain that coursed through her. Lethia uttered a curse under her breath. She tossed the key and cuff to Scarface.

Lethia snatched Alima's arm and quickly brought it to her lips. Alima cried out, jerking on her arm to bring it back to her, but Lethia's grip was strong.

"What are you doing?" Alima gasped.

Lethia's warm tongue skated around the mangled skin of her right wrist.

"Stop moving," Lethia growled.

Alima halted her struggle at the sight of Lethia's iridescent eyes. Her breath caught in her throat. The way Lethia stared at her had her experiencing what a small animal would feel when knowing a predator had caught sight of them.

Her lungs screamed for her air, but she dared not move. Lethia continued, moving to her other wrist. Alima gasped. If she hadn't seen it with her own eyes, she wouldn't have believed it.

Her skin was slowly restoring to its former state. There wasn't even a scar.

"How—? What the—?" Her gaze met Lethia's. Shock filled her. What sorcery was this?

Hunger burned in Lethia's eyes. Her hold on Alima tightened. A growl rumbled from her chest. She licked the small traces of blood from her lips, her sharp fangs peeking from underneath her lips.

"Your Grace. Let's allow Ms. Morgan a chance to settle in and get cleaned up." Zetta sidled up beside the princess. Her voice was soft, but there was a weird expression in her eyes.

Lethia blinked, coming out of whatever trance she was in.

"But of course." Lethia released Alima abruptly and stepped back. She ran her hands along her pants. The princess appeared rattled. She marched to the door. "See that she is bathed and dressed. There is much for us to do today."

Alima stared at her wrists in amazement. The

damage done by the handcuffs was no longer visible.

"Come, Ms. Morgan. Allow me to assist you." Zetta offered a strained smile.

Alima watched the door shut behind Lethia.

What in the world was that?

CHAPTER EIGHT

Lethia tried to rein in the bloodlust coursing through her body. Her intention had been to heal her mate. She'd sensed Alima was experiencing pain from the handcuffs. Her skin had been mangled, raw, and bleeding slightly. The enzymes in her saliva would heal her, but it came at a cost.

One taste of her mate's blood was throwing Lethia into a frenzy. The need to drink from Alima was intense. Thankfully, Zetta must have sensed that Lethia was on the verge of the blood madness. Not many vampires experienced it, but few did who could not consume the blood of their mates.

This may happen if the mate held out on sealing the bond. Or if the mate died before the bond could be sealed. Whatever the reason for not consuming the blood of a mate, a vampire could go insane, and in their blind lust, they could do some damage to their mate.

Why would it hit her so fast?

She'd had only a few licks of Alima's wrists, that shouldn't have triggered it.

She would have to offer Zetta a bonus for recognizing that Lethia may do something like biting her unwillingly.

Lethia stalked away from her mate's private quarters and went into her own. She slammed the door and leaned on it, trying to catch her breath. There were many things she wanted to do to Alima, but Lethia would have to stay in control.

She needed Alima to want to mate with her. That would make the bond between them blossom. It was already growing. Lethia could feel the pull to be near Alima. Soon, her human would experience the need for Lethia, she'd want the bite of her mate.

Lethia could not wait to teach her the joys of being with a vampire. Once they had completed the bond, Alima would enjoy a long life and live beside Lethia.

Pushing off the door, she continued on into her master suite. She took in the room and couldn't wait for the day she would share it with Alima. For now, she would remain in her own room until she was ready.

Lethia changed her clothes. There was only one thing that could take her mind off mating, and that was training. Within minutes, she no longer resembled a wealthy member of the royal family.

She paused in front of the floor-length mirror and took in her reflection.

Her black leather tunic showcased her well-defined bicep muscles, and her matching pants looked as if they were melted on her. Her knee-high boots gave her additional height. She restrained her hair then grabbed three favorite daggers, arranging them along her body.

Today was training for new recruits in her army. She wanted to go observe her new vampire warriors. One thing her father had taught all of his daughters was they had to make their presence known to the vampires who wore their colors and fight for them. The Riskel princesses all rode alongside their warriors.

They were very hands-on, and it helped the morale of the army to see their commander fighting with them. Neither Lethia, Velika, nor Hegna would send their warriors to fight without them joining in. Even the king donned his armor and picked up his sword.

The royal family would all die to protect their people.

This was a tradition and how she and her sisters had been raised. Any vampire with the Riskel name was a protector of their race.

Lethia stepped out of her quarters and glanced in the direction of Alima's door. The urge to return to her was strong, but she pushed it aside. Turning away, she marched off, focusing on what she had to do today. Zetta would take care Alima, that was why she'd been hired.

Lethia forced herself to leave that level of the castle. Since it was still daytime, her warriors would be training in the indoor facility.

She made her way through the castle. Most of the workers she passed here human. A few vampires lingered around. For them, this was the late shift.

She arrived at the lower level that would take her to the tunnels. A century ago, tunnels were built that connected the facilities in the grounds. The warriors would be in the training facility. It, too, was outfitted with steel window coverings that allowed them to safely use the building without the sun's harmful rays attacking them.

The tunnels were constructed to allow them to move around during the day.

In Maine, the sun wasn't as strong as the southern parts of the continent, but it still did damage to vampires.

"Your Grace." Lane stepped from the darkened entrance. He lowered his head in a bow before meeting her gaze.

"Lane. What are you doing up?"

"Figured I'd train and beat up on the new recruits." He grinned, showcasing his fangs. The former human had certainly taken to vampirism. It was almost as if the gods had gotten his former life wrong. He embodied vampirism. Once she had turned him, he had gone through the horrific changes, but he'd come out stronger.

He was a natural-born hunter.

Lethia had never regretted making him into what he was today. He had been a great asset to her and was a loyal friend.

"Leave any of them for me?" She arched an eyebrow.

He motioned for her to join him. "Of course."

They walked down the darkened tunnel. It was formed during a time before modern technology was available. Stone walls, and sconces lit with fire provided light for them. The tunnels were narrow but sturdy.

"What do you think of them?" She was always looking for improvement, and speaking with Lane allowed her to get insight on someone who had been through the process as an outsider. He'd had to shed the little bit of humanity he had when transitioning to a vampire and to be a guard for the royal princess.

In order to assume the honored role of guardian of a princess, the vampire had to be deadly and pledge their life to their charge. Lane had proven himself countless times. When it was discovered that his sister was alive and well with Velika, Lethia had allowed Lane the choice.

Go and be with his sister—Velika would have welcomed him to her coven—or he could remain with her. She'd been honored when he'd decided to stay with her coven. Lane was not a prisoner, and since his sister was the mate of *her* sister, he was allowed to go and visit. With the upcoming birth of Velika and Quinn's child, they would be traveling soon to meet the first of the new Riskel generation.

"There are a few who have great potential. Fast. Hungry for battle and blood."

"You shall point them out to me when we arrive." She grinned. This was just what she needed to keep her mind off Alima and the sweet taste of her blood. Lethia's smile disappeared, the hunger for her mate reappearing.

The desire for her was already coursing through her. The need to take her was strong, and the universe was demanding she do what she was born to do. She was not going to have as much as time as she thought she would have.

Take, mate, and cherish.

It was the way of vampires.

Her fangs descended with the thought of piercing Alima's soft flesh. The sweetness would fill her mouth then flow down her throat. She'd drink it in, then in return, give Alima a gift of her own.

Eternal life.

"Can't wait to see you whip them into shape. Their cockiness needs to be brought down to another level." Lane's chuckle broke through her thoughts.

She inhaled and channeled the energy that

burned inside her for her mate to having her warriors on the mat.

She increased her pace.

Fighting was just what she needed now.

"I won't have any problems with that."

* * *

"DO YOU YIELD?" Lethia growled. She rested her foot on the chest of the new warrior. The tip of the sword she'd stolen in the fight was now pressed against another warrior's throat. The young vampires needed to be educated on who they fought for.

They, like the enemy, had taken it for granted that she was a female.

Forgetting her last name was Riskel.

But that was all right. She'd completely proved why she was their commander and hadn't even broken a sweat. The two warriors stared at her. One had fear in his eyes while the other held a look of envy.

"Yield," the one under her boot mumbled.

"Aye. I yield, too." The one under the sword raised his palms to her.

She grunted, stepping away from them. Turning, she nodded to Dru. Her second-in-command was fighting a smile. Lethia had bested the two cocky warriors in under five minutes. She held the sword in her hand and saw it was a crude practice one that wouldn't even slice a strand of her hair.

"What mistake did they make?" Dru asked. She stepped from the sideline and faced the sea of warriors.

The two vampires dragged themselves off the floor. The confidence they once had was now gone.

"Getting in a fight with the commander?" a light voice came from the middle of the crowd.

Chuckles went around.

"Who said that?" Lethia asked. She tossed the sword to the mat. A hand went up. "Come forward."

The men parted to reveal a short female who was sweaty and in her fighting leathers. Her dark hair was pulled up in a high bun, and a sword was sheathed on her hip. Her eyes were wide and full of fear as she met Lethia's gaze.

"Now why would you feel the answer was to battle the commander?" Lethia asked.

The young female swallowed hard. She tore her attention away and looked around at her fellow warriors. No one would meet her gaze.

"Because they are inexperienced and were too full of themselves. Before fighting you, they should have watched you spar with someone else first. Did their research first."

The silence in the room was deafening. No one knew how she was going to respond. Dru gave a nod to the young warrior.

"What is your name?" Lethia asked. She was impressed with the female's insight. She was correct that they should have watched her. But they were too anxious to get in the circle with her to prove themselves. There was always one or two who believed they were the best to ever wield a sword. Lethia wasn't too surprised since Lane had given her a heads-up about a few of the warriors.

But Lethia was only too happy to put them in their place.

"You are correct, Sunni," Dru answered, jumping in.

The girl relaxed as if she had thought they would punish her.

"A good fighter would know when to engage an enemy," Dru went on. "A good warrior would know when to avoid an enemy that is too great."

Nods went around as understanding dawned on them.

This was a learning curve for their new recruits. It would be a while before any of them would be put on the front lines in battle. Lethia's army was mighty, and it took much training. Even the most experienced warriors still trained to keep their skills sharp.

"That is true." All eyes fell on Lethia. She motioned to the two young vampires. "When you have your brothers or sisters fighting by your side, you are to work together. That is how we defeat our enemies. Through teamwork. On the battlefield, it is not just one warrior running off to battle but an army. We will stand together."

"Partner off. Three to each group," Dru ordered. "In the next week, teams will battle. We're going to test your ability to work together."

Lethia was satisfied with her second-in-command's process for new recruits. As they began finding others to partner up with, Lethia motioned for Dru and Lane to join her. They came to stand at her side.

"What do you really think of this group?" she asked. Both of their opinions mattered to her.

The new recruits sparred with each other. Lethia, being the trained warrior she was, saw plenty of room for improvement. These young vampires had a long way to go.

Years ago, Dru had asked for permission to work with the new recruits. It would give Lethia's captains a chance to focus on the more experienced warriors and planning battle strategies. It was a great idea that Lethia had endorsed. Her army was stronger, and those who made it through Dru's strict training were allowed to join the ranks of warrior.

"Just give me some time. We have some good prospects," Dru said.

"I agree," Lane murmured. His gaze moved around the training room. "Give them time. We have huge expectations for them to meet."

"But of course we do. If we don't set the bar high, then we will all be killed. The enemy will exploit our weaknesses. My army is what protects our people." Lethia's gaze landed on the young female. Her form with a sword was damn near perfect. She almost reminded Lethia of a younger version of herself. "This Sunni, I want you to keep an eye on her. She has much promise."

At that moment, the tiny female flipped her much bigger opponent over her shoulder and pressed her sword to his neck. Her gaze moved across the room and met Lethia's. A blush stole across her face before she turned away.

"I figured you would say that." Dru gave an approving nod. "I'm almost tempted to test her on a small special team."

"I read most of your report you submitted." Lethia folded her arms in front of her chest. Everything about the lycans being in her territory didn't sit well with her. "I want you to leave a team to keep an eye on the lycans. I want to know every move."

"You're wanting to know if their alpha arrives." Dru chuckled.

"Yes. Whoever you send, I want Sunni with them. Let her get a taste of reconnaissance work." Lethia gave a nod. She remembered a time when she'd got her first break as a young warrior in training. There had been an older vampire who'd extended a hand to her. Lethia only felt it was right for her to do the same for a new recruit.

"Won't be a problem. I know the perfect vampires to take her under their wings."

They turned and took in the teams sparring with each other. Lethia's sharp gaze roamed the room. She had a good feeling about this group.

"Want to show them how it's done?" Lane murmured. His eyes held a twinkle in them.

"You sure you want to embarrass yourself?" Lethia arched an eyebrow at him.

She had personally trained Lane under her. He had been an eager student and a natural fighter. Maybe sparring with her guard would be just what she needed to keep her mind off Alima. The human kept creeping into her thoughts. Maybe fighting a tough opponent such as Lane would keep her from entering her mind.

"Look, if you don't want to lose in front of—"

"Pick your weapon," she growled. The fierce competitor in her flared to life.

Lane knew she hated to lose. His grin widened as he backed away.

Dru laughed and called out for everyone's attention. Soon, Lethia was facing Lane on the main mat. Her two daggers rested on her waist. This fight would include real weapons. Lethia didn't worry about injuries. Being a vampire allowed her to have swift healing.

The air was filled with excitement as the recruits watched. Lethia took notice of how the females were separated from the males. Lethia grinned. Women always stuck together.

"My royal guard has taken it upon himself to challenge me." Lethia smirked.

They circled one another. They had trained and fought each other many times, and she was well aware of his habits, just as he was familiar with hers.

"The point I want to prove is that with much practice a vampire could be worthy to protect their princess," Lane said. A growl ripped from him as he dove toward her, attacking her first. He pulled his sword out of the sheath on his back, swinging it at her.

Lethia blocked his advance with her daggers. Gasps went up at the display of sheer force Lane showed. Lethia wouldn't have it any other way. If he were to try to go easy on her, she'd punish him for it.

Advice she'd always lived by was to *practice as of this was real life.*

Lethia clenched her teeth at the power Lane had when his sword landed on her blades. If one did not know his story it would be assumed he was a born vampire. He used power, she used speed and wit. Spinning around, she slipped behind him, but he already anticipated her move and spun with her. His sword blocked her daggers.

Their speed increased as they fought.

Lane managed to draw blood, just as she did. They didn't hold back from each other. They were both excellent fighters, and neither of them would want to lose.

She moved in close, but he caught her by the arm, sending her flying to the mat. She rolled to the side, missing the edge of his sword as he buried it into the mat. The energy in the room grew electric. She was sure the warriors were shocked that Lane would be so bold as to put his hand on her, much less toss her like a doll.

But Lethia wasn't one to stay down. She was a dirty fighter and wasn't above using anything she had to win.

Lethia bared her fangs and swept her legs near his, connecting with his ankles. Lane tripped over her and fell backward onto the mat.

She refused to lose.

Losing was not in her nature.

Using her speed, she landed on top of him, her blade to his neck. She grinned, pressing it deep into his skin, enough to draw blood.

The room fell quiet.

Lane growled his disappointment. Apparently,

even her guard thought he would best her in front of the group.

"Do. You. Yield?" she ground out through clenched teeth. Tendrils of her hair broke free and fell into her eyes.

He held her gaze, and she could read all of the emotions passing through his eyes. She pressed harder, daring him to move. He didn't flinch at the blade piercing his skin. She arched an eyebrow, waiting for him to answer.

"Yield."

CHAPTER NINE

She shouldn't like it, but she did. In fact, she loved it. Alima snuggled down under the covers and breathed in sharply. She had never had an entire bed to herself. Especially not one this comfortable, with plush pillows, silky sheets, and a heavy blanket that kept her warm. Sleep had claimed her almost immediately.

She'd closed her eyes and remembered her shower she'd had. Back in the compound they were limited, and the water was always lukewarm. But the one she'd taken last night was long, luxurious, with steam filling the room. Alima had scrubbed her skin until it glowed. She was embarrassed by the dark water that flowed down the drain when she had rinsed off.

Zetta had a small tray of food delivered, and she'd eaten everything but the plate, bowls, cups, and silverware. There was no shame in enjoying the wonderful food that had been cooked.

Alima opened her eyes and stared at the ceiling. She could not get used to this. Life in a castle was not meant for her and certainly not as the mate of a vampire.

She was going to escape.

There were many obstacles that would stand in her way.

First off, her room's windows were secured with thick steel coverings. Alima rolled over and stared at the monstrosities. They were on automated timers according to Zetta. Which would mean at night, they would lift.

Then there were the guards posted outside her door. There would be no sneaking out of her room via that entrance. Her only option would be the window, but she was on the third floor, and there was no telling what was outside her room.

Rolling back over, she sighed.

Any escape would have to be calculated and put

into play when she was not in her room. Patience was going to be something she'd have to learn.

Bringing the covers up higher, she nestled against her pillow. She was unsure of the time and thought maybe she could go back to sleep. She hadn't realized how tired she'd been. The last twenty-four hours had been taxing.

But if she went back to sleep then those dreams would plague her again.

All of them had included Lethia.

The blonde had been in each one. Alima couldn't even remember ever having such vivid sex dreams. Her body was tense with sexual need. Her core clenched remembering the sight of Lethia licking her wrists. Her tongue had snuck out and trailed along the markings of the handcuffs.

It had been so damn erotic.

She should have been turned off by it, but she just couldn't shake the memory of Lethia's eyes transforming, her fangs peeking from underneath her lips, and the flames of desire that burned in her gaze.

"Nooo…" Alima murmured.

How could she be attracted to the vampire princess? The woman was the most powerful person in their town, state, and territory.

She was the daughter of the vampire king.

But right now, with the memories floating through from her dreams, Alima's body was craving a release. The visions that came to her were downright sinful. It had been a long time since she'd had sex, and it hadn't even been a thought when trying to save humanity. Helping her fellow humans had been her purpose. Saving all of those when her own sister's life had been taken.

Would it hurt to indulge in fantasies that only she knew about?

Her body was overheating.

In her dream, Lethia had her naked and spread out on a massive bed that was large enough to fit six adults comfortably. That tongue of hers had slid through Alima's folds, teasing her clit and her core.

Alima tried to control her breathing but was unable to. The scene was too vivid as if it had really happened. Had she not known better, she would have said it had been real.

She flipped onto her back and tried again.

Inhale slowly.

Exhale.

These fantasies were wrong, but her traitorous body apparently didn't know any better. Without even checking, she knew her pussy was slick with desire.

Frustrated, she dove her hand underneath the covers and slipped it beneath her nightgown. The cotton material was tangled around her legs. A strangled moan escaped her at her confirmation that indeed she was aroused. Her folds were slick, and her clit was swollen and achy. Her back arched off the mattress when her finger connected with her little bundle of nerves.

Alima snatched her hand back.

No, she couldn't do this.

Sexual release was not as important as escaping and gaining her freedom.

No matter how sexy the vampire was. Or how many orgasms she'd given in a dream.

Alima's heart pounded. Her body screamed for her to continue, but she had more important things she had to do. She tossed her legs to the side of the bed and sat up.

What was wrong with her?

A knock sounded at the door before it flew open with Zetta entering her room. She shut the door behind her and paused, offering her a slight bow of her head.

"Good evening. I hope you slept well," Zetta said.

"Surprisingly, I did," Alima murmured. Her cheeks warmed thinking of what she had just contemplated doing in her bed. Now she was glad she had resisted. That would have been embarrassing to be caught giving herself pleasure.

"Well, I am to get you ready and give you a tour of the castle." Zetta zipped over to the closet and disappeared inside it.

"Really?" Alima perked up at this information. Getting to know the layout of the building would certainly aide her in her plans.

"So I'm not a prisoner?" she asked. She hopped down from the massive bed and walked over to the entrance of the closet.

Zetta pulled items off the hangers and placed them on the island that sat perched in the middle of the room. "Of course not. But the princess has ordered the guards to remain with you." Zetta avoided her eyes.

"That sounds like a prisoner to me," Alima said dryly. She leaned against the doorjamb, watching the vampire put an outfit together for her.

"Well, you threatened to leave, and we can't

have that." Zetta turned to her with clothing draped across her arm.

"Why does it matter?"

Zetta brushed past her and went over to the bed, dropping the items on to it. Alima followed, ambling behind her.

"Why does she care? She can go back to the draft and find another human to drink from." Alima shivered. Her hand went to her neck automatically.

What would it feel like to have Lethia sink her sharp fangs into her skin? Would there be pain? Alima had heard of some humans who got a thrill of being bitten, signing up to be live donors. What was the draw? Wasn't it painful?

"Do you know anything of vampires?" Zetta asked. She narrowed her eyes on Alima. She folded her arms. "If you did, you would know that vampires only ever have one mate. That person is perfect for them. Fate has deemed their mate is to be with them for all eternity. Now that she has you, my princess won't have to spend her life alone."

Zetta's chest rose and fell swiftly. Longing was evident on her face.

"You've entered the draft," Alima stated.

"I hope, wish, and pray every day to be

matched. I've saved up money my entire life so that I'm blessed by the gods to have a mate and we will be able to live a good life."

"How old are you?" Alima asked.

Zetta didn't look a day over twenty five.

"I am seventy-five," Zetta replied.

Alima walked over to the edge of the bed and took in the clothes laid out for her. She touched the soft fabric.

"But what about what the human wants? Do you know anything about us?" Alima arched an eyebrow at the vampire. "If so, then you would know that humans don't like having their rights and choices taken away."

"Neither of us will win this argument." Zetta sighed. She cupped Alima's elbow and guided her toward the bathroom.

Alima had the urge to shake her off, but she decided to behave. She didn't want to let on that she was going to rebel.

* * *

ALIMA GLANCED AROUND, taking in the grounds of the castle. It was much more than she had expected. This was the first time she'd ever been here. The moon was high. After assisting her to get dressed, Zetta had taken her around to showcase the beautiful building. Alima had to admit the castle was breathtaking. It reminded her of the fantasies she had when she was a young, innocent girl dreaming of becoming a princess.

It was hundreds of years old and still kept in immaculate condition. History surrounded her at every turn. Even though she was silently memorizing the layout of what was shown to her, she couldn't help but appreciate what she saw.

Now they were outside walking through the courtyard. Parts of the castle surrounded it. It led out to a beautiful garden, fields, and even a stable. There were other buildings that came in sight as they continued on their stroll.

Alima glanced behind her to find one of the guards trailing her and Zetta.

"Does he have to walk so close?" she asked. "It's not like I can outrun him."

"Not only are the guards here to make sure you don't run away, but for your protection, too," Zetta murmured. She strode along beside Alima with her hands clasped in front of her.

"What do you mean, my protection?" Alima

eyed the vampire. Who would try to harm her here?

"There are plenty of people, human, vampire, and others who will know the princess has found her mate. Because of that, you will have a target on your back."

"What does that mean, and why would they come for me? Just because I am her mate? How would they know that?" Alima paused and faced Zetta. Something else she had said captured her attention. She stared at the vampire. "Others? I'm confused. If not human or vampire, who else would want to hurt me for being Lethia's mate?"

She hated to ask the question. She didn't want to consider herself Lethia's mate at all.

"You humans just don't get it, do you. There are more than just humans and vampires roaming this world." She stepped closer to Alima. She gave an exasperated sigh and shook her head. "You should be honored that fate chose to give you Lethia Riskel as a mate. The moment your name became connected with hers, your life was in danger. Vampires have had many enemies since the first vampire was documented. One enemy that hates vampires more than humans has surfaced. They are more powerful than your people could ever be, and if our princess and her sisters can't stop them, then we will all be in danger, including humans."

"Who is that?" Alima whispered while her heart raced. This was craziness that she had never heard. She wondered if Reed knew there was something out there besides vampires.

"Lycans. It is rumored that they are growing in numbers and will want a war. You think you hate vampires, you wouldn't want to try your luck with those wolves."

Alima froze in place, watching Zetta walk away from her. She blinked and scurried to try to keep up with her. That couldn't be true. She was sure Reed or some of the other human leaders would have shared this information with them.

"Are you serious? You expect me to believe that there are people out there who can change into a wolf?" Alima said incredulously.

The guard behind her snorted.

She spun around and flared at him.

"Is there something you want to say?" Alima growled. She was tired of these vampires telling her how she should be grateful, that she should be honored to be matched with a princess bloodsucker, and how her choices basically didn't matter.

"I'm just surprised you don't believe there are such a thing as lycans. How can humans be so ignorant?"

"Remus, be careful of how you speak to Ms. Morgan. She is the mate to your princess." Zetta leveled him with a hard glare.

"I mean no disrespect." Remus gave a brief nod to Alima. He was tall with dark hair braided back away from his face. His electric-blue eyes were vivid even with the moonlight shining down. The courtyard was lit with soft lights that hung from the building. "As the future princess who will sit alongside our very own Princess Lethia, I am honored to be a part of your protection detail. Please know that myself and Magna will protect you with our lives."

Alima's glance jerked over to the other vampire guard standing back farther than Remus. Her attention was captured by another figure. A tall black man walked alongside her, dressed in a formal uniform.

Lethia.

Her long blonde hair flowed behind her as she confidently made her way to them. She was dressed in a black one-piece ensemble that looked as if she were poured into it. She drew closer, and Alima could see her eyes were darkened with eyeliner, flawless makeup, and ruby-red lips. Her hardened muscles appeared softer in the outfit.

She arrived in front of Alima and reached out a gentle hand, tipping Alima's chin up so their eyes could meet.

"My mate," she breathed. Her crystal-blue eyes studied Alima. "How goes the tour?"

Alima found herself tongue-tied in Lethia's presence. Her heart rate increased, while her breaths grew faster. The memories of her dreams came rushing forward.

What was wrong with her? She found herself stepping closer to Lethia.

Lethia's smirk had her jerking back. Alima was unsure what this was between them, but she didn't like it. Just like she didn't like how Lethia's gaze seemed to see into her soul.

Those dreams of hers were going to remain her secret.

Why wasn't she being mean to Alima? Weren't vampires supposed to be driven by the need to feed?

"The tour was going just fine," Alima replied. She cleared her throat, suddenly finding it dry.

Lethia gave a nod and turned her gaze to Zetta.

"I can take her from here," Lethia said.

"Are you sure, Your Grace?" Zetta asked.

"Yes, I'm sure. It would do me some good to spend some time with my mate." Lethia looked behind at the two guards and jerked her chin to them. "We will be fine from here. My mate won't be able to escape me."

The three hesitated at first but must have seen something in Lethia's eyes that had them bowing to her.

"Yes, Your Grace," they echoed.

Lethia rested her hand on the small of Alima's back, drawing her close. She guided her away from the castle.

"Come, *miere*. Let's take a walk," Lethia murmured.

Alima's muscles tensed. This was the first time she would be alone with the princess, and she wasn't sure what to think. They continued through the courtyard where a few people strolled along. Alima tried to relax, but the warmth of Lethia's body was drawing her to her.

"Where are we going?" Alima asked.

They rounded a corner that led to an area with

a beautiful garden on the outskirts of the yard. The castle walls no longer covered them. Past the garden were a few other structures that were resting on the property.

From afar, Alima had always assumed it was just a castle on a hill. But the structure was like a little town on its own. Since leaving the inside and coming outside, she had seen plenty of vampires and humans alike on the grounds. They all appeared to get along, some even working together.

This was a scene she had never expected to see.

Her entire life she had been told vampires were the enemy.

She inhaled, enjoying the scents of the flowers that were planted along the trail. The wind blew, and even though it was warm, she still felt a chill. Zetta had chosen a light white shirt with a pair of soft linen pants that tied at the waist. She had refused to allow Zetta to do her hair. Alima had chosen to re-braid it into her two plaits she normally wore. Her hair was in its natural state. She usually kept it washed, oiled, and braided. She was proud of its length. It had taken her years to grow it to her mid back.

She turned and hadn't realized they had walked so far from the castle. They approached a wooded area near one of the structures. The rays from the moon was the only light that allowed her to see. She turned back and found Lethia watching her.

"Why are you staring at me?" Alima sniffed.

"I want to know what you think of the castle. This is to be your home." Lethia shrugged. She motioned to the path that disappeared into the woods.

"Well, it's beautiful, but it will not be my home." Alima folded her arms. Darkness sealed them into the woods. Alima slowed her pace, taking in the area. She glanced where the moon would have been, but it was hidden by the tops of the trees. "I can't see. Maybe we should turn back."

"There's nothing for you to be afraid about," Lethia murmured. She drew closer to Alima, closing the gap between them. Her hand slid along Alima's arm. "There is nothing in these woods that will hurt you while I'm here."

Her massive grin showcased her fangs.

"Let me guess, you are the big bad predator?" Alima arched an eyebrow. She stepped back from Lethia. It was dangerous being too close to her. Again, her body was responding to the vampire. Her nipples pressed against her bra, begging to be let out. Her core pulsated while her skin was covered in goosebumps. The scent of Lethia's perfume drifted through the air. Alima found herself wanting to bury her face into the crook of Lethia's neck to inhale it.

She walked backward away from the vampire, trying to put some space between them. Her thoughts were jumbled when near her.

"Then you would be correct. Did you notice you don't hear any animals in the woods? Not even the nocturnal ones?" Lethia stalked toward Alima, her body moving as a predator would.

Alima looked around and saw the path led farther into the woods. She wondered what was on the other side of it. Would it lead her to town? There may never be another chance for her to find out.

"I'm not afraid of you," Alima whispered. She took off running. She pumped her arms as fast as she could.

The sound of Lethia's laughter echoed through the air behind her. She gasped, trying to draw in as much air as she could. Her feet pounded on the dirt path. Her heart raced while she strained to hear Lethia.

Alima did something stupid and glanced over her shoulder and didn't see any sign of Lethia.

The base of her stomach seemed to drop away.

Shit.

Where was she?

Lethia's laughter carried along the wind, but there was no sign of her. Alima faced forward and tried to push herself faster. She broke through a clearing. The trees parted, allowing the moon's rays to shine down on her. She spun around in a circle, seeing four pathways.

"Fuck," she whispered. Which way did she go?

"So determined," Lethia said.

Alima rushed toward the path nearest her. She panicked, now realizing this was a bad idea.

She couldn't outrun a vampire.

How the hell had she forgotten about their super speed? Alima came to a halt when Lethia suddenly appeared in front of her.

"I can hear your blood rushing in your veins." Lethia's devilish grin spread wide. "Did you really think you could run from me?"

Alima headed toward another path but skidded to a stop when Lethia appeared before her again.

"Stop doing that!" Alima screamed. She backed away from Lethia. Her heart was practically in her throat.

"I think it's so cute how you think you can fight

what fate has designed in the stars for us. We will be together." Lethia loomed in front of her, her silhouetted figure highlighted by the glow from the moon.

"This isn't right. I'm not your mate."

"But you are, *miere*." Lethia ambled toward Alima.

The vampire appeared cool and collected like she hadn't even run, while Alima was out of breath and had started to sweat. Lethia, on the other hand, still appeared as if she had just walked off a cover of a magazine.

Alima backed away from her. Lethia tossed her thick blonde hair over her shoulder, sauntering toward her.

"I just want to be left alone to live my life."

"But what kind of life is it without the one who will love you, cherish you, and take care of you for eternity?"

Alima continued stepping away from Lethia until her back hit something hard.

Dammit!

A tree, and it was too late for her to move. Lethia stood close, trapping her against it.

"Like vampires cherish humans. If they did, then why are humans killed by vampires every day?

Their throats ripped out and left to die?" Alima hiccupped, almost crying.

Lethia paused, her gaze unwavering.

Alima closed her eyes and inhaled the tantalizing scent of the woman. She tried to ignore it, but it was tempting her. She trembled with a need unlike anything she had ever known.

Deep inside, she wanted this woman.

Wanted to get a taste of what she offered.

But she couldn't.

Vampires had ruined her world, her life, and had taken her sister away from her.

Because of vampires, human lives were in disarray.

"Someone close to you has died by the hands of a vampire." It wasn't a question but a statement. Lethia's hand cupped Alima's cheek. Her warm breath skated across Alima's face.

Alima closed her eyes and tried to hold back the need to cry and scream. She had promised herself a long time ago that she wouldn't cry any more for her sister. That was not what Joslin would have wanted.

"Tell me."

"Does it matter?" Alima sniffed. She inhaled

and tried to get herself together. She blinked back the tears that rested on the edges of her eyelids.

"It does. If I am to get to know my mate." Lethia tipped her face back, rubbing her thumb along Alima's cheek. "You assume the worse about me without wanting to even get to know me."

"You vampires are—"

"What? All alike? How do you know? What vampires have you gotten to know?"

"Well, um…" Alima stuttered.

"The answer is none. I don't even need you to answer to know the answer." Lethia's thumb reached Alima's bottom lip.

"And you don't even know me, but you are so certain that I am your mate. You would want to spend an eternity with me? Someone you don't know and who won't live that long?" Alima scoffed. She leaned her head back against the tree, trying to put some distance between her and Lethia.

"Oh, but you are, and you will." Lethia leaned down and brushed her lips across Alima's.

Alima's breath stalled in her chest at the soft caress of Lethia's lips.

"You feel the draw between us," Lethia said. "I can feel the slight tremors in your body, the way your pulse quickens when I'm near you, and how your scent calls to me."

"My scent?"

"Your sweet arousal." Lethia's lips ghosted over Alima's ever so softly. Her hand traveled along Alima's jawline and trailed to her neck. "Soon you will beg for my bite."

"No, I won't." Alima tried to push Lethia away, but the woman was solid as a rock. She shook her head in denial. She would never beg a vampire to bite her. No matter how sexy and desirable that vampire was.

"And you're so sure?" Lethia's fingers gripped Alima's chin and forced her to turn her face away.

Alima stiffened at the feeling of Lethia burying her face in the crook of her neck.

"You think that you can fight against fate."

"A draft designed by vampires is not fate," Alima stated. She bit back a whimper at the sensation of Lethia's tongue skating along the column of her neck. She fought to keep from resting her hands on Lethia. If she did, she might do something as crazy as trying to take her clothes off. Instead, she gripped the tree behind her.

"Oh, but it is. Every match that has been made

has been one hundred percent accurate," Lethia said.

Alima's back arched at the sensation of her sharp fangs sliding along her skin. She held her breath, waiting for the pain, but it never came.

Lethia rested both hands on Alima's face. "You know inside you feel it, and I can't wait for your instincts to take over."

"It won't happen. I'll find a way to escape," Alima breathed.

Lethia lifted her head and gripped Alima's face in a tight hold. A growl rumbled in her chest.

"You keep saying that and I will lock you away forever until you submit to what we have," Lethia growled.

"Lock me away, and that will guarantee that I'll hate you forever," Alima whispered.

Silence drew out between them. Lethia's fingers dug into Alima's face briefly before she lightened her hold. Alima watched the emotions play out on Lethia's face.

Anger. Rage. Uncertainty, then strangely enough, vulnerability.

"Get to know me." Her thumb caressed Alima's skin softly. A deep yearning appeared in her eyes.

"You'll see that I'm not a bad vampire. I'm powerful. Strong. Loyal and will love you for all eternity."

"How can you speak of love?" Alima ignored the other qualities. Her heart did a funny little dance at the thought of having someone totally devoted to her. To be by her side and always want her, but it seemed too good to be true. "We don't even know each other."

"Then it is done. We will spend as much time together as possible and we'll let fate prove what I already know."

CHAPTER TEN

Lethia settled back against her desk, holding a goblet of her favorite blood type. Alima sat perfectly on the chair in front of her desk. Her human appeared calm, but Lethia knew better. Her pulse at the base of her neck gave away her true feelings.

Lethia's gums burned, her fangs wanting to descend. She was craving her mate too much, but the human still fought her. She took a sip, and normally it would quench her thirst, but today, it was only getting her by. The blood she needed was coursing through Alima's curvy body.

After their little tryst in the woods, Lethia had taken her mate back to the castle where they could relax and chat.

As much as it went against her very nature, she was going to have to court her human. She remembered things about humans. They courted the ones they were interested in. Outings called dates had been popular. She wasn't sure if they still did it in these days after the war, but it was something she remembered before the new millennium.

"Since you have so many preconceived notions about vampires, ask me any question you want." Lethia leveled her gaze on Alima. She liked how her mate didn't hesitate to meet her gaze. Alima was a strong human with so much fiery passion. Lethia couldn't wait to unleash it.

Alima remained quiet at first. Her gaze traveled down Lethia's body, sending a wave of desire rushing through her. Lethia felt her body respond. She had to draw back on her emotions.

Who would have thought she had almost been about to grovel to a human?

Being outside in the fresh air, the moon high, and her mate triggering her most basic sense to hunt by running, Lethia was so close to getting on her knees and begging her mate to accept her.

"A pure-blood vampire isn't the least bit disappointed to have been matched with a female human?" Alima arched an eyebrow. She settled back in her chair and eyed Lethia. "Wouldn't you have preferred a male? A vampire male where you can have little vampire babies to keep your family lines pure?"

"No, not at all." Lethia sat on her desk and raised her goblet again. The warm, copper fluid flowed down her throat. She held it with both hands to keep them from reaching for Alima. "I've lived a very long time and have seen how fate has taken care of us. There is no use in fighting it. Fate has a way of making us see things her way. As for the purity of my line, if a human was deemed to be the other part of my soul, then it means we each have something the other needs. There is always a purpose for what fate decides, and it's not for us to question it."

"But you wouldn't want a strong male vampire?"

"I've always preferred women. Not that I have anything against men." She finished off the blood and licked her lips. Placing the goblet down on her desk, she focused on Alima. "But I love the softness of women, the sweet taste of what lies between her thighs, the feel of her thighs tightening against my face when she reaches her climax."

Lethia stood and sauntered around to stand behind Alima. Her mate watched her with wide eyes. Her chest rose swiftly. She was affected by Lethia's words. She nervously licked her lips, and it took everything Lethia had to not grab her and pull her up so she could claim them. The softness of them was still etched in her mind from the brief kiss they had shared.

Lethia rested her hands on Alima's shoulders. Her mate's muscles tensed underneath her fingers.

"And as for my line, that will be taken care of when it's time. Any child born to our mating will be loved and a member of the royal family." She trailed her fingers over Alima's long dark braids. She would love to see her hair spread out on her pillows. "My sister, Velika, and her mate will be welcoming their first child any minute now. We will be traveling soon to see them and meet my new nephew or niece when they arrive."

"Your sister's mate is human, right?"

"Yes, Quinn is human. She's the sister of my personal guard, Lane."

"So she mated Quinn, and you entrapped Lane to work for you?"

Lethia tightened her hold on Alima's braid and tugged on it to force Alima's head back. Lethia held in a snarl. Her assumptions were wearing her patience thin. None of the people who served her were forced. They all did it because they want to.

"It was quite the coincidence. Quinn and Velika were matched by the draft, and Lane…his story is unfortunate and not mine to tell. But because of me, he is able to continue living his life. I gave him the choice. I've never forced anything on him. It is his will to stay and serve me."

She released Alima and moved back to her desk.

"You turned him." It wasn't a question but a statement.

"As I said, it was his choice, and he took it. He is a free man to leave if he wants."

"And what do you get out of him being a vampire and serving you?"

Lethia stared at her while she contemplated what she had gained from turning Lane. She could have certainly left the human to die. He had been weak, broken, and moments from death. Alima watched her, waiting for her to answer. Lethia sighed, knowing she should just tell her mate the truth. She wanted Alima to trust her, allow them to be close and let the bond develop between them.

"A loyal friend. Someone who will have my back, someone I know will tell me things I need to hear and not what I want to hear. He's the brother I've never had," Lethia answered.

Alima's eyes widened at her honesty.

"I will never lie to you, *miere*. Lane and I are close."

"And you've never…" Alima allowed her words to fade out.

Lethia knew what she was asking. She bit back a smirk at the little bit of jealousy appearing in her mate. She was sure Alima didn't even recognize her face was broadcasting her emotions.

"Never." Since they were talking of men, Lethia just figured she'd ask the one question she was dying to know. "Before you came to be here, was there a special person in your life? A boyfriend? Girlfriend?"

"No." Alima shook her head.

Her steady heartbeat was confusing. Lethia had expected it to spike when she lied, but it remained the same. If there was no special someone in her life, then who was the male she'd always been around? By her reports, Alima spent a lot of time with him.

"Why is that?" Lethia found herself asking. Alima was a very beautiful woman. How had the humans resisted her?

"My choice. I've dedicated my life to—" Alima shut her mouth tight and glanced down at her hands.

"Fighting vampires." Lethia smirked. She wasn't bothered by her mate's former job.

Velika had spoken of how Quinn had helped the humans in her territory. She'd insisted that having a human mate helped with the relationship between vampires and humans. Maybe she could get Alima to see that she could do the same thing once they sealed the bond. Her human was so passionate about her people, and maybe this would work out.

Fate certainly knew what she was doing, Lethia mused.

A knock sounded at the door. It opened with Lane peeking inside.

"They are waiting for you," he announced. His gaze landed on Alima for a moment then returned to Lethia.

She gave him a quick nod, and he backed out the door and shut it.

"Come. You are going to go to this meeting with me." She held her hand out to Alima.

"I am? Why?" Alima hesitated before taking her hand.

"Because as the mate of the warden, you will have decisions to make as well." She towed Alima behind her.

"Decisions like what?"

Lethia faced her again, and Alima almost ran into her. She reached up and trailed a finger down her cheek.

"Because you will rule these lands with me. You will have a say in things for not only my people, but yours as well." Alima's sharp inhale was the only sound in the room. "There is a problem that I must handle, and I want you there with me."

She turned back around and opened the door. Lane gave the formal greeting by pounding his fist on his chest.

"My ladies. I will escort you to the meeting," he said. He was dressed in his standard uniform with the blue royal crest embroidered on it. The blue signified that he served under her. Each sister's crest was a different color. Velika's red, Hegna's purple, while their parents' was gold.

"What could I possibly assist you with?" Alima whispered.

She had yet to collapse her fingers around Lethia's. Her hand remained stiff and awkward, but Lethia wasn't going to let her go. They followed Lane through the castle, headed toward the war strategy room where she was to meet Dru and her captain, Kane.

"I'm curious as to what you will think. Just sit back and observe." This would be a test for her mate. Being the warden gave Lethia the great responsibility of keeping all those who depended on her safe. With a human mate, she would be happy to entertain any thoughts Alima had. It would be refreshing to get a human's perspective on matters that concerned them.

The lycans would affect both vampire and human.

* * *

"CAPTAIN THADDEUS, I'm sure you have been briefed on what this meeting is about." Lethia breezed into the room with Alima and Lane behind her.

Izora stood on watch outside the room. The guard pounded on her chest as they walked past her. The door shut behind them.

The strategy room was one of the most secure locations in the castle. It was enforced with not only stone and steel but magic as well. If war was to break out, this was where she and her army captains would meet.

She had been very selective of her captains, and the one she wanted to meet with was Kane Thaddeus. He was one of her most experienced vampires who had fought in many wars over the centuries. His loyalties ran deep with his father serving her father. Kane was older than her, and there was no one else she would trust to guide and prepare her army. He reported directly to her and Dru.

Lethia led Alima over to the chair next to hers at the head of the table. Alima curiously took in the room. Dru, Aubrey, and Kane were patiently waiting for her arrival. Along the walls were maps, past battle plans, and weapons. The large table in the middle was where she had strategized plenty of attacks on the enemy.

Kane's gaze landed on Alima as he stood. His eyebrow rose slightly at the recognition that Alima was human.

"That I have," he answered, his focus moving to Lethia while he thumped his fist over his heart.

She saw the questions in his eyes. He was of the older generation where he kept quiet, never questioning his superiors. He was a handsome vampire, not looking a day over fifty. His long brown hair was tied at the nape of his neck. He wore his official uniform, his swords on his waist.

Lethia stood proud next to Alima, a small smile appearing on her lips. There were only a few people who knew that she had been matched with her mate.

"Captain, please allow me to introduce you to my mate, Alima Morgan." Lethia rested a hand on Alima's shoulder.

Kane turned to face Alima and offered her a deep bow.

"It is a pleasure, my lady," he murmured. He lifted his head and thumped his fist over his heart again.

Lethia was satisfied with his show of respect for her mate. There would always be vampires against mating with humans. There had even been an uproar about the royal family mating with humans. She was glad to see so far there was no opposition from those who were close to her.

"Alima, *miere*, this is Captain Kane Thaddeus." Lethia gave a slight squeeze to Alima's shoulder.

"Um, it's nice to meet you," Alima replied with a shaky laugh.

"Alima, the silent one over there is my second-in-command, Dru Moldark." Lethia motioned to Dru who was standing at the opposite end of the table.

Dru, already standing, gave a bow of her head toward Alima. Aubrey stood from her seat, a small smile in place on her lips.

"It is a pleasure to officially meet you, my lady," Dru said. "I'm sure the fates have matched the two of you well."

"Thank you," Alima whispered.

"And to your right is Aubrey Lafayette, my personal advisor." Lethia motioned to Aubrey.

"It is a pleasure to meet you, Ms. Morgan. I've read so much about you." Aubrey bowed her head.

"I'm not sure how to take that, but hello." Alima stared at Aubrey for a brief moment before looking away.

"Please have a seat." Lethia motioned for Kane

and Dru to sit at the table.

Lane moved to stand before the door. Between him and Izora, they would guard them to ensure they were not disturbed.

Lethia sat at the head of the table.

"Now that the formalities are taken care of, I want to get to the matter at hand," Lethia began. She crossed her legs and settled back. "Dru and her men have confirmed that the lycans are here."

Alima's short gasp was the only sound in the room.

Lethia didn't glance over at her, for she assumed her mate was unaware of the existence of lycans.

"The reports that Dru submitted were disturbing. There is a large number of them here, but their alpha has not been spotted. My sister, Velika, provided us with information regarding this pack and the alpha. We will not tolerate these beasts moving in on my territory." Lethia gave Dru a nod, encouraging her to share the information of what she had already gathered.

"There are around one hundred members of this pack. They have settled on outskirts of town near the ocean."

"Isn't that where the sewer tunnels begin?

There is a wooded area in that direction that anyone rarely goes into since it is surrounded by the water," Kane interrupted.

"Yes. Our number is just a guesstimate. There is no telling of the number that may be hidden underground," Dru said. "From the details that Princess Velika shared, they have a new alpha who has organized these wolves. We are on the lookout for her. With this amount of wolves, the alpha has to be around."

"How did their numbers grow so much? If there are the amount here that you say? How many are around the country, or the world?" Kane sat forward.

Dru slid him photos and copies of her report. Lethia had already memorized each word on them.

"Who knows, but this alpha is the key. There had been rumors before, but no one took them seriously," Lethia said. She hated to think she had been one of those vampires who had thought they had taken care of their lycan problem.

The vampires and lycans had gone to war centuries ago when she was just a young vampire, training amongst her father's army. They had driven them down to almost extinction. Lethia suspected that their number was rising. A hundred wolves would be what was needed to protect the alpha.

If she had been hiding for years, she'd take a hundred vampires for protection.

"And this alpha's name?" Kane spat out. He stared at the photos, anger evident in the tone of his voice. He had fought in that war, so she was sure he was taking this personally.

"Azura Michaels," Aubrey replied. She slid a few papers around the table. "The princess requested the blueprints of the sewer system."

Lethia took her copy and eyed the design of the sewer system that was hidden beneath the earth's surface. It would be the perfect place for lycans to hide. It was dark, below ground, and a low-traveled area.

"As I've shared with Dru, I want a small team to watch them. I want to know the moment the alpha shows her face."

"Do we have any photographs of this alpha to know what she looks like?" Kane asked.

"No. That's the thing. No one has pictures of her." Dru sighed. "At least not clear ones."

"That's why I want a team to go and keep an eye on them. The moment the alpha appears, I want to be notified."

Lethia glanced over at Alima who had remained quiet. Her wide-eyed gaze looked around the table.

"What are your thoughts, *miere*?" Lethia asked her.

"This is a lot to take in. So you're telling me that lycans, wolf shifters, exist and they are here and can possibly be going to war with vampires here." Alima cleared her throat and sat forward.

"*Miere*, be prepared to have your eyes opened with the knowledge you will gain. My hope for you will be that you are able to use your experience to help other humans." Lethia could already tell the mating bond was changing her. She was becoming softer toward her. She wanted her mate to succeed in her new position. She still had a lot to learn, and once they sealed the bond, she would be needed to help rule not only the vampires in their territory but the humans as well. "Defending the lycans will protect not only the vampires but humans, too. Lycan attacks have not been reported yet."

"Yet?" Alima gasped.

"You think to fear vampires? Lycans didn't give a shit about rules and laws in the past, and I doubt they do now. Any rules they follow are lycan-based," Aubrey interjected. "Besides the struggle for power, lycans were biting and turning as many humans as they could two hundred years ago. It was vampires who saved humans, and your people never even knew."

"That's true?" Alima turned to Lethia. Shock, fear, and disbelief were written on her face.

"Kane and I both fought in that war." It had been one of the most memorable battles Lethia had entered. At the age of thirty, she had ridden under her father's banner into war against the lycans.

"Aye, that we did." Kane turned to her with a grim look. "This fight with the rogues will be pushed aside. This is top priority, Your Grace."

"That I agree."

"Shouldn't the humans be warned?" Alima asked. "They should be made aware that a new enemy is out there. They would need to prepare."

"We would need more information before we make this public," Lethia replied.

"What more do we need? Lycans are here. Humans need to know there is another predator on the loose that can kill them." Alima pushed back from the table and stood. "When vampires revealed themselves, we were taken by surprise. I can't stand by and see my people go through that again. They have to know. Now."

CHAPTER ELEVEN

Alima was shaken to her core. She had to warn Reed. He would know what to do. He would alert the proper authorities on this lycan issue. Humans couldn't go through another wave of attacks from these paranormal creatures. How had they lived centuries before without knowing that vampires and lycans were among them?

"What is it, *miere*?" Lethia asked.

They exited the room, and Alima slowed to a stop. Her breaths were coming fast, and she was having a hard time inhaling.

"I need…I need air," Alima gasped. Her thoughts were swirling around in her head.

Javari.

She had to warn him, too. He would need to know about this so he could protect himself. Her dear friend had to leave Crystal Cove. If the lycans were here, then he would be in grave danger. Maybe she could convince him to go where her parents were.

"Come." Lethia cupped her elbow and guided her down a series of hallways.

Footsteps sounded behind them. Alima didn't look behind to see who trailed them. They jogged up a small stone staircase and exited through a heavy door.

Cool air hit her.

Alima inhaled sharply, the fresh scents of the outdoors surrounding her. They traveled a short distance and stood beside a large stone wall. Alima glanced at the sky and took in the beautiful artwork that painted it.

Daylight would be coming shortly.

"The sun will be rising soon," she murmured. She leaned back against the cool wall, mesmerized by the details of the sky. Would she ever be able to see the sunlight again? If she was the property of a vampire who was nocturnal, would she ever be able to allow the warm rays of the sun to kiss her skin?

"I'm not worried about the sun," Lethia replied softly. She moved to stand next to Alima, following her gaze.

"Isn't it harmful for you? Won't it kill you?" Alima's breaths were slowing.

"Yes, but I never fear death," Lethia said. She turned, leaning her shoulder against the wall.

Alima had to tilt her head back slightly to meet her gaze. Her icy-blue eyes watched Alima. There was something hidden in them that she couldn't decipher.

"There are other things that I fear, but the sun is not one of them, nor is death. It comes for us all eventually."

"For me sooner than you." Alima snickered. She was starting to feel more like herself. The thought of another predator out there hunting her people was triggering fear and anxiety. She was going to have to find a way to escape. This solidified it. No matter what Lethia did to her, she would have to get word out.

She wasn't convinced Lethia would notify the human leaders in Crystal Cove or the state of

Maine or even the entire country. How long had they known the lycan numbers were rising?

Lethia had promised she would share information, but would she?

How could she be trusted? She was a vampire.

But she hasn't harmed you yet, a voice whispered in the back of her mind.

"Death won't come for you for a very long time." Lethia lifted a hand and ran it along Alima's cheek.

Alima unconsciously leaned into her touch. Her soft finger sent a shiver through Alima. How could this woman be cold, calculating, and a killer one moment, then gentle, almost loving another? Her fingers stopped on the pulse of Alima's neck.

"Once I place my bite here, you will live a long, fulfilling life. No sickness to worry about, and you will be well taken care of and loved."

Alima blinked and returned Lethia's stare. She wasn't sure what type of spell the vampire wove around her, but she was falling for it.

"You mentioned love again. How is it that you could possibly love me?" she whispered.

A small smile graced Lethia's mouth. The tips of her fangs peeked from underneath her lip. Alima's gaze dropped to them. Her breath caught.

What would it feel like to have them pierce her? Her stomach clenched at the thought.

Lethia's fingers trailed along Alima's collarbone, coming up to cup her cheek. Alima wasn't sure who had moved, but somehow there was no room left between them.

"It is the way of the vampire. The moment I saw your picture when I received notification of the match, I felt a strong pull to you. Everything inside me screamed that you are my other half. It is as natural as breathing for a vampire once they see their mate. The moment you stood before me solidified it. The scent of you, the feel of you, and the taste of you will all but drive me to protect you and cherish you for life."

Alima's heart stuttered. She'd never had anyone say such beautiful things to her before.

"But us humans, we don't have anything inside us that reveals our true mate."

"But you do. You just have to listen to what your heart is telling you." Lethia's hand dropped to Alima's chest. She tapped on it right above where her heart sat. "You know you feel the connection to me. Give in, Alima. I promise you, there will be nothing but pleasure."

Lethia leaned down and covered Alima's mouth with hers.

The kiss was explosive.

Alima gasped, her lips parting, allowing Lethia's tongue to push inside her mouth. The vampire was demanding, her tongue stroking Alima's. Lethia turned them, backing Alima to the wall. Her body covered Alima's as the kiss deepened.

A moan slipped from Alima. Her body trembled with the touch of Lethia. She pressed close to Lethia, returning the kiss. A growl spilled from Lethia as her hand slipped behind Alima and gripped her two thick braids. She tugged, tilting Alima's head back to present the column of her neck. Lethia's lips burned a hot trail over Alima. Her fangs scraped along, urging a ripple of fear and anticipation through her, but the bite never came.

Alima groaned, secretly wanting to experience the bite.

Would it be pleasurable as Lethia had led her to believe?

Or would it be painful? She had seen so many humans with their throats ripped out.

Lethia would never harm you, that same voice whispered. *She will be your protector.*

Lethia's lips were back on Alima's, coaxing them open. This kiss was harder, more dominating as she claimed them. Alima shivered when their tongues met.

This kiss was like a drug.

Addicting.

Alima needed more.

Their breasts brushed each other. Alima suddenly had the urge to strip her clothes off so she could feel Lethia against her, naked. She wanted to feel the soft mounds, her hard nipples sliding over Lethia's. She lifted her arms, her hands entwining into Lethia's thick blonde tresses to bring them impossibly closer. Alima pushed her tongue toward Lethia, trying to tease her, eliciting another rumble from the vampire.

Power flowed from Lethia. Her strength and heat overwhelmed Alima and her senses. All that filled her mind was this vampire. Her fair skin, her crystal-blue ices, her toned frame, high, full breasts, and her fangs.

Pure visceral need ripped through Alima.

She desired the release of pleasure that Lethia promised her.

Lethia tugged at the belt of Alima's pants. Her hand slipped inside, diving between Alima's thighs.

Alima widened her legs, a cry escaping her lips when Lethia's fingers parted her labia. Her pants fell down to her ankles, but she didn't care.

"Yes," Lethia hissed.

Her fingers dipped into Alima's wet heat. Her core was drenched with desire. Lethia trailed her fingers through Alima's slit, drawing her moisture up to her clit.

"Lethia," Alima moaned. Her head fell back on the wall as the vampire rubbed her sensitive nub. Her hips thrust forward to meet Lethia's fingers.

Lethia's face nuzzled her neck, her lips brushing Alima's skin.

"Yes, *miere*. Give me your release," Lethia murmured. She lifted her head, watching Alima. Her fingers quickened, drawing out Alima's pleasure. Her eyes grew eerily iridescent, her fangs on full display while she took Alima in.

Alima was unable to look away. Her body grew feverish, and she rode Lethia's hand. She panted, trying to catch her breath. Her hands rested on Lethia's biceps, squeezing her tight, the waves of her release teasing her.

"Lethia," she whispered.

"Give it to me, *miere*." Lethia pressed a kiss to her lips.

Her finger slipped away from Alima's clit. Alima cried out. Lethia raised Alima's leg to rest on her forearm, opening her fully to her. Alima was greedy, not wanting Lethia to stop, but she was soon rewarded with Lethia pushing a finger inside her.

"Oh," Alima cried out. "More."

Lethia gave her what she demanded, adding another finger. Lethia's mouth covered hers, her tongue fucking her mouth just as her fingers did her pussy.

Alima dug her fingers deeper into Lethia's arms, her body trembling. Lethia's fingers pumped her slick channel while her thumb pressed down on Alima's clit.

Alima tore her mouth from Lethia's, panting. She squeezed her eyes tight, basking in the sensations coursing through her body. Her head fell back again, allowing Lethia to trail kisses down the column of her neck. Her finger slipped out of her core and arrived at her swollen bundle of nerves. She strummed the sensitive flesh.

"Come for me now, *miere*. Give me what I want," Lethia growled. She nipped Alima's skin with her fangs.

Alima's body detonated.

Her cry ripped from her, echoing through the air. Her body shook, her release washing over her. The only thing holding her up was Lethia's firm grip.

"That's what I want to see," Lethia purred. She pressed an open-mouthed kiss on Alima's lips, sliding her fingers back into Alima's slick opening. "Look how you grip my fingers after you reach your pleasure."

Alima whimpered. Lethia's fingers felt so good to her. She didn't know why she craved this woman's touch so much. Her core pulsated, clamping down around Lethia's fingers.

"Lethia," Alima whispered. It was the only word she could form at the moment. She slid her hands along her vampire's strong arms and up to cup her face. She brought Lethia to her, offering up her lips.

"Yes, *miere*. Your body is recognizing me as yours." Lethia placed a chaste kiss upon her lips.

Alima cried out, wanting more. Lethia withdrew her fingers from Alima and brought them up to her lips. Alima's leg slipped down, her foot coming to rest on the ground. She watched with bated breath. Lethia licked her fingers clean. A growl rumbled from the vampire. Her eyes fluttered closed before snapping back open.

Alima's gaze moved to over Lethia's shoulder.

"The sun. It's rising," Alima breathed.

Lethia stiffened and glanced back.

"Come, *miere*. Let's get you inside." Lethia kneeled before Alima and reached for her pants. She paused, eyeing Alima's center. She leaned forward and kissed Alima's plump mons pubis. She glanced up, her eyes riddled with lust and desire. "The next time you reach your climax will be on my tongue."

She helped Alima with her pants, sliding them up. She stood before Alima, a small smile playing on her lips. She knotted the two ties together and leaned in for another kiss.

The sun was moments from breaking through the clouds. Steam slowly rose from Lethia's skin. Alima's heart raced.

"You have to get inside," Alima cried out. She wasn't sure why, but she didn't want the sun to burn Lethia.

"I'll be fine." Lethia took her hands and tugged her behind her, heading back to the castle door.

They rounded the corner and entered the doorway. Lethia slammed it behind her, sealing them away from the burning rays of the bright-yellow orb in the sky.

"Are you okay?" Alima asked. She forced Lethia to stop and turn toward her. There was low light in the crammed hallway from sconces lining the walls with flicking flames of fire. She waved the steam away from Lethia, seeing a few reddened areas on her cheeks and forearms. "You're burned."

"It will heal. I've had worse." Lethia smirked. Her eyes held something Alima couldn't read. She hated that the vampire could hold secrets in her eyes. In front of her, the redness faded away.

"You're healing," Alima whispered. She had heard of vampires' quick healing, but to see it in person left her amazed. She flicked her gaze to Lethia's. "What do you mean you've had worse?"

"I've lived a long time, *miere*. There have been many attempts on my life because of who I am and what I am." She bent down and pressed a hard kiss to Alima's lips. "Now, let's go up to my quarters so we can finish what we started."

Alima was rendered speechless. She leaned into Lethia's hold, wanting what she offered.

"Your Grace," a deep voice rumbled behind them.

Lethia's eyes closed, and she rested her forehead on Alima's.

"What is it, Lane?" Lethia asked without looking.

There was another figure beside him, a female dressed in a formal uniform. She had been standing outside the meeting room earlier.

"You are needed. Something urgent," he said.

Lethia uttered a curse in another language. She lifted her head and gazed down on Alima. Her fingers slid across Alima's bottom lip. She kissed Alima again, this time soft and slow. Alima fell against her, sinking into the kiss.

Lethia raised her head, brushing the few tendrils of hair away from Alima's face that had escaped the braids.

"Go meet with Zetta for a lesson before bed. I'll come find you later," Lethia whispered.

Alima could do nothing but nod.

"Izora, take my mate to Remus so she may go meet with Zetta for her lessons."

"Why can't I go with you?" Alima whispered.

"Not this one. Your lessons are more important." Lethia took her hand and guided her up the stairwell. She released her to the female warrior and gave a nod.

Alima stood frozen, watching her vampire walk away with her guard.

"Please come with me, Ms. Morgan," the guard said.

Alima stared after Lethia wondering—when did she become her vampire?

CHAPTER TWELVE

"What do they want?" Lethia growled, stalking beside Lane. Her fangs were still descended. She'd had her mate right where she'd wanted her. Alima had crested on her fingers and hand, but Lethia had wanted her mouth on her mate's cunt when she'd reached orgasm. She'd wanted to taste her mate as her body softened and released her sweet juices.

But that moment had been taken from her.

She had to go meet with the human representatives of Crystal Cove. Lethia's hands balled into fists at the notion of being interrupted with her mate. They had made great progress. She had witnessed the need in her mate's eyes. The bond was growing between them. She could feel it and taste it on her fingertips.

Alima was breaking.

Soon, Lethia would be able to sink her fangs into her mate's neck and drink in her sweet blood. It called to Lethia, and it took all of her strength to keep from biting and claiming her mate.

But that wouldn't have been right. Her mate had to give herself to her.

To want the bite for the bond to solidify.

Forcing a mating was against the laws of vampirism.

Lethia would never force herself on Alima.

This meeting would have to be quick so she could find Alima and take her back to her quarters. She had meant what she'd said. They would finish what they'd started. She would have her face buried between her mate's thighs before the day was over.

She passed some of her servants, human and vampires, nods and curtseys given to her. She acknowledged them all. She was a fair employer and appreciated every one of them who was loyal to her house. The castle was buzzing as it came alive. Even though the vampires would be winding down, the human employees were arriving for duty.

"The humans are calling for a meeting with you regarding an increase in the number of missing people," Aubrey answered, stepping out of Lethia's office. She shut the door as Lethia and Lane arrived.

"Then why are you stopping me from going in there?" Lethia folded her arms.

"As your advisor, I would think you would want to speak with me first before going in there to talk with the governor and mayor." Aubrey raised her eyebrow.

Lane chuckled and moved to stand by the door. He faced forward, keeping his eyes averted. Her friend would keep watch as he had always done.

"You said that they want to speak about missing humans. That has nothing to do with me." Lethia shrugged. "What do they want from me?"

"All the recent humans who have gone missing were all chosen as mates to vampires. Your meeting tonight at eleven will be with representatives of said vampires. All of the humans missing are from our territory. Being the warden—"

"I got it." Lethia held up and hand. She ran a

hand through her hair and tucked some of it behind her head.

Aubrey eyed her suspiciously.

"What?" Lethia said.

"What were you doing before you arrived here?" Aubrey asked.

"I was with my mate outside." Lethia met her advisor's gaze head-on.

Aubrey had been a close friend and someone she could count on since they were teens. Aubrey had gone off to college while Lethia had joined her sisters in training in her father's army. When she was appointed as warden, it was only natural for her to choose Aubrey as her advisor. Her friend had studied human politics and government. Over the years she had continued schooling, officially and unofficially learning strategies that had come in use with overseeing her people.

"And are we making progress in that area?" Aubrey asked.

"Great progress, but unfortunately, I was interrupted with a meeting I didn't know was added on," Lethia snapped.

"Don't take that tone of voice with me. If you would use the tablet I had set up for you, then you would see everything that is on your schedule."

"Why would I need that when I have you?"

"For the millionth time, I'm your advisor, not your secretary. You need to get one." Aubrey motioned for Lethia to follow her. "One of these days you will listen to me."

"If I haven't done it in over two hundred years, why would you think I'd do it now?" Lethia smirked.

Lane opened the door for them. Lethia strolled into the room with her head held high. Enoch stood off in the corner. Not that she needed protection from the humans, but it was customary for her personal guards to be present.

She hated meetings with the human leaders. They always whined about everything. She never understood how some of these men had come to power. If a woman ran the show for them, she was sure their lives would be so much better.

"Gentlemen," Lethia said, heading toward her desk.

The two men sat in their chairs, turning to look at her. She held back a sneer. They obviously had no home training about respect for a woman or a royal. Neither of them stood in her presence.

"When in the presence of royalty and a lady, you should stand when Princess Riskel enters the room," Enoch growled as if reading her thoughts. His sharp gaze landed on the men.

"My apologies," they echoed.

They scrambled out of their seats and stood. Their wide eyes jerked from Enoch, then their attention landed on her.

Lethia took her seat behind her massive desk in her comfortable leather chair. Aubrey took her spot behind her to her left.

"Please have a seat." Lethia motioned for them to return to their chairs. "It's a fine morning, is it not?"

"How…how would you know? The windows in the castle are all sealed shut," Governor Masters said. His gaze flicked to her steel-covered windows.

"I have just come from outside, breathing in this morning's sweet air," she replied haughtily. She crossed her legs and met both of their wide-eyed stares. "Now, my advisor has updated me on the nature of this meeting. Please, explain what is going on."

Lethia leaned back and waited for the whining to begin.

"Then I'm sure Ms. Lafayette has shared with you the concern we bring," Nathan Bell replied.

The mayor of Crystal Cove was an overweight, balding gentleman with beady little eyes.

Lethia didn't trust him as far as she could throw him.

"Humans, male and female, who were chosen by your draft—"

"It is not my draft," Lethia interjected calmly.

"Oh, but was it not started by your father, the king?" Bell questioned. His eyes narrowed on her. His lips pressed firmly in a grim line while he watched her.

She remembered to remain calm. These human leaders were always looking for a reaction from her. They wanted to have the chance to say she was a brute, a menace, and a danger to their people. Relationships between vampires and humans were already strained. She and her sisters were working hard to smooth it out.

That was why her mother, Mira, had felt it would be best to enter her three daughters into the draft. If they matched with humans, the queen felt this would help how the royal family was viewed. It would also help to bring the two species together.

First Velika was matched with Quinn, now Lethia with Alima. Would Hegna be matched with a human? Her elder sister, the heir to the throne, was against mating. She would probably disappear herself before taking a mate. Lethia held back a chuckle at the thought.

She was the only one of her siblings who was not opposed to mating. Ever since meeting Quinn, Velika had changed her mind and was very much in love with her human mate.

Once Lethia announced to the world that she and her mate had completed the bond, she was sure this would affect the vampires' decision to enter the draft just like Velika's mating had.

It would appear her mother's decision was paying off.

"That it was, but the results are science. Proof that our two species can cohabitate and even fall in love and procreate," she replied dryly. She leaned forward, resting her arms on her desk. "Now tell me. What is it exactly you want?"

"We believe someone is targeting the humans who are chosen in the draft. Once their names are picked, these people have disappeared, never to be seen again," Masters said.

Lethia paused, keeping her face passive.

Her mate had disappeared when her name had been chosen.

Alima would know.

Maybe she should have brought her to this meeting.

"Is that so? Are you sure the Rebels didn't have anything to do with their supposed disappearance?" Lethia asked.

It didn't get past her the way the two of them glanced at each other.

"Um, the Rebels?" Bell sputtered.

"Yes, don't act like the human rebellion group is supposed to be a secret. There is not much that gets past me." Lethia sighed. "Now, have you spoken with them? It would seem they are in the habit of helping humans escape their matched mates which breaks the treaty between vampires and humans. This, I'm certain, my father would be very interested in hearing about."

"No, please." Masters pushed up from his chair. His eyes widened in fear. "You mustn't take this matter to the king."

Of course they would be frightened by the threat of the king. Her father was a tough, fierce vampire who would ensure the humans held to their part of the treaty. Breaking their agreement could send them back to war.

The humans wouldn't want that.

"And why shouldn't I? My very own mate was

being whisked away by the group after our match was announced."

Their eyes grew even wider at her announcement.

She sneered at them, brandishing her fangs. "I'm a little insulted that you looked past your own people and bring this problem to me when you should be questioning them."

"We have." Masters flopped back down in his chair. He shook his head and settled back, his shoulders slumped. "None of the humans have reached their destination. It's as if they disappeared off the face of the earth."

Lethia paused.

"Ten people have disappeared from this area. Even their drivers who were helping them. Abandoned cars found by the road, but no sight of them anywhere."

"WHAT DO YOU THINK? Are they telling the truth?" Lethia asked.

Aubrey, who had remained silent for the entire meeting, came around from behind Lethia and took a seat in one of the abandoned chairs in front of her desk. She pulled her notebook from a pocket and opened it.

"I do believe they are telling the truth," she replied.

"What of you, Enoch. What do you think?" Lethia glanced over at her guard.

"Aye, they spoke the truth." He gave a nod.

Lethia steepled her fingers. She didn't want to voice what she was thinking, but she was sure it was the case.

"If the vampires did not receive their mates and the Rebels were involved, we need to find out what they know. How they work and where they were headed," Lethia said.

"And how do you imagine we do this? Just walk up to the human Rebels and demand they tell us?" Aubrey snorted. She shook her head and closed her notebook. "They hate us. We will be the last people they would turn to for help."

"Why would I need to go speak with the Rebels when I have one of their own here?" Lethia grinned.

Her mate.

She would question her on everything she knew about the missing humans.

"And you think your mate will tell you things

about her former life?" Aubrey arched an eyebrow. She tapped her pen to her lips. "Have you gained her full trust so fast?"

"I have my ways…" Lethia waved a hand in the air. "She will speak."

"Yes, I'm sure you have your ways around women. You always have, but I'm asking you if she trusts you." Aubrey leveled her with a firm gaze. "Bedding someone and having them trust you are two different things."

Lethia glared at her friend and trusted advisor.

"You don't think trust comes along with taking pleasure from someone?" she asked. Lethia thought back to the sight of her female taking pleasure from her. The mask of emotions on Alima's face as she'd ridden her hand.

"Trust to get pleasure from someone and trust with secrets that could betray her own people? Not the same thing, my friend."

Lethia looked away from her and stood from her seat. She folded her hands together at the base of her spine and strolled from behind her desk.

"When did you become so wise?" she asked.

"A long time ago, but you've never paid attention. I'm not the type of woman you're into." Aubrey chuckled.

Lethia leaned back against her desk.

"We need to look into this. If you are telling me that I have a meeting with the vampires who were supposed to receive their mates, then we need to be able to have answers for them."

"That we do. I'm sure they will demand some form of retribution for their missing mates," Aubrey said, the smile falling from her face.

Lethia thought of Alima and where they had found her. What if they hadn't? What if when the guards arrived, the car was empty and abandoned?

What would she have done?

She had received the files on her mate, seen her picture, learned of her.

How would she have felt had Alima not arrived to her unharmed?

Lethia already knew.

She would have torn this world apart to find her.

"What are you thinking? I saw in your eyes when the humans spoke of how they found the vehicles abandoned, you already have a guess."

It was amazing how well her friend knew her. Lethia had thought she had hidden her feelings and expressions, but Aubrey knew her too well.

"I don't even want to contemplate it, but my

gut is telling me this is the lycans," Lethia stated. She glanced between Enoch and Aubrey. "Humans disappearing. Lycans' numbers rising. Anyone catching a pattern?"

"Shit," Enoch uttered.

"Look into human disappearances in the last five years." Lethia turned back to Aubrey. Her gut was telling her this was the right decision.

"You're thinking there's going to be a correlation between the missing humans and the rising number of lycans." A light went off in Aubrey's eyes. She flipped over her notebook and scribbled a few things down.

"It's the only answer. I doubt their numbers would jump up due to births. Turning humans would be the only way," Lethia murmured.

"I'll get on this immediately."

"You do that, and I'll go have a conversation with Alima." She pushed off her desk and headed out of the office.

She would go search for her mate.

They needed to have a conversation.

CHAPTER THIRTEEN

"Mistress. It's time to rise," a soft voice chimed.

Alima yawned and turned over. She snuggled down into the blanket, trying to hold on to sleep. Her dreams had been plagued with visions of Lethia again. This time they were even steamier than the last time. Her body tingled in places that demanded to be touched and caressed.

"Mistress Morgan."

Alima sighed. She opened her eyes and found Zetta standing at the side of her bed.

"What time is it?" Alima sat up, rubbing her eyes. She raised her arms above her head to stretch.

The mattress was so soft and alluring. She glanced around and had to think hard on how she'd ended up in bed. The last thing she remembered was going into her room and lying across it. She was going to wait for Lethia to come for her. She had promised she would after her meeting.

"It's a little after eight in the evening, mistress." Zetta folded her hands together, a slight smile appearing on her lips. "It would seem that you were extremely tired. I came in to check in on you and found you asleep."

Alima's gaze fell on the windows and found the steel coverings had lifted.

"Wow. I guess I was more tired than I realized." She glanced down and still had on the same clothes.

"I've laid out your clothing, and after you are dressed, I will escort you to the dining room for your evening meal."

"Oh, um, sure." Alima slid along to the edge of the bed. She paused, swinging her feet in the air. The bed was tall, and she hated how she had to run and jump onto it. Her cheeks warmed as she fidgeted with her hands. "Where is the princess?"

"I'm sure she's already up and attending to

business." Zetta walked across the room and paused in the doorway. "Bath or shower?"

"I think I'll take a bath today." Alima hopped down from the bed and stretched one more time. She would have to admit this was the best sleep she'd had in years.

She walked into the bathroom, still not used to someone waiting on her hand and foot. Zetta had the water running, filling the clawfoot tub. The scent of chamomile filled the air. Alima inhaled, taking in the soft, soothing scent. She eyed the tub and couldn't wait to soak and relax in it.

"Do you need assistance with bathing, ma'am?" Zetta asked. She shut off the faucet and stood back, waiting.

"No, I don't. I've been bathing myself since I was a child. I can do it."

"Very well then. I will alert your guards to call me when you are ready. I will go and check in with the chef. What would you like for your meal?"

Alima's stomach rumbled at that moment. She was a little thrown off, acclimating to a vampire's schedule. She wasn't sure if she should request breakfast, but she was craving some fluffy pancakes.

"Do you think the chef could make me pancakes?" she asked.

"The chef will make you whatever you want."

"Okay, then yes. Pancakes. Some eggs and bacon." Alima's stomach rumbled again. Yes, she was starving. This was definitely a change. When she was living in the compound, she would visit the food pantry and get some dry cereal or oats for breakfast. It would be something she could ration out and keep for a few days. Pancakes were a luxury she couldn't afford before.

"Anything else?" Zetta asked.

Her eyes held a twinkle of mischief in them, but Alima didn't care. If she could splurge now on food and not have to pay for it, then she would.

"Hash browns, too, please."

"Um, okay. I'm not sure what that is, but I'm sure the chef will. He is human." Zetta bowed and moved toward the door. She paused before crossing over the threshold. "When you are done, open your door and ask for the guard to escort you to the dining room. I'll meet you there."

"Sure." Alima turned away and stripped her clothes off. She dropped them all in a pile on the floor and slipped her first foot in the water. The temperature was perfect. She sank down with a loud sigh. The tub was abnormally large, but she didn't care. At least two full-sized adults could fit in it comfortably.

Alima rested back, allowing the warm water to work its magic on her. She closed her eyes and tried to relax, but thoughts of the meeting she'd gone to plagued her.

Lycans. Wolf shifters. People who could morph into wolves. Their bites could change a human to what they were.

While she was safe behind the walls of the castle, her people were in danger. She was going to have to find a way to slip out and go warn someone. Maybe she could get word to the Rebels. Reed would know what to do.

Alima couldn't live with herself if something happened to Javari or anyone she knew.

Things with Lethia had taken a turn. Their moment outside would be etched in Alima's brain forever, but she couldn't allow it to go any further. She would have to leave, and sealing the bond with Lethia wasn't an option for her.

Somehow, she was catching feelings for Lethia. She was going to have to distance herself, put the wall back up that the vampire had broken down. She thought of the door that led to Lethia's room.

Was she in there?

Did she sleep alone?

Alima's heart rate increased. She had stayed away from the door ever since she'd learned that it led to Lethia's personal bedroom. Leaning back, she stared at the ceiling. She was not going to go over there and test to see if it was unlocked.

Her people were more important, their survival was necessary. Sacrificing what could be for something that had to be, needed to be top priority.

No matter how good the kisses were or how amazing the orgasm, she was going to have to cut it. She was going to have remember that it was Lethia's people who'd taken her sister from her.

She sat up.

God.

How could she have forgotten her sister was no longer walking this earth because of vampires?

And here she was, almost sleeping with one. She had allowed one access to her body. It was a vampire whose kisses had taken her breath away, a vampire whose talented fingers had pushed her to ecstasy.

Alima swallowed hard. She sat back, her vision blurred. The pain of losing her sister burned in her chest. She couldn't forget that.

She couldn't stop fighting for her sister.

Joslin's death would not be in vain. She was going to break free and help her people. They had to know about the new threat.

Vampires or lycans, which was worse?

She didn't want to find out.

But from the sound of it, Crystal Cove was no longer safe.

A war would soon be breaking out, and humans would be in the midst of it.

Alima washed herself. The water had cooled, and goosebumps formed on her skin. She basked in the feel of the water sliding along her skin. Baths were nonessential back at the compound. She wasn't sure where she was going to go when she escaped, but the compound would be one of the first places Lethia would look.

No, she would have to carry out the original plan of escaping. She'd go to Reed, and he would help her. She would share with him everything that she had learned while being here so he could take that information and work with other Rebel groups.

She stepped from the tub and grabbed a towel. She quickly dried off and wrapped it around herself. She padded into the bedroom and took in the outfit Zetta had laid out for her. It was a beautiful dress, but it wasn't something she would want to wear. If she had the opportunity to slip from the castle, then a dress wasn't suitable.

Turning on her heel, she went into the closet and searched for something else. She soon found a pair of dark leggings and a long cotton shirt. It was more her style, or at least close to what she'd worn before coming to the castle. She snagged a pair of shoes and went back into the bedroom.

Once dressed, she went back into the bathroom and stared at herself. She almost looked like her former self. She breathed a sigh of relief. The longer she stayed, the more she would get used to the lifestyle of fancy clothes and endless amounts of food. Everything that her people did not have.

She didn't want to lose herself here.

Alima snagged a comb and brush from the vanity's drawer. She undid her long braids, needing to touch them up and redo them. Combing her hair always relaxed her. Even when she was little girl, she'd enjoyed her mother brushing her hair. There were plenty of nights where she had fallen asleep while her mother braided it.

With a sigh, she gave it a few good strokes with the brush then began the task of braiding it again. Her twin braids were her signature style. Once she was done, she put everything back then left the bathroom. Her stomach was grumbling. She hurried to the door to alert her guard that she was ready to go eat.

"Hello," she said, twisting the knob. At least she knew the door was kept unlocked.

The guard in front of the door turned toward her.

"I'm ready. Zetta said to let you know so you could take me to the dining room."

"Yes, my lady." He gave a nod and motioned for her to step from the room.

She walked out and closed the door behind her. He guided her toward the stairwell.

"What is your name again?" she asked.

"Magna, my lady."

She gave a nod, remembering that Remus was her other guard. The princess had assigned two men to guard her, plus a servant. She noticed that Scarface was no longer on her detail.

She would basically never have time alone where she could disappear. She was going to have to figure out a distraction in order to slip free. They arrived on the first floor with Alima taking in the route from her room. There were many turns and halls to get to where they were now. She just prayed she remembered the correct ones.

Magna pushed open a double set of doors and ushered her in. The dining room was massive. If she yelled out, she was sure her voice would echo. A large crystal chandelier hung above the long table. It was decorated with fresh-cut flowers in magnificent vases. A single setting was placed at the head of the table.

"Please have a seat, Miss Morgan. I will alert the staff that you are here." Magna pulled out her chair for her.

She gently sat, taking in the room while he walked over to another door. He peeked his head in, his voice low as he spoke with whoever was on the other side.

The dining room was tastefully decorated, but it was too big for just her to dine. Why would they have her eat here alone? This table was large enough for twenty people. Magna stepped back into the room and pressed his back against the wall.

Alima sighed, unsure what to do. Within a minute or so, a short female rushed in pushing a cart.

"Greetings, Miss Morgan. Would you like coffee?" she asked.

Alima took in her golden tan, big brown eyes,

and brown hair that was pulled up into a bun on top of her head.

"Um, yes, please."

The woman took a porcelain mug from her tray and filled it with hot coffee. She placed it on the table near Alima.

"Cream or sugar?"

"Please." Alima nodded.

The woman set a little jug of creamer and a sugar bowl on the table with a small spoon.

"Feel free to doctor it how you like, unless you'd like for me to do it for you." She offered a smile and stepped back from the table.

"I can do it. Thanks." Alima leaned forward and fixed her drink.

"We've received your request. The chef will be done shortly. If you need anything before I return, please feel free to ring this bell." The woman set a silver bell down on the table.

"What's your name?" Alima asked.

"Gail, ma'am." She bowed to her then pushed her cart back toward the door she'd come from.

Alima was left alone with a guard who didn't really speak much. She sighed and reached for her coffee. She brought it to her lips and took a sip. It was wonderful. It had been a long time since she'd had such good coffee. She was used to a watered-down version from them trying to ration out food.

"There you are."

Alima jerked and turned, finding Lethia waltzing through the doorway. Her heels clicked on the floor while she made her way to the table. Magna thumped his chest when the princess passed him. Lethia gave him a nod but didn't take her eyes off Alima.

"Hello," Alima murmured.

She stared at the beautiful sight of her vampire coming toward her. Lethia's long blonde hair was left free, flowing down her back. She wore a blue sleeveless shirt dress with a belt secured around her waist. It stopped mid-thigh, putting her gorgeous legs on display with four-inch heels covering her feet.

Alima's mouth grew dry.

"How was your slumber?" Lethia asked. She took the chair to Alima's right. She tossed her hair over her shoulder. Her crystal-blue eyes were enhanced by the color of her dress. She leveled her gaze on Alima while waiting on her to answer.

"It was really good. I don't even remember falling asleep," Alima admitted sheepishly.

"I saw. I came to see you, and you were at the foot of your bed." Lethia offered her a fangy smile.

Alima had a brief memory of someone shifting her to the pillows and covering her with the blanket. "Was that you who moved me?"

"It was." Lethia leaned forward and took Alima's hand in hers. "As much as I wanted to wake you so we could continue what we had started, I decide to let you sleep. You needed it."

Alima swallowed hard. Had Lethia showed up before she'd dozed off, she was sure they would have certainly finished what they'd started. She had been in a euphoric state ever since she'd climaxed.

"About that," Alima began. She drew her hand back and lowered her eyes to her drink. How did she break it to the vampire that they couldn't move forward? Lethia had changed recently. Alima recognized that Lethia was gentle, nice, and even appeared to actually care for her. She wasn't the cold, calculating warden she'd presented at first.

She almost appeared humanized.

"What is it, *miere*?" Lethia glanced down at the hand Alima had pulled away. She focused on her, a softness appearing in her eyes.

"What does that mean? *Miere*?" Alima asked. It was a word that Lethia used quiet frequently when referring to her. It wasn't English, and Alima was curious.

"It's a term of endearment, but that is not the issue."

Alima sighed, not sure she wanted to bring this up. Maybe it was best that she didn't share her feelings with Lethia. If she caught on that Alima was still wanting to leave, she'd enhance the security and do whatever she could to keep her.

Alima sat forward and shook her head.

"I was wondering how the meeting went? It looked as if it was going to be important." There, she'd gone with that. It would keep the heat off of her and prevent Lethia from becoming suspicious.

"I'm glad you brought that up. I was actually going to speak with you about it," Lethia mentioned. She rested back and crossed her legs.

Alima's gaze dropped down to the span of creamy white thighs that were on display.

"Oh?" Alima's eyebrows arched high. This wasn't what she'd expected. Lethia was turning to her for her opinion. This wasn't the first time, but now, again, she wanted Alima's point of view on something.

She really is a good person who cares for her ward, a voice said in the back of her mind.

"Sure. What is it?"

The door to the kitchen opened again, and Gail came through. She paused at the sight of Lethia sitting at the table.

"Oh, Your Grace. I didn't know you would be joining us." Gail's eyes widened. She gripped the handle of the tray. "Would you like something?"

"Hello, Gail. Yes, please. Type B for me. Warmed." Lethia offered a small smile at the servant.

"Give me a second." Gail blushed.

Alima watched in amusement as the woman disappeared back through the door with her cart.

Hmm…it would seem the human servant had a slight crush on Lethia. Alima didn't blame her. Lethia was quite gorgeous.

Alima turned to Lethia and took her in again. Jealousy reared its little green head in her chest. She bit her lip and wondered if Lethia had taken any liberties with any of her servants. Did she fancy a woman like Gail? Did she know Gail was crushing on her?

"You are so kind to your employees," Alima said.

"How should I act? Scream and yell that I didn't notify them that I would be joining my mate for her evening meal?" Lethia appeared amused. It was then Alima realized Lethia had only paid Gail a moment of her attention before putting it all back on Alima.

Alima's cheeks warmed at the assumption she had made. She had believed the worst about Lethia. From a distance, the only thing she had known about the vampire princess before coming here was that she was hard, deadly, and a fierce warrior. Everything she had learned about the princess was from the human media and from her Rebel organization's intel.

"Well, no. I guess not. It would seem they all love you." Alima had taken notice of how the warriors, guards, and servants all acted around her. There was an air of respect and admiration that came from them when Lethia was around.

"I care for my people. Everything I do is for them. Even the humans who live in my territory. I try to keep their best interests in mind. Are all of my decisions I make sound? Probably not, but I try my best. Out of my sisters, I was the only one who didn't mind our mother entering us in the draft."

Gail burst through the doors again. She had a wide smile on her face as she pushed her cart to the table. Delicious aromas floated through the air and assaulted Alima's nose. She inhaled, a smile appearing on her lips. Her attention went to the cart. Her stomach grumbled, announcing it was famished.

"Here we go," Gail announced. She paused beside the table, lifted a large goblet, and placed it down in front of Lethia.

"Thank you, Gail." Lethia smiled at her.

"And for Miss Morgan." Gail's smile widened. She hefted up a plate that held a silver dome over it and set it down in front of Alima. "I believe this is what you requested."

She removed the dome and revealed three fluffy pancakes, eggs scrambled to perfection, crispy bacon, and a pile of hash browns. Alima breathed in the scent and moaned.

"God, this smells amazing," she gushed.

"Here's butter, syrup, and ketchup. Anything else you require?" Gail asked, setting the table with the condiments. She stepped back and folded her hands before her.

"I'm not sure." Alima slathered her pancakes in butter and syrup. She looked around the table and saw she had everything she would need. "I think I'm good."

"Very well. Please ring the bell should you

think of something." Gail bowed her head to Alima and then turned to Lethia with a deep curtsey. Her blush deepened as she raised her head. She guided her cart out of the room and disappeared.

Alima took her first few bites before remembering Lethia had come to her for a reason.

"What did you want to ask me?" Alima reached for her coffee and took a hefty sip.

Lethia held her goblet, sipping on it while she watched Alima eat. Alima felt a little weird that Lethia didn't eat any food.

How could blood sustain her?

By the look and feel of her, she was toned and fit. There was barely an ounce of fat on the vampire.

Alima sighed. There was no way she could give up food, and the way this cook had laid out her meal, she was going to have to go meet this person to give a personal thank you.

"My meeting held a great concern. Something I was sure you would be interested in hearing. I think even you would be able to help with the issue the governor and mayor presented." Lethia lifted her mug and took another hefty sip. Her lips were covered with a thick red film.

Alima had the certain urge to go over to her and lick them clean.

She shuddered.

Where did that thought come from? She wasn't squeamish when it came to blood, but she didn't think she would want to consume it.

She watched with bated breath as Lethia licked her lips, cleaning them.

Her heart pounded, and she remembered the sensation of that tongue traveling along her neck. A shiver worked its way through her body.

"What situation with the humans?" she murmured.

"It would appear that humans have begun to disappear," Lethia announced.

"What are you talking about?" Alima averted her eyes and glanced down at her food. She stabbed her fork into her pancakes and brought them to her mouth. They were fluffy, buttery, and soft. She chewed, enjoying the flavors that exploded on her tongue.

"I know all about your little organization and them whisking humans away who were matched," Lethia said.

Alima's food stuck in the middle of her throat. She coughed, trying to free it. She reached for her coffee and took a swallow, trying to dislodge the lump. It finally went down. She coughed again to clear her throat.

"What are you talking about?" she wheezed.

"Don't play me for stupid, *miere*. I know you were on the run from me. You made that very clear when you first arrived here." Lethia narrowed her gaze on her. The kindness was fading from her face. She was slowly transforming back into the vampire Alima had first met. Coldness entered her gaze. "Imagine the humans not wanting to hold up their side of the bargain."

"The leaders of this country do not speak for us all." Alima took another swig of her coffee. Her hand tightened on the handle.

"Oh, but they do. I believe you humans elect certain officials to lead you, and those people who are voted in to office do, in fact, speak for the general masses. The agreement was at the end of the war, humans and vampires alike would enter the draft."

Alima bit her tongue. This argument about the draft would continue between the two of them. At the moment, she couldn't afford for Lethia to get pissed off and have her locked up for fear she'd try to leave.

"I don't want to argue," Alima said, trying to defuse the situation. She relaxed her muscles and took another bite of her food. "Well, since you are aware, yes, the Rebels help humans who want to leave. That's it. We don't take anyone who wants to stay."

"Are you sure?" Lethia asked. She studied Alima while holding her goblet. "Ten humans have disappeared recently."

"Ten?" Alima paused. That was extreme for their area. With their small town, five may have been matched in a month.

"Yes, all ten people were matched in this past month and all were taken. You would have been eleven."

"They will be safe. When I drove—" Alima clamped her mouth shut. She had said too much already.

"You drove humans away, didn't you." Lethia leaned forward, her gaze narrowing on her. "You participated in helping humans escape their duties to the draft?"

Alima stared down, moving her eggs around the plate with her fork. "Listen, you are passionate about your people, I'm passionate about mine. I will always fight for my people." She looked up at

Lethia and shrugged. "I don't know what else to tell you, but if a fellow human is desperate to get away from the vampire they are matched with, then yes, I will help. I have helped, and yes, I've driven people away."

"To where?"

"I never took them the entire way. I drove them to a point, then they switched drivers. I only ever drove a certain distance. I never saw them to their destination," Alima admitted.

"Was it the same point each time when you did the handoff?" Lethia asked.

Alima sighed, knowing the information she was about to give was more than she should. This was a betrayal to the Rebels, but at least she only knew so much. That was why Reed organized the escapes the way he did so if any of them were ever captured, their strategies would still be safe.

"There were three routes that I rotated between. I'd drive there, the person would then get into another vehicle, whose driver would take them to another drop point."

"Where was your destination when you attempted to escape?"

"I don't know. They don't even let the escapee know because they aren't allowed to tell family and friends where they are. This is a very secretive plan. Everyone was blind to another step. You're only told the information you need to know because what they want is to disappear. Completely." Alima suddenly felt as if she were being interrogated by the princess. Gone was the person who had kissed her so passionately and brought her to orgasm. Sitting next to her was the warden of the east, commander of an army and a lethal vampire.

Lethia's cold eyes were narrowed on Alima.

"Well, they have been successful. The last ten people disappeared as well as the drivers. Their cars were found abandoned along the highway."

"Oh." Alima stared at her. She swallowed hard, unsure what this meant. She had made plenty of handoffs in the past. Just the thought that she could have been one of them who had disappeared, either as a driver or a passenger… "The drivers aren't supposed to disappear with them."

"That's what I figured. I've had a meeting with the human leaders, and now, tonight, I will meet with some of the vampires whose mates are missing."

"Are you going to try to find the humans?"

"I am, because I believe wherever they are, they are in danger."

CHAPTER FOURTEEN

Lethia sighed, staring down at the screen of the tablet Aubrey had set up for her. She hated the new technology. Gone were the days where they could send messengers to get information to different houses. Now, they received emails that arrived almost immediately with files and reports.

As she'd lived through the changing times, she'd tried to keep up. If it wasn't for Aubrey, she would be stuck in the old days. A few messages came through, and an electronic mail alert popped up. She grew frustrated and thought about sending the tablet out of the damn window.

She eyed the window showcasing the dark night sky.

"Don't you think about it." Aubrey breezed into her office with Lane trailing behind her. She dropped the tablet down on the desk and growled.

"How is it you can acclimate so easily to these things?" Lethia muttered. She tucked a wayward strand of her hair behind her ear.

"Because I want to and I find them fascinating." Aubrey grinned, displaying her fangs. "And you are just one old vampire who is stubborn and set in her ways."

"The old ways were good," Lethia muttered.

"The old ways are ancient, and no one uses them anymore. You must come into the future." Aubrey sat on the edge of the desk. "Just think. Without the modern-day technology, you wouldn't have your mate. You would continue living in the same town as her and never know it. She'd go off and get married to some human—"

"Silence," Lethia growled. She leaned back and knew her friend spoke the truth. How lucky was she that her mate had been right up under her nose? She didn't even want to imagine Alima marrying, growing older, and dying without her. Lethia would have continued to walk this earth until either she was killed in battle or took her own life out of loneliness.

Lethia's focus turned to Lane who stood formally in front of her desk. She had given him permission to drop the formality when they were alone, but he still stood waiting for her to address him.

"What is it, Lane? You can rest at ease," Lethia announced.

"I come bearing news of the male who was a known companion to your mate," he said.

Lethia pushed back from her desk and stalked around it. There were some things she was willing to do to ensure her mate would want her. Getting rid of the male who held her attention before was the start.

"Where is he?" she asked.

"He's in the dungeons." Lane cut his gaze to her. "What would you like me to do with him?"

"Leave him for now. Once I've sealed the bond with my mate, I will decide what we will do with him." Lethia was a jealous vampire. She didn't want to think of her mate being touched by another. Anyone who had would die by her hand. "Have the kitchen send two meals a day."

"Yes, ma'am." Lane gave her a nod, then

thumped his chest. He exited the room.

"Are you going to kill the human male?" Aubrey asked.

"If I find he's lain with my mate, then yes." Lethia held back a growl. If he had so much as kissed Alima, he was a dead human.

"Speaking of your mate, where is she?"

"With Zetta. I've charged Zetta with her education of vampirism. If she is going to be my mate and rule this territory with me, I thought it was best she learn about our people."

"That a fabulous idea. It would help her feel more comfortable around us."

Lethia had taken a page out of her sister's playbook. Velika had done the same for Quinn, and it had paid off. Her sister's mate dove in to learning about vampires, and it appeared to help curb her fears of them. Together, Velika and Quinn had become one hell of a pair ruling the northwest together.

Lethia glanced at the clock on the wall. Her meeting with the vampires would commence soon, and she was sure Aubrey had information for her. "What of the vampires who are coming for this meeting."

She pushed down the strong urge to go to the

dungeon and interrogate the companion. That would come much later.

"They are not happy at all about this situation." Aubrey picked up the papers on the desk she'd put down.

Lethia sat in the chair in front of her desk. She pinched the bridge of her nose, already tired of her day. It was only after ten, and she was ready for this night to be over with.

She just wanted to say fuck everything and go to her mate.

Alima.

She had looked beautiful while she had eaten. Lethia had a feeling she had angered her. She hadn't liked the way Alima had pulled her hand from her. What had caused her to back away? They had made such good progress. The way she'd fallen apart in her arms had Lethia wanting to go to bed with her, but duty had called.

She wanted to go to her and take her away. Lethia wanted to whisk her to a secluded area where it was just the two of them. If she could get Alima underneath her, she was sure her mate would succumb to the mating bond.

"Hello. Lethia. Come back to me." Aubrey snapped her fingers.

"What?" Lethia blinked and focused on her advisor who was propped up on the edge her desk.

"Are you listening to me?"

"I'm sorry. I was thinking of something important I need to attend to." Lethia sat up and blew out a short breath.

"Important, my ass. You are thinking of your mate."

"Why would your ass be important?" Lethia asked, completely confused. Why would she need to mention that?

"It's a saying, Lethia. I really need you to catch up with the time period we are living in." Aubrey rolled her eyes. She handed the papers to Lethia. "Review these quickly. To sum it up, the four vampires who will be meeting with you will be pissed and demanding their mates or the blood of the person who took them."

Lethia scanned the papers. It didn't matter who they were. All that mattered was their mates were missing and they wanted her to solve the problem.

"Were you able to look into what I asked about the other missing humans?" Lethia glanced up from the paperwork.

"I have, and it's not looking good. Not only have humans who were escaping the draft disappeared in the past, other humans have been reported missing as well. All across the country, there has been an increase in the number of victims. And you know who they are blaming, right?"

"Vampires," Lethia murmured.

"Yes." Aubrey reached behind her and grabbed the tablet Lethia had abandoned. She opened it and tapped on the screen. "Out of the ten thousand missing person cases filed in the last five years, one percent were found dead, throats ripped out, and it was blamed on vampires."

"And you're telling me that thousands of humans are still missing, that we know of, but there are no traces of them?" Lethia's breath snagged in her throat. This was not looking good.

Fuck.

This was how the lycans were growing their numbers.

Aubrey nodded, her eyes giving away that she was thinking the same thing Lethia was.

"Have you shared this with anyone yet?" Lethia asked.

"Not yet. I wanted to present it to you first. Lethia, this is worse than we thought. I only dug back five years. If I go further back—"

"There will be more," Lethia whispered. This was something they were going to have to act on immediately. She couldn't be the warden who allowed the lycans to infiltrate her territory. She flicked her gaze back to Aubrey. "I need to meet with my captains and Dru. We need to devise a plan of attack."

"We are going to have to notify the council." Aubrey's quiet words pierced the air.

Lethia froze. She shook her head and stood. She paced the floor, not ready for the council to be involved. She just had to keep this quiet for now until she could gather more details. She needed to confirm her suspicions were true.

Were the lycans snatching humans and turning them?

"Not yet." Lethia held up a hand. She shook her head again and addressed Aubrey. "You know how they will be. This will be handled by me."

"There has been a meeting request for you to see them," Aubrey announced.

"Shit," Lethia cursed. What could they possibly want? She had standing quarterly meetings with them, and it was not time yet. "Why do they want to meet with me?"

"Um, have you forgotten that the council will

want to meet your mate? There will need to be a formal introduction of your mate to not only the council but to your ward. They will need to meet Alima."

"She's not ready for the council."

"It won't matter. As the warden, you have a duty to seal the bond and present your mate."

"I'm working on the bond," Lethia growled.

"Well, you will need to work faster." Aubrey hopped down from the desk and stood before her. She pushed her thick hair back away from her face and offered up a smile that didn't quite meet her eyes. "You know how politics works. I can only stall for a little while before their demands will escalate."

"I know." Lethia covered her face with her hands. The weight on her shoulders was growing, but it wasn't anything she couldn't handle. She was a Riskel, she would solve all of the problems of her people.

"Have you even told your family yet?"

Lethia stared at her friend. No, she hadn't spoken with her family. Her last conversation with her sisters had been about the lycans the night she had purchased the company of the whore.

"No, I haven't." Lethia walked over to the window of her office. She stared out into the night.

Her gaze roamed the property before flicking up to stare at the large moon.

"Well, that is one notification I can't do. You'll have to call your mother. I'm not getting my head bitten off by the queen." Aubrey chuckled. She glanced down at the tablet, her fingers flying across the screen. "I will put reminders in for tomorrow. We'll regroup and get all of the notifications sent out. Don't worry. I'll make sure it's all taken care of."

"I really do appreciate you, Aubrey." Lethia turned around and leaned against the window.

"I know you do. That's why you made me your advisor. For the millionth time, you need a secretary. But what I need for you to do is to claim your mate."

* * *

"WHAT ARE you going to do about it?" Aleister James demanded. The disgruntled vampire stood near the fireplace in the parlor and faced her.

"I hear your concerns and I'm very thankful that you have brought it to my attention." Lethia hated playing politics, but the vampires all had a right to be heard. This was a serious issue. If their mates were disappearing, then that would affect the next generation of vampires.

Their meeting had been going on for about an hour. The servants were keeping them stocked with the best blood while the vampires shared their complaints with her. Each of their stories started as her own with Alima had. They had been notified of their mate, received their packet of information, and then no mate had showed. The guards who were to escort the humans to their vampires were unable to locate their mates. It was as if the humans had disappeared into thin air.

Her personal guards were present. Lane, Enoch, and Izora were spread around the room, posted along the walls. Their duty was to ensure her safety and keep order with this meeting. So far, the vampires were calmer than she would be had Alima not been found.

"We've waited so long for this day. When it should be the happiest moment to finally be able to meet the one person fate has gifted me, then to find out she went missing, it's devastating," Virgil Rankins said. He ran a hand through his hair and lifted his goblet to his mouth. He downed the blood and set the cup down on a table near him.

"I want you to understand that we are going to

work around the clock until we find out what happened to your mates," she promised. Lethia held her goblet to have something to keep her hand busy. She wasn't truly interested in drinking it.

The scent of the blood wasn't as sweet as her mate's. The bond was growing between them. The taste of Alima was still a memory on her tongue. Her body was aching to have more of her sweet, copper blood. Aubrey was right. She was going to have to claim her mate soon. Once she had her first full drink from Alima, she wouldn't need to receive blood from anyone else. Her mate's blood would sustain her for all eternity.

"In the meantime, what are we going to do about other mates for vampires? I just wouldn't recommend anyone go through what we are going through," Cleon Wilkes spoke up. He was the calmest of the men standing before her. A haunted look hovered in his eyes. "I can't help but think that my mate is somewhere injured and needing me. He had just moved to Maine, and from what my report said, he had no family nearby."

The door to the parlor opened with a servant girl entering. She went around with her tray, exchanging the men's goblets for full ones.

"My men won't rest until we have word on

what is going on." She offered a tight smile to Cleon. She handed her unfinished goblet to the servant who took it then disappeared from the room. Lethia collapsed her hands together and glanced between the men. "Is there anything else we haven't discussed?"

"Are there any leads?" Virgil asked.

"I'm working on a few at the moment, but nothing solid. As soon as I hear something, we will be in touch with you. I pray the fates will allow us to deliver your mates to you unharmed." She gave a nod to him and turned to see if the other two had anything else they wanted to discuss.

"I do appreciate you taking the time to hear us out personally," Aleister mumbled. He blew out a deep breath. "It's not like they disappeared into thin air. Someone knows something."

"I'm looking into all avenues." Her gaze flicked to Lane, signaling she was done with this meeting. They would stay and repeat everything. She understood their fears and she hoped she would be able to find all of the missing mates. The longer it took, the chances they would find them unharmed would decrease.

"Gentleman, we are going to have to cut this meeting now," Lane's deep voice echoed through the room. He strode forward and came to stand next to her. "The princess has another meeting after this."

"Well, we thank you for being so open with your hospitality," Cleon said. He set his empty goblet down.

Lethia didn't miss how quickly he had downed his blood the servant had just brought.

"We have your contact information and will be in touch. Please stay and finish your drinks," Lethia offered.

The men gave her a quick bow, murmuring their appreciation.

Lethia walked out of the room with Enoch and Izora flanking her. Lane would take care of the vampires and notify her butler, Sterling, that their meeting was done. She kept quiet until she was far away from the room.

"We need to find the missing humans," she said, her pace quicker as she headed back to her office. She needed to get a hold of Dru and receive an update.

"Yes, Your Grace," her two guards echoed.

CHAPTER FIFTEEN

"Thank you for bringing me out here." Alima stared at the starlit sky.

The moon shined down on them while they enjoyed the outdoors. Zetta sat across from her at the table. She'd lost track of how long they had been outside. Zetta had arranged for their lesson to be held in an outside seating area. The views of the property were breathtaking.

Large arched stone columns surrounded them, allowing them to walk out into the plush grass. The seating area was decorated with a tasteful table and chairs. Rich history of the old castle lay around them. The sconces along the wall held large flames that highlighted everything. Potted plants lined the area, giving it a cozy feel. Alima felt as if she had been transported back in time.

A gentle breeze blew. She shivered and glanced around. Her two guards were posted on the outskirts of the columns. They were dressed in their uniforms with long swords sheathed on their waists on one side and guns on the other.

Zetta was a very thorough teacher, ensuring that Alima was learning much about the vampire culture. Tonight's focus was history. Alima felt as if she were back in school with the way Zetta was teaching her. It was sort of interesting, but that wasn't what she really wanted to know.

"It is my pleasure. You are doing well," Zetta said. The vampire offered her a small smile. She motioned to Alima's empty glass. "Would you like for me to have them refill your glass?"

"Sure." Alima peered down at her notes. They had covered the sixteenth century, but that wasn't what she was interested in. History had never been one of her strong subjects when she was in school.

A servant appeared and refilled her lemonade.

Alima offered the young woman a smile. "Thank you."

Alima took in her scrambled notes. King Niall had ascended the throne at the young age of one hundred and twenty-eight. It still amazed Alima that vampires could live as long as they did. According to her notes, the king had met his mate, Mira, a year before he became king. His now wife had been a warrior for her father who served his father. She smirked at the story of the royal couple's meeting.

Mira, a strong warrior, had challenged the warrior who was so infatuated with her during a training session. Mira had not realized that the warrior she had bested in front of his men was the heir to the throne. They were destined mates, falling in love with each other. They were mated immediately. A year later, Niall's father was killed in battle. Niall and Mira had ascended the throne.

It was a beautiful story, but Alima wanted to hear about Lethia and how she became one of the wardens. Naturally, she would assume it was because she was a princess, but Zetta immediately shot that down. All three princesses had to prove themselves.

But according to Zetta, they were going in order, and learning of Lethia would come later.

"Will the king and queen want to meet me?"

Alima asked. She suddenly realized that if she was to mate with Lethia, she would have to meet the other royals. She gasped at the thought of seeing the vampire king and queen. From what she'd read of the couple, they were vicious and ruthless when it came to their enemies. Their subjects were extremely loyal to them, and they ruled their kingdom with an iron fist.

"Of course they will. You have been matched with their daughter. I'm surprised the queen hasn't already showed up," Zetta said. She flicked the pages in the book before her then slid it across the table toward Alima. "Now let's take a moment to discuss the seven kingdoms."

"Did you hear that?" Magna spoke suddenly.

Alima looked over at him, surprised he had spoken, but his attention was on Remus.

"Yeah, I heard it."

They both stepped away from their post.

Remus turned and stared at her and Zetta. "Stay here."

Alima and Zetta eyed each other before turning back to him with a nod. The guards disappeared from their post.

"Did you hear anything?" Alima murmured.

Zetta held up her hand while she listened. She

stood from her chair and walked to the edge of the stone floor. Alima wasn't sure what caught her attention, but she joined the vampire. She stared out into the night, not seeing anything.

"There was a growl," Zetta murmured softly.

"It was probably just an animal." Alima rubbed her arms as the wind blew again.

"I don't know. It didn't sound like anything that normally is around. The only animals that come this close to the property would be rabbits, raccoons, and squirrels. Nothing that would growl." Zetta blew out a deep breath and faced her. The vampire tried to appear cool, but Alima saw the worry in her eyes. "I'm sure everything is fine."

Alima squinted, but she couldn't see anything in the darkness past the spotlights that shone on the building.

"Of course. The royal guards are the best," Alima said, trying to convince herself. Lethia wouldn't assign two men who weren't good at what they did to protect her. She eyed the yard again, a sense of dread filling her.

"I'm going to walk out to see if I can spot the guards," Zetta said.

"Are you crazy?" Alima gasped. "Remus said

for us to stay here. I'm sure they will be back shortly."

"I don't like how quiet it is," Zetta muttered. She offered a smile and patted Alima on the arm. "I'm not going far. A few steps, then I'll be right back. They should have returned by now."

Alima shook her head as she watched Zetta step out into the yard. The woman was insane. Maybe it was the vampire in her, but if a guard said to remain, then that was what they should have done. Zetta was no warrior from what Alima could tell.

Alima took a step back. Goosebumps appeared on her arms as she waited.

Something was off.

Zetta's cry echoed through the air. Alima jumped, her heart galloping. Footsteps raced away from her. She wasn't sure what Zetta saw, but Alima froze in place.

This would be the time for her to disappear.

She glanced around and took in that for the first time she was left alone. It was cowardly to not go after Zetta to make sure she was unharmed or to see if she needed help.

She wouldn't get this chance again.

Spinning on her heel, she raced to the opposite side of the patio away from the doorway and the safety of the castle. She skidded around a thicket of bushes and sped across the grass. She entered the woods, trying to keep her breaths silent. If there was one thing she knew, vampires were fast.

This was her one time she would get to escape, and she was going to have to succeed. Who knew she would be presented with a moment where she would be unguarded and outside?

Thank goodness she had worn something comfortable. Once she made it to the bottom of the hill, she would have to be swift. She tried to think where she would go, and the first thing that hit her was she had to notify Reed or Nolan. She had to share with them everything she had learned.

One of the things that had been ingrained in her mind when she had joined the organization was information was power. What she now knew, Reed would know what to do with it. If the lycans were about to be a problem, then this was something she would have to notify them of.

She skidded to a halt, holding on to a thick tree. A howl echoed through the air. She shivered at the sound. The noise of fighting came from the direction she had just left. The vampires would be distracted by the lycans.

Shit, they really did exist.

Lethia.

Alima hesitated for a brief moment. Maybe she should go back. Lethia would be pissed if she escaped. She shook her head. No, this information was too important not to share it with her human counterparts. She would have to risk the wrath of her vampire.

Pushing off the tree, she kept moving forward.

ALIMA KEPT TO THE SHADOWS. She had made it to the bottom of the hill and was making her way through town. She had to find Javari. He would know where Reed and Nolan were. She hated going back to the compound, but it was the only way she could get the information to the leaders of the Rebels.

She cut through the alleyways she had been all too familiar with. She was used to sneaking around town in the darkness. Even though it was dangerous for a human to be out during that time, she had mastered the art of hiding in the shadows.

Downtown Crystal Cove would be alive with the vampire population. Their fancy clubs, bars, and shops opened at nightfall. Naturally, she avoided this part of town and stuck to the human side. Not many human establishments remained opened after dark. There were a few that braved being open, though. With downtown being so close to the royal castle, not many rogue vampires chanced being this close to the warden. The farther away from downtown, the more rogue activity increased.

Alima paused at the mouth of one alleyway, listening to the sounds that were coming from it.

A gasp, a growl, and a moan.

A feeding.

She held her breath and didn't look as she slipped past. She didn't want to alert the vampire and interrupt. It must be a feeding that was consensual, listening to the moans that echoed along the walls and followed her. She tried to put the groaning out of her mind. Her footsteps quickened. Her place wasn't too far from downtown.

Once she turned down the road that led to the compound, she took off running as fast as she could. Her gaze remained locked on the building. She came to a halt at the corner and tried to catch her breath. Three men sat in front of the building as they aways did. She smiled, recognizing them.

She inhaled sharply and walked toward the building. The men turned at her approach.

"John. Tim. Newton," she said. She offered them a greeting with a small wave.

They stared at her as if they had seen a ghost.

"Alima." John paused, gawking at her.

"What is it? Why are you looking at me like that?" Alima barked a nervous laugh. She came to stop in front of them. She eyed the building and glanced at the window that was Javari's apartment. He had better be home, she hadn't risked her life coming here for him not to be.

"Weren't you captured? How are you back?" Tim said.

She glanced down at his hand and took in the bowl of food he was eating. All three of them were consuming food. This was not the sort of thing she was used to seeing.

"Where did you get that?" She pointed at the bowl in Tim's hand.

"This? Well, that lady vampire who had been searching for you gifted us food," Newton said. He raised his spoon to his mouth, stuffing his face. He paused to swallow then grinned at her. "She gave us enough to last for two months."

Alima's mouth dropped open at this information. Lethia had given her commune food? Everyone who stayed here was living on a strict budget, low income, or no income. Times were hard. Even Alima had to make do with what she had. Not being able to find a job after she'd lost her last one had left her having to use the food bank and barter for her necessities.

"What are you doing back?" John asked.

"I have to find Javari. Have you seen him?" she asked.

"Now that you mention him, I haven't seen him come or go in a day or two." Newton scratched his head.

That wasn't good. She believed Newton. He sat out here and always knew who came and went. If he said Javari hadn't been here in a day or two, then something was wrong.

"Maybe he's used the back door." She didn't know who she was trying to convince, her or them.

"Maybe." Newton shrugged. He returned back to his food.

She gave another wave and hurried inside the building. She rushed up the stairs to Javari's floor and went to his apartment. She banged on the door and waited. She held her breath at the sound of footsteps approaching. She closed her eyes and prayed he'd open the door.

The door opened, and disappointment filled her when she saw Javari wasn't standing there. A young guy stood before her. She couldn't remember his name, but he was tall, slim, with a mop of curly blond hair.

"Yeah?" He leaned against the door.

"Is Javari here?" she asked.

"Nah, he ain't here." He swung the door closed, but Alima pressed her hand against it to keep him from closing it. "Do you know where he is?"

"Hell if I know." This time he was successful in shutting the door in her face.

Alima turned around. Where the hell was Javari? He couldn't be at work. The miners only worked during the daytime. If not at work, then he should be home.

She hesitated as to whether she should go up to her apartment. She'd been gone long enough where they'd probably replaced her with someone else.

Blowing out a deep breath, she raced down to the first floor. There was a phone in the lobby she could use. She would call Reed. That would be the best thing she could do at the moment. His location was always kept confidential, but there was the number of the Rebels' organization she could use to check in.

At the bottom of the stairs, she saw the old-fashioned landline telephone sitting on the table. She picked up the receiver and dialed the number. It rang twice before it was answered.

"What is it?" a gruff voice said.

"Yes, this is Alima Morgan. I need to speak with Reed," she announced.

The person on the other end went silent.

"Hello?"

"Alima? This is Terry. Where are you? Aren't you at your new location?" he asked.

"What? No, I never made it to my location. My vampire found me. Why does everyone keep asking me that?" She exhaled. Hadn't the driver said that she'd been taken from him? It was protocol for drivers to give feedback on any disturbances or interruptions in the plan. A passenger being taken should have been reported.

"Alima, we were told you were handed off fine when you left Crystal Cove." Terry's voice dropped low.

Alima's hand shook as she pushed wayward

strands of her hair from her face. Why would the driver submit a false report?

"I need to speak with Reed. It is important. I have information I need to share. Is he or Nolan around? I don't know how much time I will have," she admitted.

She spun around at a sound coming from the stairs. A young kid who looked about fourteen came down. He shuffled his way toward the front door. She watched him exit the building before turning back to the phone

"Hold on." There was muffled conversation on the line.

Her heart raced as she waited. A sense of dread filled her. Her gaze landed on the front door, not moving. She half expected Lethia to stride through.

A sense of anger and rage appeared in her.

Confused, she pressed a hand on her chest. Where were these feelings coming from? It pained her and made it very difficult to breathe. She'd never felt anything like it before.

Was it the bond Lethia spoke of?

Were they connected?

How? They hadn't completed their mating yet.

"Alima?" Reed's voice came on the line. "Oh

my goodness. Are you unharmed? Terry said your vampire captured you?"

"Reed. Yes, I'm fine, but I don't have time. I was able to escape from her. I need to share something with you that I learned."

"Where are you? We will come get you," he said.

"I'm not sure there will be enough time. I think she's coming for me," Alima whispered. She closed her eyes and tried to inhale and exhale through the emotions taking over her. She ran a hand along her face. If these were the emotions from Lethia, then she would be in a world of trouble. The vampire was wanting to kill someone.

"Where are you?"

"I'm at the compound, but I have to tell you that Lethia is investigating lycans. They are real and they have moved in to Crystal Cove. We have to—"

"I'm sending someone for you now," Reed interjected. His voice lowered back to the calm tone he used when consoling someone. Many of their people trusted him, believed in him, and considered him a fighter for humans who wanted nothing to do with vampires. "You haven't told anyone about this, have you?"

"No, I wanted to share this with you. I knew you would know what to do," Alima replied. She leaned against the wall, the emotions coursing through her too strong. If Lethia captured her again, she doubted she would be able to get any other information out to Reed.

"You did very well, Alima. We wouldn't want to start a panic." Reed's voice was calm as he spoke.

Alima released a sigh of relief. He would do the right thing for their people.

"Has your vampire bitten you yet?"

"No." She closed her eyes, holding back the comment that she almost wanted Lethia to, but she couldn't allow that to happen. She couldn't complete a mating with one of those who had taken her sister from this world.

It would betray the memory of Joslin.

"Is there somewhere safe you can wait? The compound will be the very first place they look for you."

"I don't know," she whispered. Her gaze flicked back to the door again. Besides Javari, she really didn't hang out with anyone. She didn't have any friends she could go stay with.

"This is what I want you to do. I want you to go to the corner of Wilshire and Cummings Avenue.

There is a small patch of woods you can hide in. I will send someone to pick you up. We need to discuss everything you've heard while in the hands of your vampire. I'm sure you've learned valuable information."

She knew the area he was speaking of. It wasn't far from the compound, and she could make it by foot.

"I'm heading there now."

CHAPTER SIXTEEN

"How many are there?" Lethia growled. She stalked through the castle, a murderous rage going through her. The alarms of the castle were sounding, alerting them of an attack.

"Not sure," Dru replied grimly, walking alongside her.

Lane, Enoch, and Izora trailed behind them. The castle was going on lockdown until the threat was averted.

Lethia's hands rested on her daggers at her waist. The moment the sensors of the property were triggered, she'd changed into a more appropriate clothing for protecting her home. The lycans were bold thinking they could walk onto her property and attack.

"Find my mate. Ensure that her guards have her and move her to a secure location," Lethia barked. Once her mate was safe, she would be able to concentrate and eradicate the lycans who'd dared step foot on her lands.

"On it," Enoch said. He broke off from them, heading down another hall.

"The castle guards have engaged." Dru held a hand up to her ear. She was receiving details through a communicator nestled there.

They rushed through a side door, greeted by the sound of fighting. Growls echoed through the air. Lethia took in the fight before her.

"Fucking lycans," Lethia snarled. "I want all of them dead except one. We need to interrogate it."

"Will do," Lane ground out around his fangs. He pulled his sword from the sheath and rushed forward with his vampiric speed, diving into the melee.

"For the crown!" Izora hollered before she and Dru raced toward the fight.

Lethia gave a battle cry and snatched her twin daggers from their sheaths. The metal was pure silver. Lycans were deathly allergic to the metal. Just as the sun was lethal for vampires, silver was the same for the lycans.

With her speed, she became a blur. She unleashed her strength, wielding her daggers around, sinking them into the furry bodies of the beasts. Rage filled her at the thought that they were attacking her home. She would welcome battle at any time, but at her own home, this was inconceivable. Each lycan who crossed her path lost their life. Lethia was a brutal and fierce warrior.

The lycans were tall, fur-covered monsters who alternated from walking on two feet to four. Their fangs and claws were as sharp as their weapons. When in their wolf form, they grew to massive heights, with inhuman strength and deadly bites.

Lethia snatched her dagger from the lycan's chest lying at her feet. The beast would eventually transition back to its human form in death. She wiped her blade on it before standing straight. Lethia brandished her fangs and spun around, sensing a presence behind her.

A black lycan made his way to her. His fangs were on display, growls rumbling from his chest. He stalked toward her on two feet, standing to his full height. His amber eyes were locked on hers, blood and saliva dripping from his fangs.

"Your alpha has sent you wolves to die tonight," Lethia snarled, pointing one of her blades at him. She dropped down into a defensive stance. She gripped her daggers tight, her gaze leveled on the beast creeping toward her. There was no fear in her heart while they circled each other.

The wolf dove toward her, slashing his claws at her. She ducked, avoiding them. She whipped around, slashing her dagger down the center of his back. He roared and came toward her, thrusting his claws at her, but she was too fast and strong for him.

She was the daughter of the king.

He was just a lycan warrior who didn't have alpha strength, which meant he was no match for Lethia.

He lunged toward her, trying to catch her in his grasp. She slid on her knees, slicing the tendons on the backs of his knees. Blood rushed from the wounds as he roared. He was tired, his balance now off, and he fell to his knees. She flew up behind him with a scream, sinking her daggers into the back of his neck, severing his spinal cord.

She ripped the blades out, blood spraying

across her face. She drew her blades along his throat, slicing both of his arteries. He fell forward, dead before he hit the ground. She quickly scanned the area and found her warriors were all who were left standing.

Lethia stood straight, throwing her head back with a battle cry. The sound was echoed around from her warriors raising their weapons to the sky in victory.

Lethia's gaze landed on Dru and Lane standing not too far from her. She stalked over to them, adrenaline racing through her. Lane held a lycan on the ground with his sword pressing to its neck.

"We have one for you, Your Grace," Lane announced. He, too, was covered in blood from the battle.

Lethia sheathed her weapons and stared down at the beast. The urge to sink her blade in its heart was strong, but she needed to question one of those wretched creatures.

"I want him in the dungeons. We will interrogate him later," Lethia ordered.

Lane gave her a nod. He and another warrior flipped the lycan over and restrained him with silver cuffs. The animal growled from the burn. A trail of smoke lifted into the air from his wrists. The silver was already searing his skin. They dragged their quarry away.

Lethia turned and scanned the area with the bodies of the lycans littering the yard. This was a message from the alpha. They were going to have to work faster to find her. She was bold, and her followers must be loyal. This was a suicide mission. "Burn the bodies of the dead. Get any of our warriors who are injured to the healer now. No matter how small, I want them checked out." Her men were stubborn and would be ready to dive right back into a fight. It had been a long time since they'd had a good battle, and her men were bloodthirsty. The history between lycans and vampires was that of a violent nature.

"Yes, Your Grace." Dru gave a nod. She walked away shouting orders to the warriors.

They got to work, lugging the dead bodies to sectioned piles.

Lethia growled. This was too close to her mate. The protective instinct inside her was flaring to life. She needed see Alima and ensure she was unharmed. Alima should have been with Zetta working on her lessons.

"Your Grace!" a voice shouted.

She darted around. Enoch sprinted toward her.

He came to a halt, his eyes frantic. Lethia immediately stiffened. She sensed something was wrong before he even opened his mouth.

"What is it?" she growled.

"We found Remus and Magna. They were injured and unconscious out on the eastern lawn," Enoch announced.

The area he mentioned was where the outer seating area was that overlooked the property near the gardens. She could imagine that it would be a spot for Zetta to take Alima. It was lit well and allowed Alima to be outside enjoying the weather.

"Where is Zetta and my mate?" Lethia clutched the handle of one of her daggers. The floor of her stomach gave way. She knew in her heart that something was wrong. If her strong guards were rendered incapacitated, there was a chance something had happened to her human.

"We found Zetta unconscious with a head wound. She's awake, and they've taken her to the healer, but there is no sign of Miss Morgan." Enoch bent his head in a deep bow.

Lethia rushed past him, sprinting in the direction he'd mentioned. There was no way that Alima would be harmed. Fear unlike anything she had ever known filled her chest. Lethia was not one to be afraid of anything, but right now, the thought of her intended being missing sent a chill through her.

Had the lycans taken her?

Footsteps pounded behind her as she raced to the patio where she was sure Zetta had been teaching Alima. She rounded the corner of the castle and came to area that was tucked away. Lethia strode onto the patio, scanning the tables and chairs. She was relieved she didn't see or scent any fresh blood. She moved to the table piled high with books, notebooks, and pens.

Lethia fingered one of the notebooks, seeing scribbles of her family tree written down. It must be Alima's handwriting. The strokes were bold and neat. Lethia looked from the table, taking in Enoch and Izora standing by waiting for orders.

"I want the entire property searched for Alima," Lethia growled. She gripped one of the books and threw it across the patio at the stone wall. Watching the book slam against it didn't take away her anger. Whoever was responsible for this would pay with their lives. Having Alima back and punishing whoever had taken her would curb this rage festering inside her.

She needed her back.

She inhaled sharply, testing the light bond link

she had begun to feel that existed between her and Alima. Her mate may try to deny they were fated mates, but Lethia knew better. She could feel it deep down inside that they were meant for each other.

"Yes, Your Grace."

She stood outside the patio walls and took in the wooded area along the property. Lethia stared at the trees. Had they come under attack and Alima had run for her life? Lethia had thought they had made great progress, but in the back of her mind, Alima's threat came to the forefront.

And I promise you that I will escape.

Lethia refused to believe Alima would turn tail and run when they were coming under attack, but then again, she wouldn't be able to survive lycans. Running may have just saved her life. If she hid on the property, they would find her.

But if she ran away like she kept threatening, then Lethia would take great joy in punishing her.

THE CASTLE WAS overrun by chaos with the topic of the attack racing through it. Lethia returned inside after ensuring the burning of the lycans'

bodies was underway. She didn't want to risk any of them surviving, so they burned them to be certain of their death.

Lethia was covered in blood and grime, but she didn't care. She needed this situation taken care of and her mate found before she worried about what she looked like. She stalked down the hall and headed in the direction of her war room.

Lane came around the corner, a hardened glint in his eyes.

"I want everyone in the war room. Now," she snapped. This meeting was imperative.

"Yes, ma'am." Lane gave a nod and fell in line with her. He raised his hand and spoke softly into his communicator.

It was time for them to officially go after the lycans. Azura Michaels was going to regret the day she sent her lycans to attack her castle. She may be a new alpha, but it was time she learned that one didn't fuck with the vampire nation.

Lane opened the door that led to the lower level where the war room was located. They arrived the same time Dru, Kane, and Aubrey did, coming from the opposite direction. They entered before her.

She swept in like a summer storm.

"How the hell did the lycans attack us?" she yelled. Lethia narrowed her cold gaze on each member. These were her top associates who should have prevented the breach. "The beasts have come onto my lands, attacking my home. This is an act of war on vampires."

She paced, growls rumbling from her uncontrollably. Her gaze flew to Lane who stood with his hands folded behind him.

"What do you have to say?" she barked.

"I'm not sure, Your Grace. The sensors were set off, and we reacted. We responded as we should have," he stated in a hard voice.

"And you, how did we not know they were going to attack if we have men on them? How did this slip by?" Lethia stalked over to Dru and stood before her second-in-command. She glared at her, needing an answer. This was too close to her mate, and now she was missing.

"I will look into this and contact the vampires assigned to watching the lycans' den," Dru replied. She met Lethia's steely gaze, unblinking. "I will get to the bottom of this, Your Grace."

Lethia paced the room, her rage growing by the second. She wanted to reach out and kill something. She flew around and glared at them all.

"My mate is missing, and no one has anything to say. How does a human just disappear into thin air?" she asked, resting her hands on her waist.

"I'm checking into the secured feeds of the property," Aubrey announced. She was focused on her tablet, her fingers swiping along the screen. She paused before looking up at Lethia. "I think I found something. Here, I'll send this to the large monitor." She moved over to the big television screen on the wall. There was a small computer connected to it. She typed out a few commands before a video of the seating area popped up where Zetta and Alima had been working.

Lethia hated that the video feeds did not include sound. She moved to stand near the screen, not wanting to miss anything. Her gaze was locked on the image of her mate sitting at the table with Zetta. Moments passed by with them speaking and referring to the books. The one that Lethia had tossed to the wall had been the one Zetta motioned to and slid along the table to Alima.

Lethia's breath caught in her throat as she watched Alima's attention be drawn to somewhere off-screen.

"What is she looking at?" Aubrey whispered.

“Remus and Magna must have been posted on the outside of the wall,” Lane murmured.

They all focused on the screen. Zetta and Lethia stood from their seats. The women walked to the edge of the room. Something was going on that had the girls shaken. Zetta motioned for Alima to stay put, but whatever she was saying to her didn’t go over well with Alima who reached for the vampire and motioned to the yard. Zetta still walked out into the yard, ignoring whatever Alima was trying to warn her about.

Lethia studied Alima who backed away from the edge. She jumped, something scaring her. She turned and ran behind a column and hid, then she disappeared off camera.

“Why didn’t she run into the building? There was a set of doors right there that would put her inside the castle,” Kane’s deep voice broke through Lethia’s thoughts.

She was wondering the same thing, but she knew why.

“Do we have another angle?” Lethia asked.

“I’m going through all of the cameras,” Aubrey said, swiping on her tablet.

“Rewind it a few seconds,” Lethia said. She

moved closer to the screen. Her gut was already screaming the answer.

Her mate had run.

Be it that Remus, Magna, and Zetta were injured, Lethia knew Alima had run just as she'd promised. She used the attack as a cover for her to get away.

Lethia was going to get her back. There was nowhere for her to run where Lethia couldn't find her. Alima must have taken what Lethia had said as a joke. Didn't she know that a vampire's mate was one of the most important things in their life? Alima belonged here with Lethia, and she was going to make her understand that. She had tried to be gentle and hoped Alima would come to her on her own.

Now, Lethia would have to do it her way.

Lethia growled thinking of how she would get her to submit.

The ringing of a phone sounded. Lethia cut her gaze around to see who would dare have a phone in her strategy room.

"That's me," Aubrey said. She pulled her phone out of the pocket of her dress and answered. "This is Aubrey Lafayette." Her eyes flicked to Lethia while she listened to whoever was on the other side of the call. "Uh-huh. I see. The princess will appreciate the phone call. You will be greatly rewarded for this."

"Who was that?" Lethia folded her arms. The room was silent while waiting for Aubrey to answer. Lethia appreciated everyone in this room. They would see to it that all would be right.

"That was Newton Jones. He's one of the men from the compound where your mate used to live. He called to inform us that she was just there. Walked in alone looking for her male companion."

Lethia gripped the handle of her dagger. Alima escaped and had run to the male?

"Get the truck. We are going to collect my dear mate."

CHAPTER SEVENTEEN

Alima was almost at the meeting point that Reed had given her. She sped up her pace, not wanting to miss her ride. It was late, and she didn't like being out by herself. A heavy feeling settled in the pit of her stomach. She just couldn't shake the feeling she was being watched. She was a block away from the intersection.

She wrapped her arms around herself and strolled along the sidewalks. She didn't like how there were so many trees and hiding places that someone could be in. Why hadn't Reed picked somewhere that wasn't so secluded? Her heart pounded. Her gaze jumped to each flicker of leaves blowing in the trees or the brush.

Alima picked up the pace. The heavy feeling that had been sitting her chest remained. It had to be Lethia, and from what Alima could sense, her vampire was pissed. How was it possible she could feel what Lethia was? Did Lethia sense her emotions as well? Alima swallowed hard and turned the corner. She hated walking along the trees. She decided to walk in the street away from them.

Her ears picked up the sounds of an engine off in the distance. She prayed it was the ride Reed had sent for her. She arrived on the corner but didn't want to stick out like a sore thumb. She backed up and hid in the trees. At least they were good for something.

Her breaths were coming fast, and she tried to coax herself to slow it down. The wait was going to kill her.

A low growl rumbled somewhere behind her. Alima froze in place. It didn't sound like a dog or any other small animal. It reminded her of the low growls she had heard before she'd escaped the castle.

She swallowed hard.

There was no way a lycan would be in the area. Her luck couldn't be that bad.

It just couldn't be.

She closed her eyes briefly and sent up a prayer.

She turned slightly, her breath catching in her throat. The small thicket of woods was thin, and she could see through it to the other side where a streetlight stood illuminating the road. There were a few homes on the other side of the woods, and she prayed it was someone's dog that had gotten loose. She blinked and squinted, scanning the trees. She froze in place again. A set of amber eyes glowed about a hundred feet from her.

A shadowy figure was high from the ground on all fours. Her gaze locked on the animal. It was bigger than any dog or wolf she had ever seen. The sound of its growls and snarls had her trembling in fear. Her mouth grew dry at the sight of those large eyes not looking away from her. Sweat beaded on her forehead.

Alima gasped and fell back against the tree. She gripped it and didn't know what to do. A massive predator was eyeing her, and she was definitely its prey.

Should she run? She sure as hell wouldn't be able to climb the tree. She knew next to nothing of lycans besides what she had read as a child in books, and she highly doubted childhood fantasy books would be accurate. Now she wished she had asked more questions before when they'd spoken of them. At the time, all she knew was she had to warn her fellow humans in town.

The beast approached her. She gasped when it stood up on two legs, stalking toward her. She bit back a scream and slid around the tree and fell out onto the sidewalk. She pushed off the ground and turned back to face the woods.

I guess running is the answer.

She cried out and took off down the road in the direction she'd come. There were a few buildings and homes when she rounded the corner. She had passed them before and hadn't seen any lights on. It was hard to tell if anyone lived in these houses. They looked run-down and abandoned as many places were after the war.

The engine she had heard was growing closer.

"Please," she gasped. She prayed this was Reed's transportation. The roar of the beast echoed behind her. She picked up the pace, trying not to look behind her. Twin headlights came her way. She frantically waved her arms. "Help!"

A howl went up in the air behind her, sending a

chill through her. She gasped and stopped as the truck drew closer. She turned. Two lycans raced toward her.

Oh God.

She was stuck between the truck driving toward her and a lycan running at her.

Alima couldn't stand here waiting on either. The lycan was going to get to her first. She ran. Tears blurred her vision. She dodged across the street and headed toward the homes.

She couldn't die hunted down by a creature she hadn't known existed until recently. She panicked and raced away. The sound of screeching tires sliced through the air followed by the sickening crunch of a collision. She looked over her shoulder. The truck had slammed into the lycan. She skidded to a halt at the side door of one of the homes. She stood on the stone driveway and watched all four doors of the SUV open. She pressed closer to the structure and prayed they wouldn't see her. Tall, muscular figures stepped from the vehicle. One in particular was very familiar. Alima knew immediately who it was.

Lethia.

The vampires rushed forward out of sight.

Lethia stood by the truck and turned in Alima's direction. The vampire princess saw her. She remained still, staring directly at Alima.

She was dressed in her fighting leathers and looked every bit the badass vampire commander. In the low light, Alima could tell the princess was angry.

Alima swallowed hard.

There was nowhere for her to go. If Reed's men hadn't showed up by now, Alima was screwed. She was not going to be able to outrun Lethia.

Alima shook her head. There was no telling what Lethia was going to do to her once they were back at the castle. She bit back a cry, her tears flowing down her face. The image of her sister's broken body came to mind. She couldn't go back to that castle and be tortured. Lethia was a deadly vampire, and Alima had pissed her off.

Lethia stalked toward her. Her stride was hard and fast. She was irate.

"Please. Don't make me go back," Alima whispered.

"You have defied me," Lethia growled.

As she grew closer, Alima saw dried blood on her. Her hair was a tangled mess, and her dark eyeliner was smeared underneath her eyelids. The vampire's iridescent eyes were locked on Alima. Gone was the patient and gentle vampire who had been trying to woo her.

Left was the cold, hard vampire warrior.

Alima's heart all but jumped into her throat.

"I can't mate with you," Alima cried out.

Lethia arrived in front of her, pushing her back against the house.

"Oh, you can, and you will. You are my mate, no one else will have you." Lethia slammed her fist into the house. The siding crumbled down to the ground.

Alima screamed, jumping as Lethia's other hand shot out and gripped her by the front of her neck. She leaned in, her fangs on full display. Her lips brushed Alima's earlobe. Her hand tightened on Alima, cutting her air supply. Panic set in. Alima clawed at her hand, trying to pull it off, but the vampire was too strong for her.

"I'm done being patient with you, Alima Morgan. I've been as nice as I can be, and if you wanted the real vampire experience, you're going to get it now."

Alima pressed her fingers into Lethia's wrist.

Her heart raced, and her lungs burned from the lack of air.

Lethia yanked her forward, releasing her throat. Alima gasped, drawing in air to feed her screaming lungs. Lethia wrapped her hand around Alima's arm and kept a tight hold on her while dragging her beside her.

"You're hurting me," Alima cried out, but Lethia ignored her. She tried to pull away, but Lethia's hand dug in her arm. Alima tugged and yanked but was unsuccessful from breaking away from her. "Just let me go."

"Did you not see those two lycans coming for you?" Lethia paused at the apron of the driveway and moved Alima around to look at her. The feral spark in her eye had Alima taking a step back away from her. "They were coming for you."

"Me?"

"Who were you waiting for? Who knew where you would be here?" Lethia demanded. She closed the gap between them, thrusting her face near Alima's. "Someone wanted you to be taken out by those wolves."

"No," Alima cried out. She shook her head, not willing to believe it. There was only one person who knew where she was.

Reed.

He had told her to go to that intersection.

Their phone call had to be bugged, and the lycans had to have heard where she would be. That had to be the reason the lycans were waiting for her. Reed was a savior of their people and held in high regard. She had worked alongside him, with him, and saw how passionate he was about helping their people.

"Who was it?" Lethia demanded. "Tell me."

"No!" Alima cried out. She struggled again to break free from Lethia. She would not betray Reed and the organization.

"Whoever it was must be working with the lycans. You'd better think long and hard who you are going to be loyal to," Lethia sneered. Her hold tightened even harder.

"How do you know they didn't follow me from your castle? How do I know it's not because of you?" Alima threw back at her. She hadn't seen the lycans before she'd run and wasn't sure if she had been followed. For all she knew, they could have tracked her down unbeknownst to her.

"You knew the lycans were on the castle grounds and you still chose to run away from me? Instead of running into the building where it was safe, you would rather risk your life to try to escape from me?" Lethia's lip curled up, her full fangs on display. She dragged Alima over to the dead lycan.

Alima whimpered, not wanting to see the dead beast.

Lethia pulled her in front of her, wrapping one arm around her waist, and her free one gripped her chin. The other vampires stood around the two dead lycans. The second one was dead in the street a few feet away. Tears poured down Alima's face, and she took in the mangled form of the lycan who'd been hit by the truck.

"They were after you. Do you see those claws? They can easily peel the flesh from your body. Their fangs would have torn into you. One bite, and they would have turned you into one of them. Is that what you want?"

"No," Alima sobbed. Her body shook, and she stared at the mangled lycan. Blood seeped out onto the asphalt around the body. The beast was large, muscular, and covered in dark fur. The claws were almost as long as her hand. One of the legs was at an odd angle, as was the head. It looked as if the neck had broken. She squeezed her eyes shut, imagining if Lethia had not arrived when she had.

She would have died.

* * *

ALIMA HELD her head down as she was helped from the SUV. Shackles had been placed on her wrists. Once again, she was escorted into the building as if she were a prisoner. The truck had sustained much damage, and they had to wait for a replacement vehicle to come. Two SUVs had arrived, with one whisking her and Lethia away while the other vampires took care of the lycans' bodies.

The ride back to the castle was made in silence.

Lethia had sat next to her and had not said a word to her. The tension between them was so thick it could be cut with a knife.

Alima's body trembled. She wasn't sure what was going to be done with her. She was probably going back to the dungeon. She had never seen Lethia the way she had been tonight. The feral vampire was something she would never want to run into on the streets, and here she was, walking alongside one.

"Where would you like her?" a deep voice asked.

"My quarters. My mate won't be escaping me again," Lethia snapped.

Alima hid her surprise at Lethia's response. She had never been inside the vampire's bedroom and didn't know what to expect. She wasn't sure she wanted to go in there.

"Why can't I go back to my room?" she whispered.

"You don't get to ask questions," Lethia snarled.

Alima pressed her lips into a firm line. She had pushed the vampire too far and decided she'd better keep her mouth shut. She didn't want to do anything to set Lethia off to bite her and drain her dry.

They took the stairs and headed up toward the master bedroom. Alima's palms grew sweaty. She walked alongside Lethia. She kept her eyes forward to keep from looking at her. Once they arrived on the level where their bedrooms were located, Alima's heart pounded. She didn't want to be left alone with Lethia, but she knew none of her guards, or servants, would be sticking around.

"I have my mate from here," Lethia announced once they made their way to her bedroom door.

"Yes, Your Grace." The guards who had accompanied them thumped their chests and bowed their heads.

Lethia opened the door and pushed it open.

She stepped over the threshold and tugged Alima through behind her before slamming the door shut.

Alima scanned the room and found it to be tastefully decorated. Nothing how she imagined. She would have thought everything would have been dark, harsh colors, but she was shocked. There was an impressive regal four-poster canopy bed that was large enough for at least five adults. The bold columns had an iron canopy with beautiful velvet drapes that hung down to the floor.

The wood-trayed ceiling was decorated with beautiful patterns that surrounded a crystal chandelier in the center. The walls were a mix of cream and lilac, the same design as on the ceiling.

The room's view was that of relaxation and luxury.

The complete opposite of what she'd expected for a fierce warrior.

Lethia pulled her behind her and headed toward a set of double doors that were floor to ceiling. Twin round crests decorated the center of each one. Lethia pushed them open to reveal the bathroom.

Alima's eyes widened at the size of the room. It was double the area of her bathroom. There was a tub in the center that was sunken in the floor. It was the size of a small pool. The water was already in it with plenty of bubbles floating around. There as a double vanity with sinks and a walk-in shower behind a glass wall. Everything about the room screamed royal luxury.

Lethia spun Alima toward her. Her iridescent eyes rocked Alima to the core. She swallowed hard, watching Lethia release her from the cuffs.

"You will bathe me," Lethia ordered.

"What?" Alima watched her turn around and strip her leather clothing from her body. Blood covered most of the items. Her weapons hit the floor hard on top of the clothing. Lethia walked over to the tub, nude.

Alima's tongue stuck to the roof of her mouth as she took in the naked vampire.

Lethia was toned but still feminine. Her breasts were full and high, a tapered waist that flared out to supple hips and ass. Alima couldn't take her eyes off the woman. Desire ripped through Alima. Her core clenched with need from the sight of Lethia's perfect body. She didn't care that there were streaks of blood covering parts of her.

Lethia took the stairs that led down to the

water. She undid her hair from the band holding it in place. Her thick locks cascaded around her shoulders. Some of the bubbles turned red as the blood that had coated Lethia's skin washed off.

"I spoke correct English." Lethia leveled her with a hard gaze. "Strip your clothes and get in the water. You will wash me."

Alima swallowed hard and took her clothes off. Lethia turned away from Alima while she disrobed. Alima wasn't going to argue with Lethia. She quickly entered the water, pausing once she stood behind her. The water was warm and felt good on her body. It came to just over her chest, the bubbles tickling her skin. She didn't know what to do. She looked around. A ledge was hidden along the tub that held a sponge, soaps, shampoos, and other items.

Lethia dipped below the water's surface before popping back up. The water rushed down her body, her hair slicked back, molding to her back. She swirled around and met Alima's gaze. Desire flared in her eyes. She didn't say a word and put her back to Alima again.

Alima gathered the sponge and pushed it in the water to wet it. She reached for one of the shower gels and opened it, sniffing. She tried a few of them until she found one she liked. She squirted some of it on the sponge and floated over to Lethia.

She brushed Lethia's hair off to the side to reveal her back. She rested a hand on Lethia's shoulder, feeling her muscle tensing. She lifted her other hand and brought the sponge to Lethia's back and began doing what she was commanded.

Her breathing stuttered. She'd never washed anyone before. This was an intimate gesture to be able to cleanse someone's body. She reached for the bottle again and soaped up the sponge and her hands. She returned to Lethia, washing her with her hands and sponge. The scent of the soap floated through the air.

Her core clenched when Lethia faced her. She remained dead still while Alima continued to wash her. She slid the sponge along Lethia's shoulders and her chest. She bit back a moan as she glided along the mounds of Lethia's beautiful breasts. Her light-brown areolas held Alima's attention. She watched with bated breath; her nipples tightened into little buds.

"I think my breasts are cleaned," Lethia murmured.

Alima jerked her hands back and blinked. She didn't know how long she had been massaging and cleaning Lethia's breasts. Her face grew warm. She kept her eyes averted but then glanced up at Lethia.

The vampire had her eyes on her.

Desire. Need. Lust.

This was what Alima saw in Lethia's eyes, and deep inside her, she felt all of those, too.

CHAPTER EIGHTEEN

Lethia inhaled sharply, watching the emotions play out on Alima's face. The anger that consumed her was still raging through her. The only thing that kept her from exploding was the fact that her mate had been found unharmed. The sight of her running for her life with two lycans after her was like a punch to the gut. If they had captured Alima, she would not have survived.

It took everything she had in her to not watch Alima strip her clothes off. Lethia had chosen to turn her back to her. She'd gripped the edge of the tub, her hands almost cracking the marble that surrounded them. Once Alima had entered the water, it covered her enough to where Lethia felt safe to face her.

She turned and watched Alima's face as she washed her.

Lethia could not push down the rage and anger that Alima would rather run away, risking her life with lycans, than stay and become her mate. Her pride took a hit, she would admit that.

But the reality was, Alima was going to come to her. She was going to be her life partner. Lethia was going to make her. She had plans for her little human that were going to ensure the bond flared to life inside Alima and she would beg Lethia to bite her.

Alima cupped her hands and brought water over Lethia, rinsing all of the suds away. Lethia's body was on fire from Alima's hands sliding along her naked skin. Her hands ached to grab Alima and shake some sense in her. Lethia saw the desire in her eyes. She wanted Lethia but was holding back for some strange reason.

Why would she resist what her body was telling her?

Lethia's gaze dropped down, and the bubbles were slowly dissipating. Alima's creamy brown mounds came into view. Her dark areolas and nipples had Lethia's mouth watering. She wanted to taste those mounds and see if they were as sweet as Alima's blood.

"If you turn around, I'll wash your hair real quick," Alima's voice broke the silence.

Lethia lifted her eyes and jerked her head in a nod. She presented her back and dipped beneath the surface again to wet her hair. Alima took her time, rubbing the shampoo through it. Her small hands made light work of the job. She washed it until it shined.

"I'm done."

"Now do yourself." Lethia swiveled around and motioned to Alima. She floated backward and took a seat on the ledge beneath the water. She leaned back against the wall so she could watch her.

Alima swallowed hard. She squeezed more of the shower gel on the sponge and washed herself. Lethia's breaths increased as Alima ran the sponge along her arms, shoulders, and her breasts. This was one of the most erotic sights she had ever seen. She had waited for the moment she would be able to see her naked.

She peeked over at Lethia who smoothed the

sponge over her breasts again. She moved on and raised her leg from the water.

"I don't think you washed your breasts good enough," Lethia murmured. Her voice was low and husky. She coughed, trying to clear her throat. It constricted when she swallowed.

Alima paused and glanced back over at Lethia. She gave a nod and lifted one breast and ran the sponge over it. Her mouth parted, and she slid the sponge along her nipple, moving to the other one. Lethia couldn't take her eyes off Alima and her beautiful brown breasts.

"Are they clean now?" Alima asked.

Lethia nodded, unable to speak. Alima's big brown eyes watched her. She bit her lip and continued sending the sponge over the rest of her body.

Lethia could no longer hold back. She pushed off the wall and flew through the water toward her. Her instinct was to complete the bond with Alima. She gathered Alima to her, capturing her face in her hands. Lethia claimed Alima's mouth in a hard, bruising kiss.

Alima gasped, giving Lethia the opportunity to thrust her tongue between Alima's lips. Lethia held

Alima's face while she plundered her mouth. Her tongue stroked Alima's, teasing her.

A growl escaped Lethia at the feeling of Alima's breasts brushing up against hers. Lethia walked Alima backward until she was pressed against the other wall of the tub. Alima dropped the sponge and brought her hands up around Lethia's neck.

Alima pressed forward, returning the kiss with the same passion as Lethia. Her moan ripped from her, sending a burst of desire through Lethia. She wanted to hear more of her moans and groans.

Lethia tore her mouth from Alima's and blazed a trail of hot kisses along her jawline. Lethia arrived at the crook of her neck. She bathed the column of Alima's throat with her tongue. The taste of her mate's warm skin had Lethia trembling. She needed to claim her. She scraped her fangs along the soft skin, eliciting a shiver through Alima's body.

"Lethia," Alima moaned.

She rubbed her body against Lethia's while her husky cries echoed through the air. Lethia's hand went on an exploratory journey, sliding over Alima's body. She cupped her breast, teasing her beaded nipple.

"See how you respond to me," Lethia rasped.

Her tongue trailed back up to nook of Alima's neck. She nipped Alima just slightly, drawing a small pinprick of blood to the surface. Lethia captured it with her tongue, the taste exploding in her mouth. She needed more. She hadn't been up to her full power fighting the lycans. Her body was beginning to reject other blood. She hadn't had a full feeding in a while. She needed her mate to accept her.

"Your body realizes who it belongs to. Who can give it the pleasure you crave."

"Lethia," Alima groaned.

Her hands dove into Lethia's hair, and she entwined her fingers in it. Her body writhed against Lethia's. She slid her hand beneath the water's surface and parted Alima's thighs. Her finger connected with her swollen clit and rubbed the sensitive flesh. Alima's head fell back, resting on the wall. Lethia's eyes zeroed in on the smooth column—the urge to sink her fangs in the pulsating artery was strong.

But she couldn't.

She couldn't force a mating. No matter who she was. She had to have Alima wanting it.

Lethia leaned down and covered Alima's lips with hers. She thrust her tongue inside her mouth.

She wrapped her free hand around Alima's braid, holding her head in place. She continued to rub and flick Alima's bundle of nerves.

Alima leaned into her, returning the kiss. Her hands glided down to Lethia's breasts, cupping them. Her small hands felt wonderful as she toyed with Lethia. She teased Lethia, pinching and tugging on her nipples. The move sent a wave of electricity to Lethia's core.

"Yes," Lethia hissed.

She peppered kisses over Alima's face, basking in the feel of Alima's hands on her flesh. Alima's hips gyrated against her hand, moving faster. The water sloshed around them. The bubbles were long gone, allowing Lethia to see her hand between her human's pretty brown thighs.

Lethia leaned in, her mouth brushing Alima's ear. "Give yourself to me, mate. Accept my bite. Be with me."

Alima groaned, then cried out. She shoved Lethia away. She scurried around to the stairs of the tub and climbed out.

"No, I can't," Alima gasped. She slipped, falling on the marble. She pushed herself up and raced over to the towels and pulled one out, wrapping it around her.

Lethia stood in the water, her breaths coming in pants. She narrowed her gaze on her. Her anger peaked inside her.

She was looking for her male companion.

The words echoed inside Lethia's mind. Her mate had left her for the male. Was that why she was rejecting her? He could never give her everything she could.

"Why?" Lethia demanded. She strode through the water and up the stairs. She ignored the water dripping from her as she stalked toward Alima.

"I can't," Alima repeated.

There was something in her eyes that Lethia couldn't read. Something more than the fear that resonated from her big brown eyes.

"You will," Lethia growled. She gripped Alima's chin in her hand. She backed her mate to the wall, trapping her with her body.

"Just kill me now," Alima whispered. Tears flowed from her eyes. She watched Lethia. Her gaze dropped down to Lethia's fangs.

The display almost thawed out Lethia's iced heart, but it wasn't enough. She narrowed her eyes on Alima and tightened her hold on her.

"Don't give me any ideas. I have plenty I'm going to do to you, but killing you won't be one of them." That was a promise Lethia was going to come through on. She had her ways she was going to use to force her to recognize and accept the bond. As much as her human thought she could fight it, fate would take over. She would just need a good shove in the right direction.

Lethia took Alima by the arm and towed her behind her into the bedroom. She walked over to a tall wall that held two doors that blended in with the decor. She pressed on them, releasing the latch. She opened them, revealing what was hidden behind.

She'd always liked to indulge in playing with her lovers in the past. Now it would seem she would be incorporating this wall sooner than she thought. It was filled with small hidden drawers and compartments. She opened one that was waist high and held soft restraints where she could keep a woman secured. She reached up and drew down the leather restraints. They were attached to long, unbreakable chains.

"What are you doing?" Alima cried out.

"Since you have a tendency to run from me, you are going to be locked here in my chambers until I see fit to release you." Lethia pulled Alima forward, pressing her back against the wall.

"No, please. Don't do this," Alima begged.

Lethia gripped her wrist and wrapped one of the leather cuffs around Alima's wrist. Alima tried to fight her off, but she was no match for Lethia's strength. She placed the other one on her, securing her. Alima leaned back, panting. Lethia's gaze dropped down to her naked body and growled.

Seeing Alima restrained in her room with her full breasts on display, her wide hips, and her beautiful pussy uncovered, it encouraged the mating bond to flare inside her. She pressed herself to Alima, their naked bodies fitting well together.

"I will do this because I can." Lethia couldn't keep her hands off Alima. She ran her finger along Alima's plump bottom lip, then her chin and down to pause between her breasts. Alima's brown nipples were puckered into little buds. Lethia captured them, squeezing them tight.

Alima gasped, her back arching. Lethia twisted them around, then tugged. She smirked at how Alima tried to deny them, but her body revealed the truth. Lethia scented her mate's thick arousal.

Lethia pressed a button, the chains drawing back. Alima's eyes grew wide as her arms were brought back, held in place.

"What is this? Why can't I move my arms?"

Alima glanced at both of her wrists before turning back to Lethia.

"You are going to give yourself to me." Lethia ignored her questions. She liked seeing her this way. Her full breast were pushed out for Lethia. She leaned down and captured one of them with her lips. She suckled the nipple into her mouth.

Alima's whimper soon switched into a moan as Lethia gripped her breast while she took her time tasting both of them. Her soft flesh was sweet and divine. She rolled Alima's nipple in her mouth with her tongue, teasing her.

"Oh!" Alima cried out. Her breasts rose and fell swiftly with each breath she took.

Lethia moved to the other one, bathing it with her tongue. She glanced up and took in Alima's head resting back, her eyes shut.

"Yes, *miere*. Enjoy the pleasure," Lethia murmured.

Alima was in a lust-filled trance. It was only a matter of time before her body would give in with Alima demanding her bite. Lethia couldn't wait for that moment. She bent down in front of her, trailing kisses along her soft belly. She didn't leave one inch of it un-kissed.

She arrived at Alima's mons and kissed it. The

scent of her arousal grew, wrapping around Lethia. Resting her hands on Alima's hips, she pressed her tongue to Alima's slit.

"Open for me, *miere*," Lethia murmured softly.

Alima's legs parted, allowing Lethia to lift one of her thighs to rest it on her shoulder. Lethia growled at the sight of her cunt. Her brown labia kept her pink pearl snug between them. Lethia parted her slit, revealing the proof of Alima's desire. Her cream coated every inch of her delicious cunt.

Lethia slipped her tongue through Alima's slit. She moaned at the taste of her. It was so addicting. She gripped Alima's leg and devoured her. Alima's cries grew louder, her hips moving as she rode Lethia's face.

Lethia licked all of her juices and arrived at her clit. She took the swollen nub in her mouth, suckling it while pushing two fingers deep inside Alima whose channel was warm, slick, and gripped her fingers tight. The muscles clamped around Lethia, and she fucked her slowly with her fingers.

"Lethia," Alima chanted her name repeatedly.

Lethia did take great pleasure in knowing she called her name. Had the male given her such pleasures? Had she come on his tongue?

Holding on to the little bundle of nerves, Lethia shook her head while tugging on it. Alima ground her pelvis down.

"Yes. Keep going. I'm so close," Alima gasped.

Lethia glanced up and took her in, her body covered in sweat, her puckered nipples high in the air. Her inner thighs were slick with her desire, as was Lethia's face.

Lethia withdrew her fingers and leaned back away from Alima, releasing her clit.

She dropped Alima's leg and stood.

"What are you doing?" Alima's eyes snapped open, shock registering on her face. She shook her head frantically. "Please don't do this to me. Don't stop."

Lethia licked her lips and sucked her fingers clean. Alima stared at her with her wide eyes. Lethia narrowed her gaze on her and stepped to her. She tilted her chin and dropped a kiss to her lips.

"Please," Alima whispered.

Lethia shook her head, not caring that bringing her almost to completion then stopping was cruel.

Her mate was going to learn who ruled her body.

"No." Lethia hit the button to give Alima a little

leeway with her restraints. Lethia disappeared into the closet. She got dressed and brushed the tangles from her hair, leaving it to air dry. She grabbed a blanket and went back over to Alima and tossed it to her. "You will sleep where you are."

Alima caught the blanket and wrapped it around her.

"Where are you going?" Alima asked.

Lethia didn't respond. She stalked from the room and shut the door. She glanced over at the guard standing outside her door. She bared her fangs at him.

"No one goes in, and no one goes out."

CHAPTER NINETEEN

"Do you need us to send aid?" Hegna asked. Her hologram figure stood with her arms folded.

She and Velika had twin scowls on their faces as they waited for Lethia to respond.

She had called a virtual meeting between her sisters. Aubrey joined her to help share the information they had learned. Her personal advisor sat at the table beside Lethia, her attention glued to her tablet.

"My home is fine. They did not breach it. I've upped security, and my warriors are ready. I have a team watching the lycans, and we are going to be the ones to attack next." She leaned back in her chair and rested her feet up on her desk. She would handle it all, even the issue with her little mate.

It took everything she had to walk away from Alima. She'd been in heaven with her face between those soft brown thighs and her tongue buried inside her wet, pink pussy. Lethia had left her quarters sexually frustrated. She'd never been so turned on and needing a release so bad. She had briefly thought of calling the madam and having a female brought over, but that wouldn't curb anything.

Her deep craving was for her mate. To take her body, then take her blood.

That was what she needed.

"Don't hesitate to call on us. I'd love to come and fight lycans with my sister," Velika said.

"Aye, me, too. It's been a long time since I've gone into battle with my sisters. It would be like old times." Hegna chuckled.

Lethia grinned at her. The three of them fighting would be unstoppable. They had grown up fighting together from the time their father had placed swords in their hands as children. Their intense training had been done at each other's sides.

It was why they were so close.

Fighting next to one's siblings helped bond them. Facing death, protecting their people, and depending on each other was what made them the women they were.

"We have one of them in the cells below," Aubrey began. She stared down at her tablet and slid her fingers along the screen. She looked back up at Lethia. She turned it around to show a video of a naked male sitting on the floor in the corner of the cell. "He's no longer in his beast form. Now would be the time to question him."

"You should have led with that when you called. I have half a mind to fly to you just so I can join in." Hegna smirked.

"We don't have that much time." Lethia gave a strained smile. Now she would have two men to question in her dungeons. Alima's male was still down there. She would be having a chat with him, but at the moment, the lycans were more important. He was secure and receiving two meals a day. He would be fine until she was ready for him.

"I could be there in less than two hours." Hegna shrugged.

"I'm confident I'll get information from him. Don't worry, I'm sure there will be more lycans to interrogate soon enough." Lethia winked at her.

Hegna was a bloodthirsty female who enjoyed torturing captives. It would be fun to have her join her. Hegna could help her with the next one. It had been a long while since she'd seen her sisters in person.

"Any word on the alpha?" Velika asked, changing the subject.

"No, but we are planning to infiltrate the lycans' den and draw them out. If she's here, she hasn't presented herself yet. She may be running everything deep inside their den." Lethia wasn't going to wait for the lycans to attack again. They wanted war, then she would take it to them. "Hopefully we'll get information from the beast that will help."

"I've tried to look her up but can't find any information on her. It's like she's never existed, or this name Azura Michaels is an alias," Aubrey shared. If she couldn't find it on her little tablet, then the information was nonexistent. Aubrey was a whiz when it came to gathering intelligence.

"Has Father been updated on the matter?" Hegna walked around and leaned on the table.

"We will be notifying him today. As I said, I can handle this. I don't think the king needs to be involved with a local lycan problem." Lethia wouldn't bother her father. She'd send notice to his personal advisor to just make them aware. Once they could confirm the missing humans and lycans were connected, then this would be a national problem that they would all have to come together to fight.

"And if it's what you are assuming?" Velika leveled Lethia with her hard gaze. The youngest sibling was bullheaded and always ready to fight.

But then, so was Hegna and Lethia.

It must run in the family.

"If my theories are correct and the lycans have been kidnapping and turning humans at the rate that I fear, then, my sisters, we will ride into battle together once again." Lethia stood and paced the floor with her hands behind her back. Their armies would have to join to defeat the lycans. They'd done it in the past and they would do it again. "I want them to assume we are clueless. Let them believe they have the upper hand."

"I like it." Hegna nodded. "We will do our due diligence to look into the packs forming in our territories just in case the alpha is not in yours. We don't know if Velika's intel was one hundred percent solid. The alpha could truly be anywhere."

"When darkness falls, I will lead a group to

infiltrate the den." Lethia paused and turned to the forms of her sisters.

Dru and Kane were already preparing her men for their mission.

"Be careful, Lethia. We don't know how these lycans compare to the ones we eradicated," Velika said.

"I've fought the ones who were released on my grounds. They are bigger. Almost as if they had been altered somehow, but they aren't as fast as we are. Same allergies to silver," Lethia said.

"But what were they after? They didn't just randomly choose to attack. They wanted something," Hegna murmured.

"I don't know," Lethia said. She shook her head and paced again, deep in thought. "My gut says that it was to study us. See how we would react, but ultimately, I think it was to reveal themselves to us." She stared at her sisters. "Those lycans sent were on a suicide mission. There was no way they were going to leave alive, and whoever sent them knew that."

"But why now?" Aubrey asked. She looked up from her tablet. "They've had hundreds of years to show themselves. What is so special about now?"

The room grew silent; no one apparently had

the answer. The war with the lycans had been brutal, the vampires wiping out most of their population. The alpha who had led them before had been deranged and had been killed in battle.

"I heard you got yourself a mate," Hegna broke the silence in the room.

Lethia's gaze flew to hers.

"I guess congratulations are in order."

"When were you going to tell us?" Velika tilted her head, disbelief on her face.

Lethia shrugged, slightly embarrassed that she was having such a hard time with Alima. "It's not going so well. My human mate is not willing to accept my bite nor the bond." She sighed. She ran a shaky hand through her hair and eyed Velika. "How did you do it? What did you do to convince Quinn to listen to the bond?"

"If I knew for certain, I would tell you, but I will tell you that you have to be persistent. Humans can be very stubborn. They truly don't know what they need. That is why fate has given them to us."

Lethia snorted.

Alima's mind didn't know what she wanted. Her body, on the other hand, knew what it wanted. It responded so lovely to Lethia. Alima's nipples, her cunt, all tasted so divine. Lethia's gums burned with the threat of her fangs pushing through them.

She blinked and pulled herself away from her memories and back to the meeting. She offered a smile to her siblings.

"If I find out anything that will be useful to you, I will notify you." Lethia gave a nod to her sisters.

They returned it and disappeared from sight.

"You're heading to the dungeons now?" Aubrey asked.

"Yes. The lycan will talk," Lethia growled.

"Well, then I'll go send the notification of everything going on to your father's office." She stood from her seat and clutched her tablet to her chest.

"What? You aren't coming with me to hear what the lycan will tell me?" Lethia rested a hand above her heart. A small smile lingered on her lips.

Aubrey stared at her without saying a word. Her advisor took a step toward her and stood before her. Concern flooded her eyes.

"When was the last time you fed?" she asked.

Lethia's smile disappeared. She looked away from Aubrey, but it was useless. Sometimes she felt the female knew her better than she did.

"Don't even try to lie, you look paler than normal."

Lethia blew out a deep breath. There was no use to lying to her friend.

"Alima is resistant to mating with me. I've tried drinking blood, but it just doesn't sit right with me anymore. I've had a few sips then I have to stop drinking it."

"It's the mating bond. It's demanding you feed from your mate."

"Don't you think I know that?" Lethia walked over to the table and rested her hands on it. She closed her eyes and inhaled. If her advisor could see the difference in her, then so would someone else. She couldn't afford to show weakness in front of her men. She had to be the powerful leader they knew her to be, so they would have the confidence to follow her into battle. No warrior in his or her right mind would get behind a weak leader.

"Well, you can't go around not feeding. You will grow weaker, and now is not the time for weakness. We have a certain lycan issue to deal with. If that alpha is here, then we will need you in top shape. You are the only around who would be strong enough to take her on."

"I know," Lethia growled.

"Why won't she accept you? What's wrong?" Aubrey pushed.

She got a determined look in her eye, and Lethia knew her friend was already trying to come up with a solution.

"Besides she's a stubborn human?" Lethia snorted. She shook her head, unsure of the answer. "I tried being nice to her, and that didn't work. I've told her how the mating bond draws me to her and that she's my focus in life, giving her anything that money can buy, and still she rejects me."

"Can you feel the bond between the two of you?" Aubrey came to stand next to her.

Lethia shuddered thinking of the emotions that reared up inside her when she was around Alima. She jerked her head in a nod, feeling so open and vulnerable with this conversation.

"Yes, and I know she feels it, too, but she's fighting it."

"Where is she now?" Aubrey asked.

"Locked in my room."

"Not sure I even want to know the nature of how she's locked up in your room, so I'm not even going to ask." Aubrey pinched the bridge of her nose. "I wish there was something I could say to make this easy, but you may want to drink from a live donor. If processed blood doesn't sit well with your stomach, then you need a live donor to try to ensure you have your full strength."

The thought had crossed her mind.

That just might work.

"It could buy you some time until Alima accepts you."

"I'll try it," she murmured. Not that she really wanted blood from anyone else. She'd had two tastes of her mate and she wanted more. The taste for her blood was what she craved. "Not now, but I promise by tomorrow if she doesn't accept my bite, I will get a live donor."

"Good. Now go do your big bad warrior stuff while I go take care of everything else." She patted Lethia on the shoulder.

"You sure you don't want to come with me?" Lethia joked, trying to lighten the mood.

"Ugh, you know I can't stand when you torture someone." Aubrey shivered. "Plus, I have to do other things like speak with the council on your behalf, continue researching so you will have all the information you need, and then later remind you to call your mother."

Lethia closed her eyes briefly. If her sisters knew of her mate, she was sure her mother would also be aware of Alima. She opened her eyes and made a note to call the queen soon.

Right now, she had a lycan to interrogate.

"WHERE IS YOUR ALPHA?" Lethia growled.

Blood coated almost every inch of her body. The lycan male was strung up on the wall, restrained with silver chains surrounding his wrists and ankles, and a collar with silver spikes was on his neck. Under each restraint, his skin was burned and torn.

His body was riddled with open wounds and bled profusely. She walked over to the table and pulled another silver stake from the box placed in the cell. Dru stood off to the corner, watching while her guards Lane, Enoch, and Izora stood outside the steel bars.

"You are going to have to kill me, vampire." He spat out blood on the floor.

Lethia turned and brandished her fangs to him.

"Oh, don't wish for death so quickly," she murmured. She hefted the stake in her hand. She had begun with her daggers. His flesh was riddled with deep cuts where she had flayed him. The loss of blood would soon weaken him. She walked over to him, holding the stake where he could see him.

His gaze locked on it.

"You vampires will die. We've heard of the stories where you vampires tried to wipe us out. But this time, you won't be so successful."

"Oh, we did almost wipe you out. We should've kept going and finished you wretched animals off." Lethia sneered. She moved to stand in front of him. She took note that he had heard stories. So he wasn't a wolf who had been around then. Little did he know he was giving her information. She reached out and pushed his head to the side, finding a bite mark on his shoulder.

He wasn't a pure-born lycan.

"He's been turned," Lethia said over her shoulder to Dru.

Her second-in-command released curse.

"Does it matter?" he gasped. His head dropped back on the stone wall. "My people will again rise to the greatness they once were."

"I wouldn't be too sure of that." She gripped his hair and made him meet her eyes. "Now I'm going to ask you again. Where is she?"

"I will not give up my alpha, vampire. Kill me," he bit out between clenched teeth. His eyes flashed their animal amber, but he would not be shifting. Not with the collar around his neck. It was designed to prevent the change. If he tried to morph, it would clamp down around his flesh, sending the silver into his neck and injecting him with argentite directly into his bloodstream.

She hefted her arm and brought it down, piercing his shoulder with the silver stake. It lodge deep inside his muscle. The burning smell of flesh wafted in the air.

"You are so loyal to your alpha, but where is she now? She left you to die. All of you were sent to die the moment she told you to attack my castle," Lethia snapped.

He yelled and screamed in pain, the silver doing severe damage to that muscle. The area around it was already dying off.

Lethia casually walked back to the table and took another stake out. This was much longer than the previous one and was serrated on the end. She tapped it on her hand as she strolled back to him.

"What are a few lycans to die for a cause? We were honored she chose us. You vampires have been too comfortable thinking you are the top of the fucking food chain," he roared. He fell back against the wall, panting. His gaze landed on the new stake in her hand.

"It's a pity you won't see the outcome. If Azura Michaels wants a war, she will get her damn war, but there is no defeating the vampires. Our numbers are too great for your pack," she growled. "Your death will be a waste, and for what? To give someone else power?"

"She's coming for you and your family. You were first. We'll tear down your dynasty for what you've done."

Lethia flew at him, sinking the stake into his abdomen. He howled, trying to buck her off him. Her aim was true; the stake lodged deep into his liver. Blood sprayed out of him, dripping onto her. His head slumped forward, allowing her to whisper fiercely in his ear.

"The bitch can come for me if she wants, but she won't be alive to go after my family. We will do as we did before and eradicate this world of you filthy animals. She will never touch my sisters or my parents." She twisted the stake around, eliciting a deep groan from him. She stepped back, taking him in.

His body slouched forward, blood flowing from his new wound. His life force slowly seeped from him. He would be dead in minutes. She growled at the news he'd announced.

The alpha could threaten her, but the second she put her sights on her sisters and parents, her death warrant was signed. Lethia picked up a rag from the table and wiped her hands on it. She lifted her gaze to Dru.

"The minute the sun has gone down, we are leaving."

"Yes, Your Grace. I have a hundred men and women fully rested and ready at a moment's notice. We will be ready."

"I want fifty more. If we are going to storm them, then I want to come like a hurricane," Lethia said. She threw the rag back down on the table and stalked toward the door, anger radiating through her body. She paused at the entryway to the cell. "Burn his body."

CHAPTER TWENTY

Alima tried to rest comfortably. The blanket she had was big enough to wrap around her. It provided little comfort on the hard floor. The restraints were proving to be a nuisance, only allowing her hands to move so far from her body. She eyed Lethia's empty bed and wondered where the vampire princess was.

She had fallen asleep for a while then had woken up. It was hard for her to adjust to the nocturnal lifestyle. But then she had woken up and found no sign of Lethia in the room.

Was she finding comfort in the arms of another

woman? Was she drinking blood from her? Alima wasn't sure why, but the thought of her with someone else was enough to make her angry. The urge to do bodily harm to the female overcame her. Another feeling was present in her gut.

Was that jealousy?

It was, but why?

Because she's your vampire, that nagging voice in the back of her mind whispered.

The vampire had all but professed her love for her. She'd shared how much she needed Alima, desired her, wanted to be with her. The look in her eyes whenever she gazed upon Alima was filled with desire and lust. She'd only ever given pleasure but had yet to ask for it.

She'd only asked for Alima to be her mate, share a long life with her, and again, offered much to Alima.

Could she let the memory of her sister's death go?

She closed her eyes. Her mind was racing. She'd spent a long time hating vampires for taking her sister and destroying the world they once knew. That was hard for her to get over. How she wished she could speak with Javari. He would always listen to her troubles. His advice wasn't always sound, and sometimes downright crazy, but she'd always felt better getting things off her chest with him. She prayed he was okay. It was unlike him to not be home when not working.

Humans just didn't fall head over heels with someone with one look.

It took time, dating, getting to know each other first.

But with vampires, it was backward. Love came first, then everything else followed. Alima groaned and turned over onto her back. Her body ached, but not just because of the floor. Her clit was still sensitive from the strength of Lethia's suckling. She inhaled a deep breath at the memory of Lethia kneeling before her, with her face buried between her thighs.

Alima bit back a whimper, remembering the sensations that had racked her body.

But then Lethia had stepped away from her, taking away the promise of ecstasy. Alima had practically gone insane being that close to her climax, only to have it ripped from her.

Even now, her body was awakening. She was still naked and wrapped in her blanket, but a shiver rippled its way through her. How she wanted that feeling back. Her nipples were pebbled, dying to experience Lethia's hot mouth and tongue on them again. She slipped her hand down between her thighs, testing how wet she was. Her finger parted her labia to be greeted by an immense amount of cream.

She sighed, dipping her finger in it. She trailed it along to her clit. It would be so easy to bring herself to completion, but she didn't want to do it without Lethia. Withdrawing her finger, she brought it up and saw the white creamy substance covering her entire finger. Not having anything else to wipe it off with, she used her blanket.

She wrapped herself up in her cocoon to keep her hands from going anywhere else on her body. She lay there forever, trying to fall back asleep. She didn't know what time it was. The shields were down on the windows, so it had to be daytime still.

Alima lifted her head at the sound of the door opening. She watched Lethia enter the room and head directly to the bathroom without even glancing in Alima's direction. Alima sat up, keeping the blanket around her. She rested back against the wall, waiting for Lethia. She heard the shower turn on.

"She already took a bath." Alima frowned.

Why would she need a shower?

Alima's heart slammed against her chest. Had she gone to another woman? Did she need to wash off the scent and fluids from that woman? Alima grew worried as she waited for Lethia to come out of the bathroom.

That sense of jealousy was back, and it weighed heavy on her.

She lost track of the time it took before the shower shut off. Alima impatiently waited for Lethia to come into the bedroom. Would she leave her chained to the wall? Would she invite Alima to her bed?

Alima was a mess of emotions. Fear filled her that the decision she would make would be the wrong one. Accepting Lethia's mating bond would be a betrayal to her family and her people.

Footsteps padded across the floor. She blinked and took in Lethia walking toward her. She was beautiful with her blonde hair wet, slicked back from her face freshly washed again. She wore a black silky robe that was left open. It billowed behind her with each step she took. She appeared paler than usual, but it could have been the play of light in the room or the black robe in contrast to her.

Alima's breath caught at the gorgeous sight her

vampire made. Her high breasts, toned abdomen, and long legs were on full display. She grew tongue-tied looking at Lethia.

Her vampire didn't say a word when she walked by. Alima felt hurt, expecting she would at least greet her, but Lethia didn't utter a single word. She strode over to a chair that was sitting against the wall across from Alima. She sat and crossed her legs. Her breasts were still on display for Alima.

Lethia leveled Alima with her icy-blue stare.

Alima returned it but then lowered her eyes, suddenly feeling shyness overcoming her. She stared down at her hands, unsure what to say. Goose-bumps appeared abruptly on her skin. She bit her lip and snuck a peek at Lethia.

She hadn't moved and was still staring at her.

She looked away, the rate of her breaths increasing. The princess' stare was eliciting a response from Alima. A heaviness settled in her core, and she shifted how she was sitting, trying to bring some relief to her center which was growing slick with need. She cleared her throat, unable to tolerate the growing tension and silence.

"Where did you go?" Alima asked, breaking the quietness of the room. She held her breath, waiting to see if Lethia would answer her. But her vampire didn't even blink. Alima couldn't even tell if she was breathing. Her gaze didn't waver from Alima.

She reached up and brushed a few wayward strands of her hair from her face. Some of her hair had fallen loose from her braids. Her gaze dropped down from Lethia's and went back to her exposed breasts. Her heart thumped along, quickening as she stared at the perky nipples that were standing to attention. She licked her lips, wanting to get a taste of them.

A tingling sensation skated along her skin. Her blanket, no longer a comfort, became an irritant. She slipped it off her shoulders, her body warming under Lethia's gaze.

What was happening to her?

Her core pulsed, growing wet. Moisture collected at the apex of her thighs. She didn't even have to check this time to see that she was even wetter than before. She slid her hands over her chest, brushing her pebbled nipples. She whimpered. The need for wanting Lethia to come to her, please her, was overwhelming.

"Lethia," she murmured. She bit her lip, trying to control herself. Her body writhed, seeking the pleasure only Lethia could give her.

But no.

That wouldn't be right. Lethia had given her pleasure, so it would only be right for Alima to return the favor. Her vampire was sitting perched in a chair, basically naked. She wondered if Lethia was as turned on as she was. It was hard to tell with the blank expression on her face.

Did she feel what Alima felt?

Was her craving for Alima anything like what she was experiencing? This burning need in her gut to be with Lethia was overtaking her.

She needed her.

Needed to know what she tasted like.

Give her pleasure.

She sat up on her knees, massaging her breasts, the palms of her hands tantalizing her hardened buds.

"I need…" Alima paused. She moaned, sliding her hands down her torso and arriving at her center. She parted her slick labia, exposing her aching clit. She brushed it with her finger, and a groan was ripped from her. "Lethia, come to me. I need to taste you."

Her voice shook as she watched Lethia. She slowly stroked her swollen bud. Lethia's gaze finally left her face and trailed over her. Alima's body went up in flames; the icy gaze of her vampire took in her hand between her legs.

Alima was losing herself to this lust-filled haze, and she wasn't sure she wanted to return. Her body had a mind of its own. She licked her lips, watching Lethia uncross her legs. She stood from her chair and sauntered over to Alima. She stopped in front of her and reached out with her hand, tipping Alima's chin up to her.

Alima removed her fingers from her dripping cunt. Lethia's hand shot out and gripped her wrist. She brought it up and bent down, sucking her fingers into her mouth. Her eyes became iridescent while she cleaned Alima's fingers. Alima's breath halted as she watched Lethia.

She released Alima's hand and cupped her chin again. Alima leaned into her hold, resting her hands on Lethia's hips.

"Please," she murmured. Alima pressed a kiss to Lethia's lower abdomen, right above her mons. She inhaled sharply, the scent of Lethia filling her senses. She glanced back up, meeting Lethia's heated gaze. "I want to please you."

Lethia blinked and stepped away from her. She headed back across the room.

"Don't leave me," Alima cried out.

Her heart raced, her body shuddering. Tears blurred her vision. She needed to taste Lethia, have her fill of her cunt in her mouth. A sob caught in her throat, and she watched Lethia lift the chair and set it down near Alima. She sat in it, bringing both of her legs to rest on the armrests, opening herself fully for Alima.

"You need a taste of my pussy, come, *miere*. Have your fill." Lethia motioned for her to come forward.

Alima scrambled, crawling on her hands and knees to Lethia.

"Yes," Alima hissed.

She rose on her knees, her gaze greedily taking in Lethia's perfect cunt. Her labia was slick with moisture, her clit dusty rose and protruding from between her lips. Her soft, pale thighs were strong yet feminine which was exactly who Lethia was. She had lived for over two hundred years, commanded armies in war, all the while remaining beautiful and extremely sexy.

Alima reached out and trailed her fingers along the soft skin. She inhaled, taking in the pure essence of her vampire.

Alima dropped her head and ran her tongue through those tantalizing folds. The taste of Lethia exploded on her taste buds, eliciting a deep groan from within her. She sucked and drank in the juices that ran from Lethia's core.

She arrived at Lethia's clit and wrapped her lips around it. She pulled it into her mouth, teasing her. Lethia's soft moan fueled Alima in her mission to bring pleasure to her vampire. She released the little bud, sending her tongue through Lethia's slit to get another taste. Rising on her knees, she wanted to get a taste of Lethia's dusky nipples. She blazed a trail of kisses over her abdomen, Lethia's hot core pressing against her stomach. Her wetness coated Alima's belly.

She leaned down and captured one of Lethia's nipples in her mouth. She cupped the mound with her hands and toyed with the swollen bud using her tongue.

"Yes, *miere*," Lethia murmured.

Alima suckled the nipple deep inside her mouth. Lethia's mounds were just as sweet as her pussy. She relished the taste and feel of them in her hands. She licked her way to the other one, sucking it between her lips. She moaned, licking and nipping at the pebbled buds. Alima's pussy was drenched in desire. Her wetness ran down her inner thighs. She released it, pressing her face between the twin mounds. She inhaled sharply, taking in the scent of her vampire.

She didn't know if Lethia had left her earlier to go be with another woman. That jealousy rose again, and she wanted to prove she was the better woman for her. Alima had this deep sense of possession for Lethia.

She didn't want her with anyone else.

She was hers.

Alima started at the realization.

Had she just claimed her vampire?

Now wasn't the time to think. She was too lost in her lust-filled haze to try to make sense of what was going on in her head. At the moment she only knew she wanted one thing.

To give her vampire pleasure.

Lethia's fingers tipped Alima's chin upward, forcing her to meet her heated gaze. She trembled and returned the stare.

"Eat my pussy, *miere*. Don't stop until I have come on your tongue," Lethia ordered. She rested her hand on the top of Alima's head and pushed her down until she was face-to-face with her slick pussy.

Alima was unable to respond. Her mouth was filled with Lethia's pussy the second she was back in front of it. Lethia thrust her hips forward, grinding against Alima's face.

She did as her vampire requested, devouring her. She teased and toyed with Lethia's clit. She raised her head and sank two fingers into her vampire's core. Lethia's channel was drenched with her creaminess. Alima pulled out her fingers, seeing Lethia's wetness coating them. She pushed them in deep again, drawing a pleased groan from Lethia. She fucked her with her fingers, slow and steady.

Leaning forward, she captured the swollen clitoris once more, continuing to work Lethia with her fingers.

Lethia's hand rested on the back of her head while she murmured encouraging words. Her hips moved in tandem with Alima's fingers. Alima, lost in the throes of her passion, slipped her free hand between her own thighs, parting her labia to find her clit. She stroked her nub.

Lethia grabbed her by her braid and forced her to lift her head. She paused her hand, leaving her fingers buried inside Lethia.

"Take that hand from in between your legs," Lethia ordered. Her gaze narrowed on Alima. "My pleasure is your focus now. Only I'm allowed to give it to you. That pussy belongs to me."

Alima whimpered, quickening her pace on her clit. How she would love to lie back and spread herself open for her.

Lethia's hold on her braid tightened. She brandished her fangs in a threatening manner.

"I said, remove it. I won't tell you again," Lethia ordered.

Alima gave a strangled cry and snatched her hand from between her legs. Her core pulsated. She thrust her hips out while she was guided back down to Lethia's center. The cool air of the room kissed her aching clit, giving her a minute amount of pleasure.

Opening her mouth wide, she covered Lethia's clit and suckled it with a force that sent her vampire's body arching off the chair. She restarted her fingers, pushing, thrusting them in and out of her slick opening.

She sucked harder, pounding her fingers into Lethia until her body trembled and shook. Her moans rang out, voicing her pleasure while her hips shot forward. She gripped the back of Alima's head, riding her tongue. Her muscles clenched, and a growl ripped from her as she reached her climax. Lethia's roar sliced through the air. Her pussy clamped down on Alima's fingers, milking them.

Alima lifted her head, her face covered with the proof of Lethia's release. She withdrew her fingers and took her time lapping at the juices, cleaning her center completely. Once done, she raised her head again and took in the sight of Lethia's body, relaxed and pliant. She rested back in her chair, eyes closed, chest rising and falling fast. Her creamy thighs were coated in her arousal. Her fangs peeked from underneath her lips as she breathed through her mouth.

Alima stared at them, wanting to feel them pierce her neck. Her heart raced, and her core clenched with the thought. Her body was still on fire, begging for release.

Lethia's eyes snapped open, and her gaze landed on her. Her facial expression was still distant. She leaned forward, dropping her feet to the floor.

"Keep those little hands away from that pussy of yours. If I catch them down there again, I will restrain them to the wall to keep you from touching yourself." She pushed back her chair and stood. She walked over to her bed, shaking off the robe, then climbed on. The curtains around the bed automatically closed, shutting her away from Alima.

Alima whimpered, not wanting to disobey her vampire. Crawling back to her blanket, she wrapped it around her and lay back down. The lights in the room shut off, basking her in pure darkness. She closed her eyes, trying to ignore the ache in her center.

Ignoring it was going to be hard. She was so aroused from licking Lethia to completion. She stared at the ceiling. It was such a task to keep her hands away from her pussy. She exhaled and begged for sleep to claim her.

CHAPTER TWENTY-ONE

Lethia opened her eyes. She wasn't sure what woke her, but she lay staring at the canopy of her bed, remembering how her mate had devoured her pussy. Her clit still pulsed from the attention it had received from her human.

Alima was coming around.

The mating bond had a hold on her. She just hadn't realized it. Lethia was only too happy to allow the bond to work on her. As much as she wanted to bring her to her bed with her, she had left her to her little pallet on the floor.

This was going to be a tough lesson for her to learn, but the reward would be the sweetest.

Lethia pushed her warm covers from her body and sat up. The cocoon her curtains that surrounded her bed created was a warm, intimate area that she loved to rest in. She only wished she could have shared it with her mate.

She grimaced, feeling weaker than she had before. Aubrey was right.

She needed blood.

There had still been a slight resistance in Alima's eyes. She hadn't understood why her body was reacting the way it was. The need to mate had been strong inside her, drawing out the most erotic response Lethia had ever witnessed. Alima's body had been ripe for the taking. The scent of her arousal had flooded Lethia, heightening her own.

Lethia had wanted to carry her to the bed, lay her down, indulge in her sweet pussy, and take her until neither of them could move.

Instead, she had walked away.

Her sleep had been restful, her dreams filled with the fantasy of Alima climaxing on her tongue. It was a welcome dream. One full of promise.

She went to crawl out of the bed but soon

paused. She listened, hearing soft pants and moans coming from the room.

Alima.

Lethia slipped her hand between the curtains and quietly pushed one back so she could step from it. She turned and found her mate lying on top of her blankets with her hand between her thighs. Her hips thrust up as she fucked herself with her fingers.

Lethia smirked. Her mate hadn't listened to her threat. She would have to prove to her who ruled her body. Lethia stalked over to her, still naked.

"You disobeyed what I commanded?" Lethia snapped.

"I can't help it," Alima gasped. Her eyes were wide and frantic with lust. She slipped her fingers from her center and brought them to her clit, drawing circles around it.

Lethia slammed her hand on the button that controlled the chains connected to Alima's restraints. They retracted. Alima cried out as her hands were yanked back, away from her. Lethia helped her to her feet and walked her back against the wall. Her body was covered in a fine sheen of sweat. Lethia pressed a kiss to her chin. Alima's face turned to hers, offering her lips up for Lethia.

She ignored her offer of her lips. She blazed a trail of kisses along her jawline and down to her neck. She bathed her neck with her tongue, wanting to sink her fangs into it, but she resisted. She lifted Alima's breasts up. She pressed them together and brought her mouth to them. She drew her tongue across them, toying with her beaded brown nipples.

Alima's whimper shot a bolt of desire through her. She suckled one nipple deep into her mouth. She flicked the bud with her tongue while releasing the mound and trailing the flat pad of her tongue along it. She licked her way to the other one, repeating the motion. Her mate's breasts were sweet and divine. She rolled the nipple with her tongue. She squeezed both mounds with her hands, pulling a moan from Alima.

"Your body needs a release, doesn't it?" she rasped. Lethia leaned down, her lips brushing Alima's ears. She rested a hand on Alima's neck while skating her other along her torso down to her core. She tightened her hold on Alima's neck to keep her in place. Her arms were held back against the wall.

She looked so beautiful restrained and at her mercy. She stood with her arms stretched out, her full breasts high, with her legs spread apart. Lethia wanted to fall to her knees and worship her body.

"Please," Alima whimpered. Her big brown eyes pleaded with Lethia.

Lethia slipped her fingers to Alima's drenched core. She gasped at how wet Alima was. Her hand became coated in her arousal. She connected with Alima's clit, circling it slowly, applying light pressure. Alima's hips thrust forward, seeking her hand.

"Yes," Lethia hissed.

Alima didn't fight against the restraints. Her eyes remained locked on Lethia, trust deep in them. Her small pink tongue slipped out and ran along her lips. Lethia growled at the sight of it. Unable to resist, she covered Alima's mouth. Alima opened hers wide, welcoming Lethia's tongue.

Lethia moved closer, flicking Alima's bundle of nerves. The kiss grew frantic.

Alima's moans and cries filled the air. Her body writhed against the wall. Her breasts jutted out, brushing Lethia's.

"Do you see how your body knows who commands it? Feel how wet you are?" Lethia pulled her fingers free of Alima's thighs and brought them up to her lips. She trailed her creaminess over Alima's lips and chin. Lethia then licked the substance away, kissing her again. "The bond has a hold of you. Give in."

She slipped her fingers back into Alima's folds, teasing her clit. She rubbed hard, drawing a cry from her mate. Alima's head was thrown back as she arched forward, riding her hand.

"Lethia," she chanted.

Lethia tightened her hold on Alima's neck, watching her emotions play out on her face. She writhed, begged, pleaded for her release. Her breaths turned into pants. Her eyes were clouded with lust, and she was lost in the sensations coursing through her body.

Lethia couldn't tear her eyes off her mate if she tried. She applied more pressure to Alima's neck and watched her body stiffen. Her mouth parted open, no breaths coming from it. Her eyes clenched shut, and her climax exploded. A warm substance shot out of her, drenching Lethia's hand.

Alima inhaled sharply the second Lethia released her neck. Pleasure flooded Lethia at the sight of her slumping back on the wall. The restraints were practically holding her up if it wasn't for Lethia's hand buried between her thighs.

"That's what I want to see," Lethia murmured.

She continued her slow strokes, lowering her head to nuzzle Alima's neck. There were dark markings forming where her hand had clenched. She pressed a kiss to them. A feral sense of pride filled her knowing it was she who had marked her. Not in the way she wanted with her fangs, but it was a start. When she claimed her, her markings would riddle her body.

Lethia withdrew her fingers and covered the front of Alima's body with hers. Their breasts were crushed between, them and Lethia loved the feeling of her mate's breasts on hers. She sent her hands along Alima's arms, gently rubbing them. Her fingers entwined with Alima's. Her lips took a hold of hers.

This kiss was gentle but probing. Lethia commanded it, thrusting her tongue inside Alima's mouth, stroking her tongue. Alima didn't hold back, returning the kiss. Her tongue dueled with Lethia's. She tilted her head to the side, deepening the kiss.

Lethia tightened her hold on Alima's hands. She lifted her head slightly, allowing her lips to still brush Alima's. The sound of Alima's blood rushing through her veins grew louder for Lethia. Her breaths came fast, just as the need to consume

Alima's blood grew. She licked her lips, then ran her tongue over her fangs.

"Give yourself to me," she whispered. She teased Alima, rubbing her breasts against hers. "How much proof do you need that we belong together?"

A shudder went through Alima. She lowered her head.

"No," she whispered faintly, but it was enough where Lethia heard her.

A growl ripped from Lethia. She gripped Alima's hands in a bruising hold before she released her. She wanted to slam her fist into the wall, but instead, she leaned in closer, her voice lethal and low.

"Is it because of him?" Lethia seethed.

"Him?" Alima's gaze flicked to hers. Those big brown eyes of hers widened. She shook her head, stammering over her words. "Who…who are you talking about?"

"The male!" Lethia shouted. She took her mate by her neck, brandishing her fangs. Alima was playing games, and frankly, Lethia was tired of all the bullshit. "Before you came here, you were known to be with a male all the time."

Alima grew still, her breathing ceasing as she stared at Lethia.

"Javari?" she squeaked.

"He has a name," Lethia rasped. She gave Alima's neck a tight squeeze. Jealousy exploded inside her at the thought of the male who was down in her dungeon. "He's the one keeping you from accepting my bite. You love him."

Lethia glared at her mate, feeling her swallow underneath her hand.

"Well, yes. I love him," Alima admitted.

Lethia crushed her mouth to Alima's, not wanting to listen to her. How could she love a male and not her? Fate surely was fucked up. How could fate bring this woman into her life, make her perfect for Lethia, only to have her woman be in love with a human male?

She forced her tongue into Alima's mouth while gripping her chin tight. She plundered her mouth, pouring all of her emotions into it. Alima whimpered, kissing her back. She groaned, brushing her breasts against Lethia's.

Lethia tore her mouth from Alima's and trailed hot kisses over her chin. She nipped and licked her way to Alima's neck.

"The male will no longer be an issue for you," Lethia breathed.

Her fangs scraped Alima's neck. Alima's muscles grew tense.

"What did you just say?" Alima whispered. Her eyes grew wide with fear.

Lethia lifted her head and glared down at her mate. She returned her hand to Alima's neck. She rubbed the marks forming on her mate's skin.

"What have you done to Javari?"

"I haven't done anything to him yet, *miere*." Lethia tightened her hold on Alima's neck. "He's here in the dungeons, waiting for me."

"Please don't hurt him." Fat tears pooled on Alima's eyelashes. She blinked, and they fell, trailing down her warm, brown cheeks.

"Why shouldn't I? When he has the love of the woman who belongs to me?"

"He's all I have," Alima hiccupped, a sob breaking through. She fought at her restraints, but they held her back. "You can't take him from me!"

"I am the warden of this territory. I can do anything I damn well please," Lethia threatened. "I will do anything to get you to love me, to accept me."

"Killing him won't get you either of those. I will

hate you forever if you harm Javari," Alima spat. She tried to move her arms, but the restraints kept them back against the wall.

"It's a risk I'm willing to take." Lethia glowered at her.

She stepped away from her. The pulse of her blood flowing was deafening to her. It was the only sound she could hear. Not wanting to do something she'd regret, she turned and walked away from her, leaving her where she stood.

"Please don't!" Alima screamed. "He's not my lover!"

Lethia paused in front of her closet. She faced forward, unable to process her emotions that had been working through her. Now her mate wanted to lie to her? She'd said she loved the male. Lethia waited to see if Alima would continue.

"He's my best friend. We grew up together. There has never been anything sexual between us. He's like a big brother. So yes, I love him, but only as if he were my own flesh and blood. He's been there for me all these years. Please, whatever you do, don't hurt him."

Her explanation did not do anything to decrease the amount of frustration and rage that filled Lethia. So Alima loved the male as a brother and still would not accept her claim. Lethia was glad that tonight she was hunting lycans.

If she could not claim her mate, then she'd go and kill as many lycans as she could.

LETHIA STORMED up to the armory where her warriors were donning their protective gear and weapons. She passed them and nodded to her warriors, acknowledging their thumps over their hearts and the lowering of their heads as their show of respect for her. She held her head high, trying to present a strong front, but inside, she felt weak. She had to concentrate to walk and not look as if she was off. Maybe she should have requested a live donor before her mission. When she came back, she would have one sent to her.

Her men and women all held fierce expressions as they prepared for battle. She walked through the throng of warriors. Some were choosing silver-plated swords, crossbows with silver bolts, and a favorite among vampires, guns with silver bullets. Her army was outfitted with the latest weapons and over the years had prepped for the chance of a resurgence of lycans. Their weapons were now more advanced than when they'd first gone to war. Her father had always wanted them to be prepared.

Unfortunately, it would seem they were at the point that he had been right to ensure vampires would be able to continue to fight lycans.

She was dressed in her fighting leathers with her two twin daggers sheathed on her waist and her gun with her silver nitrate rounds. Even though she preferred to fight with her daggers, guns proved useful. Her silver rounds were quite effective against lycans. These bullets that had been developed were silver-plated with liquid silver nitrate on the inside. The liquid invaded the lycans' bloodstream, carrying the deadly metal throughout the beasts' bodies, killing them within minutes.

Lethia headed toward the room at the back. Dru and Kane bent over a table, studying and discussing whatever they were looking at.

"Your Grace."

Lethia paused and turned. Aubrey walked toward her. The advisor rushed, her hair flowing behind her. Her blue eyes held an expression of concern.

"Aubrey." Lethia gave a nod to her advisor.

"You sent word that you needed to speak with

me immediately. What do you need?" Aubrey asked.

"Walk with me." She motioned for Aubrey to follow her.

They cut through the room and exited out of a side door that led to a hallway. Lethia shut the door.

"You look like shit," Aubrey said immediately. She rested a hand on Lethia's arm. "You didn't drink from your mate?"

"No." She shook her head. She stood tall, trying to draw on her internal strength. "How have Zetta and Alima's guards faired?"

"Zetta has made a smooth recovery. I gave her another day or so to make sure. She was mentally traumatized by the attack. As for the warriors, they are ready to reassume their duties."

"I will need to speak with them before they do," Lethia murmured.

"They didn't do anything wrong," Aubrey said.

"I didn't say they did. Their actions kept the lycans from my mate." Even though Alima had run, the lycans were too busy fighting the guards to leave and run off after her. Lethia inhaled sharply, trying to draw in a deep breath.

"Are you sure you are up to going out on this mission?"

"I'm fine, Aubrey. I've been fighting my entire life, I know myself," she barked. She closed her eyes, immediately regretting her outburst. Aubrey was only after her well-being. "I'm sorry."

"I'm just worried about you." Aubrey ran a hand through her hair and leaned back against the wall beside her. She clutched her tablet to her chest. "What do you need me to do while you're gone?"

"Send a servant up to my room to see to my mate."

"She hasn't been harmed, has she?" Aubrey whispered.

"What? No. Why would you think that?" she scoffed. She turned and rested her shoulder on the wall so she could look at her.

"I just needed to be sure."

"No, see to it that she's fed and there is someone who can help her bathe. She is not to be released from her restraints."

"Fine, I will send someone." Aubrey sighed and reached up to pinch the bridge of her nose. "I wished you wouldn't go under your current circumstances."

"I'll be fine." Lethia pushed off the wall and

rested a hand on her friend's shoulder. "Also, have a donor available. I'm going to try drinking from one when I return."

"You'd better. I don't like seeing you this way." Aubrey tucked her hair behind her ear. "Just so you know, while you were resting, I was able to get a photo of Azura. It took some workings and dealings, and don't ask, but we have it. I sent it to Dru."

"Good job, Aubrey." Lethia was impressed as aways with Aubrey's workings. She had contacts all over the world, and Lethia was sure one of them had paid off. "Have I told you how great you are?"

"Not nearly enough. Also while you were sleeping, we've received two reports of unidentified attacks on humans out in the open, and they were not vampires."

Lethia released a curse. "Who reported it?" she asked.

"The mayor. He's already demanding something be done. The humans are in uproar. The council has caught whiff of it, too, and are demanding to move up the quarterly meeting to discuss. They would have come today, but I was able to buy you time."

"When will it be?" Lethia asked. She hated convening with the council, but this meeting she dreaded. They were going to demand to see her mate, see proof that they had sealed the bond. They would want to formally introduce her to the coven and the entire territory. Her time would soon be running out.

"Next week."

Lethia nodded. That was more time than she'd assumed she'd get. Aubrey didn't take any shit, and Lethia was sure she'd pushed back the council without even breaking a sweat or a nail.

"Very well then."

"I think that is all the updates for now." Aubrey turned and opened the door, waving her hand in. "Come, let's go send you off to battle properly."

Lethia stepped through the threshold, and she thought of what Aubrey had said. The proper way to send her off to battle would be for Alima to allow her to drink from her to give her the strength and power she would need to meet her enemy head-on. Alima would stand by the door and watch her drive off, then would greet her when she returned. Lethia imagined what it would be like. Her human would welcome her home, bathe the remnants of the fight from her body, then go to bed with her, making love all day. There would be kisses, bites, and feedings.

It would be the perfect ending to her night.

One day she would get that. Her stubborn human would give in to her. Sooner or later, her mate would beg for her bite.

She marched into the room where Dru and Kane were in a heated discussion.

"What's going on?"

They abruptly ceased and glared at each other. Dru turned to her and gave her a nod.

"Your Grace. We've had a sighting of the alpha. It's confirmed. She is in Crystal Cove," Dru announced.

Aubrey's gasp filled the air. Lethia didn't look her way. She already knew what Aubrey's face would reveal and what she was thinking. Lethia would be fine. She was the daughter of the king, one of the most powerful vampires around.

"Good. Then we will settle this shit tonight. The alpha is mine."

CHAPTER TWENTY-TWO

Alima closed her eyes and wiggled her fingers. Her arm was asleep. The painful numbness in her upper extremities ached. Lethia had left her tethered to the wall. Alima knew she had pissed the vampire off again.

She had come out of her lust-filled haze, heard the vampire whisper for her to give in, and her first response that left her lips was "No." Alima leaned her head back on the wall and searched within herself.

Could she give herself to a vampire and still

fight for her people? Still avenge her sister's death? Take care of her parents?

Tears flooded her vision. She hadn't spoken with her parents in months. It had been agreed upon they would keep communications to necessary contacts only.

And then there was Javari. Lethia had said he was down in her dungeons. She hoped he was safe. She didn't know how long he had been down there, but it would explain why he hadn't been at home when she'd gone to his apartment.

Was he being treated fairly?

Was he already harmed?

Javari had been the one constant in her life, and she didn't know what she would do if Lethia took him from her. The feral look in Lethia's eyes had left her worried.

Alima's eyes snapped open at the sound of the bedroom door opening. Her breaths quickened as she waited to see who walked through them. Her gaze landed on a woman that was not her vampire.

It was Lethia's advisor, Aubrey.

The woman took one glance at Alima and rolled her eyes.

"This is how she left you?" Aubrey blew out a deep breath and shut the door. She stood there for a moment, studying the room, then walked toward Alima.

"Are you here to release me?" Alima asked. She warily eyed the vampire.

Aubrey stared at her, keeping her gaze on her face. She never wavered below to Alima's nakedness. Aubrey hadn't even batted an eye at the fact that Alima was chained to a wall that was littered with compartments. Alima wasn't sure what else was stored in them.

"Oh, I was given strict instructions that you were not to be freed."

"Then why are you here?" Alima cleared her voice.

She tried to push down the feelings of embarrassment. Aubrey, on the other hand, appeared cool as a cucumber, as if seeing a naked woman chained to a wall was an everyday occurrence for her. It left Alima wondering who else Lethia had tied up in her room. With Lethia away from her, she was starting to think a little clearer.

"I wanted to come look in the face of the human who would get my friend killed." Aubrey paused a few feet from Alima. Her cool blue eyes held a hint of disappointment, and fear. Unlike Lethia, her face was easy to read.

"What are you talking about?" Alima hadn't done anything to get Lethia killed. How dare this woman come here and accuse her of such a thing. She grimaced at the shooting pain that radiated down both arms when she went to move them.

"Lethia hasn't fed from anyone in a while now. The mating bond that you refuse to acknowledge takes hold of a vampire immediately. We are driven to want to bite our mates to not only make them ours but to give them life longevity so they can walk beside us for as long as we may live. Our sole purpose when it comes to our mates is take, mate, and cherish. It's burrowed down in our DNA. Doesn't matter the vampire. Their only goal is to treasure their mates."

Alima swallowed hard, unable to speak around the lump in her throat.

"But because you haven't accepted her bite, you withhold your blood from her. She's a stubborn woman who would probably kill me if she knew I was here tonight." Aubrey tucked her thick dark hair behind her ear and glanced away. She folded her arms and paced in front of Alima. "But I'm here because I care about Lethia Riskel. We've been friends for well over two hundred years."

"What is the point of this lecture?" Alima eyed the vampire.

"The point I'm making is that you are the key to everything for Lethia. Her happiness is centered around you. Relations between human and vampires can be smoothed out because of you. Her leadership of her territory can be enhanced because of you, and her life is in your hands."

"I have not done anything to Lethia to hurt her."

"Oh, but you have. The fact that she has not had any of your blood or anyone else's, she grows weak. She is not the same powerful vampire I know. She's paler, her mind isn't as sharp, and she just left to ride into battle to face the lycan alpha."

Alima's heart stuttered. She had noticed Lethia had seemed a little paler than normal but had dismissed it.

"She'll be just fine, won't she? She's a strong fighter," Alima whispered.

"We don't know this alpha. Lethia's going up against this wolf blind. I've begged her not to go, but she's the only one who can face an alpha." Aubrey faced her. "Why won't you accept her?"

Alima turned away and stared across the room. She didn't want to have this conversation with this woman. It wasn't any of her business what went on between her and Lethia. The silence stretched out. Alima heard Aubrey move around, the tap of her heels echoing on the floor.

"Was it because of the death of your sister?"

Alima jerked her head around to meet Aubrey's gaze. Aubrey folded her arms and walked toward Alima.

"It was tragic. We've all lost someone in this war and through the transition of trying to get used to this new way of life. You can't harbor all this hatred toward all vampires."

"You don't get to speak of how I should feel or what I should be doing. You don't know me." Alima blinked back the tears that threatened to spill. She inhaled sharply and stood to her full height. She had to have some pride, even though she was chained to her lover's wall, naked.

"I know that blaming an entire species for one or two vampires' actions is wrong. If a human male had killed your sister, would you hate all human men? Would you fight against all of them? You are punishing Lethia for something someone else did, and you will get her killed."

There was a knock at the door.

Aubrey strolled over to the door and opened it.

A young vampire with mousy-brown hair and wide eyes entered.

"Please see to her needs and that she is cleaned. The princess does not want her unchained. She's a flight risk," Aubrey instructed.

"Yes, my lady." The young girl nodded. She turned to look at Alima and she, too, didn't appear to be surprised by Alima being restrained to the wall.

"I will loosen the restraints where she can move around sightly." Aubrey went over to the wall and tapped on a button on the panel.

A whirling sound came from behind Alima. The slack in the chains loosened. Alima groaned at the sharp pain zipping through her arms. She shook them out, trying to get the circulation flowing.

"Where is Zetta?" Alima asked. She eyed the new servant who stood waiting.

"She was injured the night of the attack. She will return in a couple of days to work." Aubrey walked toward the door. She smirked, glancing over her shoulder. "I'm surprised you asked, since when you ran away you left her for dead."

Alima didn't have a snappy comeback for her. She watched the advisor slip through the door and shut it behind her. What she'd said was the truth. She hadn't wanted Zetta to go out there, but the vampire was stubborn. She'd disappeared into the darkness, and Alima had taken advantage of being alone.

She lowered her head and sighed. She fell to the floor and sat on top of her blanket. She hoped Zetta was okay. The vampire's job had been to see to her needs and help her understand vampires better.

Alima glanced up and looked at the servant girl. "Thank you for coming to take care of me."

"But of course, my lady. It is an honor," the girl replied in a soft voice. "My name is Gerty, and I'll go draw some hot water and snag some towels." She headed into the bathroom.

Alima sighed and thought of Lethia. Had she really been starving herself since she couldn't drink from her? Had Alima sent her to her death unknowingly? She didn't know much about the lycans, but she prayed Lethia was strong enough to take the alpha wolf down.

ALIMA FELT LIKE A NEW WOMAN. Gerty had worked her magic, bringing in buckets for Alima's needs. She had ensured her body was squeaky clean along with her hair. She'd even helped Alima empty her bladder with a bucket. It was slightly embarrassing but necessary.

This time, Alima had braided her hair in a crown around her head. She wanted to be different today, and to be honest, she wanted to look pleasing to Lethia when she came back. She opted to stay naked, even though Gerty would have tried to finagle something for her to wear on her chest, but she knew deep inside, her vampire preferred her naked. Gerty brought her fresh blankets and helped her make a little cocoon out of them to cushion her back when she lay down.

Food had been delivered from the kitchen for her. She'd eaten everything on the tray, not realizing how hungry she had been. Once she was clean and fed, she had lay in her nest of blankets and fallen asleep.

She woke, confused slightly. She didn't know what time it was, but the window shields were lifted, allowing moonlight to shine in through the windows. A few lamps were left on, illuminating the suite.

Alima sighed and burrowed down in the blankets. She couldn't wait to see Lethia. They would have plenty to talk about when she returned.

If she returns, a voice said.

"She will," Alima murmured. She had faith in Lethia. She was a fierce warrior and would defeat the lycans.

She sat up at the sound of the door opening. Her heart rate quickened, hopeful it was Lethia, but instead, a slightly older woman who was the exact image of Lethia entered. Her dress accented her curves but then flowed out around her feet. Her blonde hair was up in an intricate updo.

Alima's mouth dropped open; she recognized this woman from television.

It was the queen.

"So it is true," the queen of the vampires murmured. Her eyes, the same color as Lethia's, lingered on Alima before scanning the room. "I won't ask why my daughter has you chained to her wall with only blankets."

"Um, Your Grace," Alima stammered. She wasn't truly sure how she was supposed to address the woman before her. Did she say my queen? Your Royal Highness? Mrs. Riskel? The only royal person she'd ever met was Lethia, and they were definitely on a first-name basis. She doubted the queen would grant her the privilege to call her by her first name.

"What is your name, my dear?" The queen turned back to her. She remained a respectful distance away from Alima.

"My name is Alima Morgan, ma'am," Alima said. She clutched the blanket around her and stared at the woman who ruled the vampires along with her husband.

"Do you know who I am?" Mira Riskel asked.

"Yes, ma'am. You're Lethia's mother, the queen," she responded. Alima glanced down at her blankets and inwardly winced. This would not be how she wanted to meet the in-laws. She had imagined it doing completely differently.

So, you have thought of a future with Lethia? Alima ignored the voice at the back of her head.

"You do know it is a courtesy for one to stand when in the presence of royalty? Or have you not reached that part in your studies?" The queen arched a perfectly sculpted eyebrow.

"I'm…I'm sorry." Alima scrambled to her feet, keeping herself covered with the blanket. She bowed her head as she had seen others do to Lethia.

"Well, you are a pretty girl. I'm sure my daughter is infatuated with you," Mira said.

"Thank you, Your Grace." Alima's cheeks warmed at the compliment. She didn't think infatuated was a strong enough word for Lethia's feelings for her.

"Since my daughter is away, I have spoken with Aubrey to get a sense of where you and my daughter stand with your mating, but she wouldn't give me much detail."

Alima swallowed hard. Worry gnawed at her. If she refused the mating bond with Lethia, would the queen take matters into her own hands and have Alima executed? She shivered at that thought.

"We are working on it," Alima replied.

The queen's gaze went to the wall behind her and the chains restraining her.

"I see." Mira didn't look too convinced. "I will have to speak with my daughter about the treatment of her mate, but if she felt it was necessary to lock you up, I'm sure there was a good reason."

More heat crept into Alima's cheeks. She dared not reveal that she was a member of the Rebel group who helped humans escape their vampire mates or that she had attempted an escape to get away from her daughter, so she didn't say anything.

She watched the queen stroll over to a table across the room that had picots and flowers on it. She lifted one and stared at it, a smile coming to her lips.

"Centuries ago, a royal taking a human mate would have been unheard of," she began. She reached for another one and held it up, studying it.

Alima hadn't had a chance to explore Alima's massive bedroom since she had been brought in. There was a seating area, fireplace, and basically all the comforts that money could buy.

"But my husband was looking into the mating issue even then. He knew that there was something we vampires were missing. We knew fate controlled who was born for us. Vampires, we live long lives, and for some, it takes hundreds of years before they find the one for them. But it was taking too long. Our numbers began to decline, and the king wanted to ensure his people did not perish.

"He hired a team to look into this, and upon finding that humans were compatible with vampires, it was a win for us. But he still faced opposition. Please note that even some vampires are resistant to human and vampire matings. It is not just the humans protesting and fighting the draft. It is a way of life where we can all come together and live amongst each other peacefully, but we must accept it. Until we learn to accept one another, there will be no peace. Matings or no matings."

Mira turned to Alima and placed the photograph back where it belonged. She offered a tight smile to Alima. It didn't appear she needed a response because she changed the subject and continued on.

"I have some business to attend to. We will meet again once my daughter has returned to discuss your mating and presentation to her coven. I have the utmost confidence that you will be welcomed with open arms. My daughter, Velika, her mate is human, too, and doing well in her new position. They are expecting our first grandchild any day now." Mira's face softened at the mention of her grandchild. It almost made her appear human. She glanced back at Alima and gave her a slight nod. She appeared to float across the room. She opened the door and left.

Alima was frozen in place. She didn't know what that was with the queen. She couldn't get a read on her, but it would appear Aubrey was leaving the details of their relationship for Lethia to tell. Alima flopped back down on her nest of blankets. The queen's words echoed in her mind.

Until we learn to accept one another, there will be no peace.

Would accepting Lethia's affections, love, and mating bring peace to her life?

CHAPTER TWENTY-THREE

Dru and Kane did well preparing her vampires who would fight for their princess. Lethia sat in the back of the armored vehicle with Kane at her side. They were spread out in the area, getting ready for the invasion of the lycan den.

"This reminds me of the war when we fought the lycans. You, a young warrior in your father's army, now look at you, leading your own army." Kane glanced at her with a crooked grin on his face.

"And you are older and still ugly," she taunted the vampire.

He threw his head back and barked a hefty laugh. The large vampire slapped his knee. A small smile played on her lips.

"Well, if you two are done reminiscing on the past, we have movement up ahead." Dru snorted from the passenger seat.

Lethia turned and glanced out the window. They were parked a block from the lycans' underground entrance. The male walking down the street kept glancing over his shoulders. He paused at the corner and stood. He scraped his hand through his hair then leaned against the light pole next to him.

"The lookout," Kane murmured.

"Get rid of him," Lethia replied. Her gums burned and stretched as her fangs descended.

They couldn't afford to let anyone alert the den that they were on the way. Kane spoke quietly in a communicator buried in his ear. Lethia reached up and clicked on the one in hers. This was one of the technologies she liked. It allowed her to stay in contact with her captains when diving into battle.

They were on the outskirts of town. There were two ways to infiltrate it. The sewers and the main entrance near the caves.

They were going in both ways.

This would keep the fight underground and

hopefully not spill out into the town. They didn't need for the human media to get a hold of the war that was brewing. All she would need was for them to catch wind of it and spread the news worldwide, instigating a panic.

Lethia watched the lycan jump at a sound behind him. He must be a newly turned wolf. Experienced ones wouldn't be afraid of their own shadows. A whip shot out of the dark and wrapped around his neck, and his body was jerked to the ground and dragged away into the darkness.

"It is time," Lethia murmured. Her hand went to the door, and she opened it.

They stepped from the vehicle and rounded it to the front.

"Kane, wait for our signal. We'll alert you when we are ready," Lethia said.

"Will do, Princess." He was leading the group that would go through the main entrance.

A warrior named Talbot walked over to join them. He was one of Kane's trusted men. He had plenty of blades strapped to his body.

Kane slapped him on the shoulder. "We'll make sure we knock on the door hard enough and wake up everyone who is sleeping."

"That we will," Talbot said. "We are ready when you are."

Lethia and Dru would go through the sewers. They would infiltrate the den in waves. They had orchestrated a sound breach, ensuring they would be victorious.

"Sync up your communicators," Dru instructed.

"For the crown." Lethia thumped her chest.

"For the crown," they all echoed with her, repeating the same action.

"We'll see you inside the lycan den." Lethia gave a nod to Kane before turning around and striding away to the point they would need to reach.

"I hate sewers," Dru murmured.

They cut down an alley that would lead to an area behind an abandoned building. The entrance was located on the small road behind it.

"They're hot, dark, and always stink."

"Life of a vampirian warrior." Lethia smirked.

Her vampires had secured the rest of the area. She took in a few of her men posted on the rooftop of the buildings. They would be her eyes and ears while they went below ground. They exited the mouth of the alley and came to the road. The first wave of warriors that would accompany her and Dru stood near the sewer plate in the ground, waiting.

They bowed their heads and thumped their chests when she stopped in front of them.

"Two hundred years ago, we went to war with lycans. They thought they would wipe us out. They didn't know how strong vampires are," she began. She met the eyes of her men and women who were ready to risk their lives for the goodness of vampires. "This alpha has made a threat to the royal family."

Growls went around.

"But we won't let them," she continued. She rested a hand on her daggers and widened her stance. "Every lycan in this den is to die tonight. We will be victorious in eradicating the threats to the vampire nation. Do this, and we will have a celebration in your honor."

Grunts went around. Her warriors were focused and knew they had to remain as silent as possible. Lycans had one hell of a sense of hearing. Even though they had the area secured, they couldn't take a chance one could hear them from blocks away. She gave a nod and headed toward the steel plate in the ground. Dru motioned for someone to come open it. Two men came over and lifted it.

Lethia pulled her gun from the sheath on her thigh. She was outfitted with knives and daggers all over body, along with two guns filled with silver ammunition.

"No, Princess. We'll go first." Dru held up her hand. She stepped forward with her rifle in her hand and motioned for a few men to follow her down. "Let us ensure the area is still clear."

Lethia didn't like it, but she had to let Dru do her job. Dru and a team dropped down in the sewers first. Lethia walked to the edge and stared down into the tunnel, waiting.

"It's clear," Dru announced in her earpiece.

"Let's go," Lethia said. She stepped forward, dropping down into the tunnel. She landed on her feet and raised her weapon, sweeping the area.

The soft thuds of her men landing behind her were the only sounds.

They jogged down the sewers. Her high leather boots protected her from the sludge and water on the ground that was ankle-deep. There was little to no light to guide them, but they wouldn't need it. Vampires had excellent sight in the dark. The tunnels were warm, moist, and dark. The stench was unforgiving.

Her warriors flanked her side as they continued. They came to a fork in the path. She and Dru would split, taking half the team with them each way. A few vampires would stay back to make sure no one snuck up behind them.

Lethia gave Dru a nod and headed down her tunnel. A few of her men went ahead of her, keeping her in the center of their formation. They stalked down and would soon come to an opening. What would be waiting for them, Lethia didn't know.

They had been unable to get their eyes on the inside of the den. The team that had been watching the lycans had given much information of the comings and goings of the lycans but hadn't been able to get any good visuals on them.

Voices echoed through the air. Lethia and her team slowed to a halt. It was hard to distinguish the distance of the voices. Growls and howls followed behind. Yes, they were close.

Her man up front held up a hand, signaling for them to pause. He pulled out a scope, slowing walking forward. He bent down and got to the ground, using the scope to take a peek. He scanned the area, and a few seconds later, he backed up and came to her.

"What did you see?" she asked.

"There's about twenty men down there in beast and human form. It looks as if they are arguing over something. The two in beast form appear to be about to engage in a fight."

Of course the beasts couldn't live together without tearing out each other's throats. They were animals after all. Personalities would clash, and they would attack each other.

"Well, I say this is the perfect time for us to drop in," Lethia brandished her fangs. She raised her hand to her ear. "Kane, Dru. Come in. My team is in place."

"We're good here," Dru came in.

"Hold your horses." Kane chuckled. "We ran into a little lycan action out here in the woods. It's been taken care of before they alerted the others."

"How much action?" Lethia asked.

"Nothing to worry about, Princess. We didn't even break a sweat. We're in place now. Shall I knock or ring their doorbell?" Kane chuckled again.

"Blow the fucking door in," Lethia breathed.

"I knew there was a reason I joined your house." Kane laughed.

At the time he'd made that choice, Lethia had been shocked and honored. He had been loyal and moving up the ranks of her father's army. She didn't hesitate to give him the title of captain when he'd followed her to her territory. He was a fierce warrior and extremely intelligent when it came to war.

"Drinks on me when we get back," she murmured.

"They always are," he said.

An explosion shuddered the tunnels. Rocks and dirt fell from the ceiling. Lethia headed toward the front of the group.

"That's our signal," she shouted. She raised her gun in the air with a battle roar exploding from her mouth.

Her men shouted the same, and they took off, racing toward the lycans.

LETHIA PULLED THE TRIGGER, holding her weapon steady during its recoil. Her aim was true, her bullets slamming into the lycans who raced toward her. The feral beasts were flooding the sewers. Her men were holding their own.

A large form barged into her from behind, sending her sprawling to the ground. A lycan snarled and snapped his fangs. She gripped his neck in her hand, holding him back from biting her. She pressed her gun to its chest over his heart and fired, emptying out the clip. His body jerked with each round, falling forward. She screamed, pushing his heavy form off to the side where he fell to the ground, dead. She rolled over and ejected her clip. She drew another one from the back of her belt and loaded the weapon again.

Lethia hated to admit she felt out of breath. She ignored it, trying to push through. She could not be weak while in the middle of the fight. She would get through this. There still hadn't been any sign of the alpha yet.

The circular area they were in opened up to many other tunnels. The lycans continued to make their way through them. Her men were putting up a valiant fight.

Dru's swords sliced through a beast. The woman was a deadly fighter. Her silver sword tore into the lycans that dared approach her. She had a set look of determination on her face as she faced the enemies.

Lethia glanced up. A single female stood in the mouth of one of the higher tunnels located nearly a story up.

The alpha.

She fit the description of the woman in the picture Aubrey had commissioned. Her gaze met Lethia's. She smirked and walked backward, disappearing into the tunnel.

"Dru!" Lethia called out.

The lycan her second had been fighting fell to the ground. She sank her sword deep inside it and glanced over at Lethia.

"She's here," Lethia said. "I'm going after her."

She took off running through the melee. The underground den was in chaos. They lycans had never suspected they would outright attack their den. She ran over to the wall and slid her gun back in its sheath. She jumped up and climbed the metal ladder attached to the wall. She flew up it and pulled herself to the ledge.

Her gaze landed on Azura. The fighting ensued below them, but Lethia refused to look backward, not wanting to take her attention from the alpha.

Lethia stalked toward her. The alpha smirked and walked in reverse.

"The great Lethia Riskel, daughter of the vampire king," Azura snarled. Her amber eyes narrowed on Lethia. "Welcome to my den."

She held her hands out in the air and barked a laugh. She disappeared from Lethia's view.

Lethia released a curse and jogged forward. She snatched her dagger from its sheath. She paused at the mouth of the tunnel. She inhaled sharply, trying to calm her racing heart and her shortness of breath. She scanned the area and found a large room with television monitors along the walls, a table in the center, a cot in the corner, and a few scattered boxes stacked up against the wall. No one was in there.

The door against the wall was left wide open.

Lethia raced across and through the door. The alpha ahead of her sprinted down the dark hall. Lethia inhaled and breathed deeply, pushing forward hard. The alpha slammed through a metal door that led them outside. Lethia was right behind her. The cool night air hit her as she jumped down the ledge onto the ground. The alpha stood near a tree. The scent of the sea was rich in the air.

The door exited through the caves and onto a

section of land near the sea cove. She stalked toward the alpha. Azura eyed her, walking around the tree, putting it between them.

"Well, it would seem you know who I am, but I haven't a clue on you," Lethia taunted. She held her dagger tight, trying to hold it steady from the slight tremors. "Not that I care. All you lycans will be dead anyway."

"Let me introduce myself to you." She bowed deeply and lifted her head with a snarl on her lips. "My name is Azura Michaels, and I assure you, me and my lycans aren't going anywhere."

"Your name means absolutely nothing to me." The only thing Lethia cared about was ending the alpha and defeating the lycans. They would destroy this pack and send a message out to the other packs around the country.

She stalked the lycan around the tree. Azura smirked, strolling away from Lethia, going farther into the woods.

"Well, it should. I am the alpha of the lycans, and you will get to know my name. How did you like my gift I sent to you?"

"Oh, you shouldn't have. All of your men are dead."

"It was a risk I was willing to take. With as

many wolves as we have, it was a small loss."

Lethia tucked that bit of knowledge in the back of her head. She was growing tired of this little game the lycan was playing.

"What, do you have hundreds?" Lethia asked, trying to get more information from the lycan.

The alpha laughed. "We've been building our numbers for years. Thanks to an initiative I instituted, I get humans delivered to me weekly. This country will be overrun with lycans soon." She gave a toothy grin and shook a finger at Lethia. "My wolves are ready and waiting for my word. There will be a war."

"You don't want a war with vampires, wolf," Lethia growled. She pointed her dagger at Azura. "You should have learned from the history books how we hunted you beasts down to little or nothing."

"I know the history," Azura snapped. "That's why I've been on a mission to bring our numbers back to where they should be. You vampires have been living a good life, and frankly, it's time for you to go."

Azura's face contorted as her body shifted. Her clothing shredded off her and fell to the ground. She grew to six and a half feet tall. Her dark fur covered her body while her claws shot out of her hands. Her shift took a matter of seconds, denoting her status of alpha. Only they could shift that fast.

Lethia pulled her other dagger from its sheath and let out a war yell.

Azura growled and rushed toward Lethia. They would be equal in strength. Lethia swiped her daggers, catching Azura across the abdomen. Her daggers were an extension of her. She'd been using them since she was a small child and learning how to defend herself.

Azura howled from the sting of her silver blades. The lycan stepped back, blood seeping from her new wound. They circled each other, their gazes unwavering.

"Come on, you mangy wolf," Lethia seethed.

She dropped down in a defensive stance, her grip tight on her weapons. The wolf snarled, showcasing her fangs. She came at Lethia with her claws swinging. Lethia barely managed to dodge them. She ducked, rising, and slashed her dagger, catching the lycan on her thigh with her vampiric speed, then spun to her, using her other dagger and slicing Azura's back.

She was much faster than the bulky wolf, but the alpha wasn't going to go down easily. Azura circled around and launched herself at Lethia. She crashed back into a tree, the lycan's claws sinking into her side.

Lethia cried out, the pain exploding through her. She gritted her teeth, her daggers falling out of her hands. One arm was pinned to the tree by the lycan.

"Your Grace, where are you?" Dru's voice came in through her communicator.

Lethia raised her other hand and gripped the lycan's neck. Azura bent down to sink her fangs into Lethia. She fought to hold the alpha back.

Azura twisted her claws around, dragging another cry from Lethia. She bared her fangs, staring up into the lycan's feral eyes.

The alpha's body jerked. Gunfire echoed through the air. She snarled and turned away from Lethia. Her claws released Lethia's side. She raced away as Dru and other vampires opened fire on her. She scurried away into the woods. Lethia slid down the tree and hit the ground.

"Your Grace!" Dru rushed to her and fell to the ground in front of her. Her eyes were wide and frantic. "Fuck. Are you okay?"

Lethia raised her hand and pressed it to her wound that was bleeding profusely. She grimaced, the pain radiating through her side and up along her body. It took her breath away. She inhaled, trying to breathe.

"I'll be good as new in a second," Lethia gasped.

"Let me see." Dru pulled her hand away and glanced at her stomach. A curse escaped her. "We need help. The princess is down."

"I'm fine," Lethia growled. She pushed up to stand, but her body wouldn't cooperate.

"Rest, my princess. We'll get someone to help you."

Vampires escaped through the door, flooding the area. Lethia shook her head. Her warriors needed to see her walk.

"I've got to get up," Lethia said.

She glared at Dru, who sighed and jerked her head in a nod.

Lethia pressed her hand to her wound and allowed Dru to help her into a standing position.

"Report," Lethia barked.

She blinked and tried to focus, but there were two of Dru standing in front of her. She stumbled to the side, with Dru coming to her right.

Lethia brushed her away. "I'm fine."

Then everything went dark.

CHAPTER TWENTY-FOUR

A sense of dread filled Alima. She didn't know what was happening, but something was wrong. The whirling mechanism of the window coverings flared to life, and she almost jumped out of her skin. She breathed a sigh of relief and leaned back against the wall.

She gripped her blanket tight, unsure of what was going on, but she needed answers. The door opened with a guard holding it open for Gerty as she pushed a cart into the room. The aroma of food floated across and hit her. Her stomach growled its approval of Gerty's arrival.

"Good morning, my lady," Gerty said.

The sun wasn't out yet, but Alima guessed it was close to it rising, hence the reason for the steel coverings sliding into place.

"Morning," Alima murmured.

She eyed the girl who stopped in front of her. She lifted a fancy tray from the cart and set it down in front of Alima. Gerty stood and stepped back toward the cart.

"Is the princess back yet?"

Gerty's eyes widened, and the floor of Alima's stomach gave way. Gerty didn't even have to answer.

"Um, yes, she's back." Gerty nervously fiddled with some items on her cart. Her eyes flicked to the door. "Is there anything else you need?"

"Can you ask for the princess to come and see me?" Alima watched Gerty's response.

"I'm not sure where she is, but I will send a message for you." Gerty scurried across the room with her cart and flew out of the door.

Alima lifted the cover on her plate. The chef had sent her breakfast. Fluffy pancakes, scrambled eggs, and sausage. There was orange juice, fresh fruit, and a bowl of yogurt on the tray. She sighed and doctored up her pancakes with syrup and butter. Even though she was worried about Lethia, she was still famished.

She ate in silence, wondering how Lethia was. She didn't like the sense of dread that stuck with her. She didn't want to think something was wrong. Was she injured? Had Aubrey been right and her decision to not give in to Lethia had put her at risk?

She set her fork down and drank the juice. The more she worried about Lethia, the more she couldn't touch the other items on the tray. She dropped the glass down and pushed the tray away. She slid her blanket back around her shoulders and sighed.

Alima stood and readjusted her nest of blankets before she sat back down. The leather cuffs around her wrists slid along her skin. She glanced at them, remembering when Lethia had restrained her against the wall where she couldn't move. There was something about letting Lethia play with her body that just aroused her.

Even now.

But she couldn't help but feel as if Lethia was harmed.

Somehow, she knew these emotions she was feeling couldn't have been her own.

Lethia was right.

The bond had her.

It could be the only thing that could explain why she had the sudden feelings of rage when she wasn't upset, the dread now, and even the shortness of breath she had experienced a couple of hours ago. She had dozed off for a moment, then had woken up gasping for breath.

She needed to speak with Lethia. They had to have a long talk, and Alima had to get some things off her chest.

The door opened, and the sounds of heels echoing on the floor had her turning. She glanced over. Aubrey headed toward her. The vampire's face was expressionless.

"I was notified you were asking to speak with Lethia," Aubrey said, coming to stand a few feet from her. She held a tablet against her chest.

"Yes, I wanted to speak with her. Where is she?" Alima asked.

"First, let me say, you don't get to demand the princess comes to you." Aubrey sniffed.

"I wasn't demanding, I asked—"

"And second, she is a very busy woman at the moment. There is a war brewing on the horizon if you knew, and she's only trying to keep it from boiling over to your precious humans."

Alima narrowed her eyes on the vampire. She didn't have to come in with an attitude. It was apparent the woman didn't care for her, and since she was making things difficult… Alima was never a person to allow someone to run over her, and today, she was not going to stand for it. She'd been through much and she didn't care if it was a human or a vampire, they would respect her.

"Listen, you don't have to like me, and I know you are close with Lethia, but you need to watch how you speak with me." Alima stood and kept the blanket around her. She wouldn't always be locked up in Lethia's room. "All I asked was to speak with Lethia, not demand. And yes, I know of the war brewing between lycans and vampires. Just as you are passionate about vampires, I'm passionate about my people. There is nothing wrong with that. We are allowed to care and fight for our people. I am grateful for Lethia trying to ensure that humans are protected in this matter."

Aubrey stared at her for a moment before releasing a sigh.

"I wondered if you had a backbone." Audrey leveled her with a glare. "The princess has returned. I'm sure she will be up here to see you soon. She has some things to take care of first."

Alima nodded. She was sure she was busy, and maybe Aubrey could help her with one of the things she was going to ask Lethia.

"Can you take me to my friend?" Alima asked.

"What are you talking about?"

"Lethia told me she has Javari locked up in the dungeon. I need to go see him."

"Oh, no." Aubrey shook her head. "You will have to speak with Lethia about that. I don't trust you to let you loose. I'll be damned if you run away on my watch."

"Please. I promise I won't leave," Alima pleaded.

"No." Aubrey's lips pressed together in a firm line. "Like I said, Lethia will be up when she's done. She'll need her rest." She headed toward the door.

"What do you mean she needs her rest?" Alima stepped forward but was stopped by the restraints. "Is she okay?"

Aubrey halted but didn't turn around.

"Do you even care?" Aubrey asked. She made her way to the door and paused with her hand on the knob. "She'll be up soon."

CHAPTER TWENTY-FIVE

"I will walk into my home," Lethia growled.

Lane had met them at the truck when they had arrived back at the castle. He held the door open, a look of concern in his eyes. It was important for Lethia to show strength when returning from battle. She didn't want any of her warriors to think she was weak.

"I wouldn't dream of trying to carry you." Lane waved his hand for her to step out of the truck.

"I've already had to carry her, and let me tell you, she's not as light as she looks," Dru said.

"Tell anyone else you had to carry me, and I'll kill you," Lethia threatened.

Her captain chuckled and came around the truck to stand next to Lane.

Lethia swung her legs around and held her hand to her wound. She wasn't healing as fast as she should. It was still oozing blood. She stood outside the vehicle and inhaled sharply. She looked around and took in everyone standing near the entrance. Her gaze landed on one person in particular.

Her mother.

"When did she get here?" Lethia muttered.

"Not too long after you left," Lane replied.

Lethia stood to her full height and began the walk to the castle. She was still in disbelief that she'd passed out. When she had awoken, she had received the report she had demanded. They had taken care of the den. A few lycans had escaped along with the alpha. She had much information to share with her parents and sisters. This fight was not over. Not by a long shot. If Azura was telling the truth, then they would all need to prepare for the war that Azura had promised.

She arrived to stand in front of her mother who

had met her halfway. Mira's gaze glanced down to her stomach.

"We need the healer," Mira said over her shoulder.

"I'm fine, Mother," Lethia mumbled.

"I'll let the healer tell me that," Mira said. She shook her head. "You are just as stubborn as your father. You should not be walking if you are that injured."

"There is nothing wrong with my legs."

"Come. You aren't going nowhere but to the healer." Her mother marched toward the door.

"Sorry, Your Grace. Your mother overrules you. Healer it is," Lane murmured. He rested a hand on her arm. He guided her into the castle. There was plenty of hustle and bustle with the warriors returning from battle.

The queen accompanied her to the infirmary as if she didn't trust that Lethia would go. Lethia had planned to go, but she was just didn't want to let her mother think she had won an argument. They arrived at the infirmary with it being chaotic, the healers and assistants taking care of the warriors who had been injured.

Ketura, the head healer, took one look at Lethia and made her way to her.

"Your Majesty." Ketura nodded to Mira and then focused on Lethia. "Princess, what happened?"

"Oh, I ran into the lycan alpha's claws." She held back a wince.

"Let's put her over there." Ketura motioned for them to follow her to a private room in the back.

Lethia stumbled slightly. Lane cursed and put an arm around her.

"Lean on me," he said.

She blew out a deep breath and allowed him to guide her to the room. He helped her up on the cot. Her mother stood in the doorway while Ketura came to stand by her.

"I'll be right outside the door if you need me," Lane murmured. He took her hand and gave it a squeeze.

She nodded then leaned back on the bed.

"Princess, let me see what's underneath your hand." Ketura lifted it. She reached to the tray near the cart and grabbed her scissors. She cut away Lethia's leather vest. Her sharp intake of breath couldn't be good.

Lethia glanced down at her stomach and grimaced. The alpha's claws had dug deep into her abdomen. She inhaled and rested her head back on the pillow. Her wound should have been almost healed by now.

"Why isn't she healing?" her mother demanded.

"Mother, let her work. We can talk later." Lethia shifted her gaze to her mother.

The queen folded her arms. Ketura poured something on Lethia's stomach. She gritted her teeth against the sting.

"I'll just place a few stitches to hold it shut until you can feed. It will heal once you have fed." Ketura moved away and turned to the drawers along the wall, gathering supplies.

"Why haven't you called me?" Mira started. She exhaled sharply and waked over to the other side of Lethia. "You should have told me that you were matched and you had your mate."

"I've just been busy, Mother. Between my mate, the missing humans, and the lycans, I've had my hands full. You were on my list of things to do." Lethia offered a strained smile.

Her mother didn't return it. "The female is quite pretty. I won't ask why she's chained to that wall of yours." Her mother's gaze narrowed on her.

Lethia groaned inwardly. There were some things that she didn't want her mother to know about, and her special wall was one of them. Her compartments contained quite a collection of toys and playthings she liked to use.

"I take it you went and met her," Lethia murmured.

"I did. She was about as close-lipped as Aubrey when I tried to get information from them. I didn't see a claiming bite on her." Mira arched an eyebrow at her.

"The blood of your mate will speed up your healing," Ketura supplied.

"I'm still trying to convince her," Lethia said.

Ketura returned to her side and injected her abdomen with a numbing medication.

"She's a very stubborn female."

"Well then, I know you two were meant for each other." Mira gripped her hand and gave it a squeeze. Her other hand came up and ran over the top of Lethia's head. "So that's the reason you're so pale."

Lethia rested back and closed her eyes as Ketura brought the needle and thread to her skin. She focused on her breathing and her mother's petting of her hair. The healer sewed her up. There was slight tugging on her skin while Ketura worked on her.

Lethia didn't want to think of Alima and her not wanting to accept her mating claim. She couldn't keep her locked up forever.

Maybe the best thing would be to let her go.

There was a risk for a vampire to not claim their mate. Lethia was a strong vampire. If Alima wouldn't be happy with her, then she would rather let her go where she could be. Her happiness was important to Lethia. She would figure this blood situation out. If live donors were the key, then that was what she would do.

"I HAVE a live donor lined up or you," Aubrey announced.

She had met Lethia and Lane at the base of the stairs. He was tagging along with her to ensure she made it to her room.

"Have her sent to my room," Lethia replied. She looked at the stairs and dreaded walking up them. She now regretted not having an elevator installed in the castle when the last set of renovations had been completed.

"Why couldn't you have listened to me?" Aubrey's eyes narrowed on Lethia as she stepped closer and lowered her voice. "This could have been prevented."

"And had I not gone, the alpha would have taken out whoever would have gone up against her. At least I'm only wounded, not dead."

"It shouldn't have been either," Aubrey snapped.

Lethia smirked. Her friend never held anything back.

Aubrey turned to Lane. "Please escort your stubborn princess to her bedroom and make sure she doesn't fall down the stairs."

"She won't fall," Lethia replied.

Aubrey spoke of her as if she wasn't standing there.

"Come, my lady. Allow me to escort you to your room." Lane held his arm out for her.

She growled and slipped her arm around his.

"I'll send up the donor as soon as she arrives. Go get cleaned up," Aubrey ordered.

"Who's the princess, her or me?" Lethia muttered.

They turned and began the hike up the stairs.

"She cares about you just as we all do," Lane said.

"I know," she murmured. She sighed and hated

this weak feeling. Her legs appeared to grow heavy with each step.

They finally made it to the level where her bedroom was located. There was a guard outside her door as she had requested. Lane guided her to it.

She held up her hand. "I've got it from here."

"You sure?"

"Positive."

The guard opened the door for her. She stepped over the threshold before closing the door. The room was slightly lit. She quietly stepped into the suite and took in Alima's form on the floor. It would appear that someone had given her more blankets. Lethia quietly padded into the bathroom and stripped her clothes off. Ketura was going to be upset, but she had to get in the shower. She would try to keep her stitches from getting wet as much as she could.

Lethia grimaced at the amount of wolf's blood that was on her, and she needed to get it off. She turned the shower on and quickly got in. The warm water felt wonderful. After a quick wash, she shut off the water and snagged a towel. She wrapped it around her and went over to the vanity. She was too tired to wash her hair. She grabbed a brush and brushed her hair so it flowed along her shoulders.

Lethia stared at herself in the mirror for a moment. She was able to see what her mother and Aubrey could see. She was paler than normal. Hopefully, the blood of the donor would be helpful. Putting down the brush, she reached for her robe that was hanging on the wall. She slid it on and tied the sash closed.

Once the donor came, she'd get a sip, then rest. When she woke up, she'd call a meeting with her sisters and father. They would need to devise a strategy for Azura. For now, she would push the alpha wolf from her mind and concentrate on getting well.

Exiting the bathroom, she made her way over to the seating area. Alima stirred underneath her blankets.

"Lethia?" she called out.

"Yes, it is I." She walked over to the seating area. Her abdomen was still tender, and she reached out and rested her hand over the wound.

Alima must have caught the motion.

"You're injured!" she gasped. She sat up, the blanket sliding off her, revealing her naked form.

Lethia couldn't help her eyes greedily taking in

Alima's curvy frame. Her brown breasts were on display with those dark areolas. She licked her lips, wanting to have her mate, but she would resist. If she were to let her go, then she should keep her hands and mouth to herself.

"I'll be fine."

"You don't look like you are. What can I do for you?" Alima said.

Lethia's heart skipped a beat. There was something she could do. Allow Lethia to claim her, accept her bite, and allow her to drink from her.

"You could help me," Lethia replied, but she wasn't sure if Alima wanted to hear what she had to say.

A couple of taps on the door sounded.

"Enter," she called out.

The door opened, and Aubrey appeared in the doorway. A small familiar female entered.

Savanah.

"Your donor, Your Grace," Aubrey said. She turned to the tiny human. "The princess has an injury. She may need to take a little more than usual."

"That's okay. Whatever the princess needs tonight, I'm hers," Savanah said. She met Lethia's gaze. A sensual smile graced her lips. She wore a short strapless dress that stopped mid-thigh. Her nipples pebbled underneath her the thin material.

"I'm not sure the princess is up for extra tonight—"

"The princess shall decide," Lethia interjected. Out of the corner of her eye, Alima knelt, watching the entire conversation. Lethia bit back a smirk. She gave a nod to Aubrey who returned it then closed the door.

"Hello, Savanah," Lethia murmured.

"Your Grace. It's good to see you. I was pleased to hear that you were requesting my services again." Savanah floated across the room toward her.

"What services do you need?" Alima asked. She was now standing, her gaze locked on Lethia.

"Vampires need blood to heal. That is what I'm here for." Savanah glanced over at Alima before coming to kneel on the floor at Lethia's feet. Her fiery red hair flowed around her shoulders. She took a tie from around her wrist and put her hair up into a high, messy bun. "I hate that our meeting was interrupted before. I so enjoyed my time with your guard before and I want to thank you for that."

Savanah reached down and pulled the dress

over her head and tossed it to the floor. Just as Lethia suspected, she was naked underneath. Her body was perfect, but sadly, Lethia didn't have the reaction to her like she had before. A certain brown-skinned female was what she craved.

"Wait a minute. You need blood to heal your wound?" Alima's voice ended on a squeak. She struggled against the restraints. Her eyes were wide and frantic as she stared at Lethia.

Lethia spread her legs to allow Savanah to kneel between them.

"Take as much as you need, Your Grace." Savanah leaned her head to the side, presenting the column of her neck to Lethia. Her pulse was pounding.

Lethia could hear the flow of her blood. She leaned forward and ran her hand over Savanah's smooth skin.

"Lethia," Alima cried out.

Lethia focused on the sound of the rushing of blood. Her gums burned and stretched while her fangs pushed through. She bent down and nuzzled the crook of Savanah's neck. Her tongue skated out along the plum artery.

"Lethia. Please," Alima screamed. She was fighting the restraints, trying to break free.

"What is it?" Lethia rasped. She needed blood. Her stomach was cramping, and her hands trembled. The rush of Savanah's blood filled her ears. Her hand came to rest on Savana's hair. She gripped it to hold her still.

"Feed from me. Take me. I'm yours." Tears streamed down Alima's face. She stood naked, her arms stretched behind her from the chains holding her back. "I'm your mate. You should be feeding from me, not her. Not anyone else."

Lethia paused. She had waited what seemed like forever to hear those words from Alima's mouth. She didn't say a word but watched her mate. She was frantically tugging at the chains. If she didn't stop, she was going to hurt herself.

Alima screamed at the chains before turning back to Lethia.

"Please. I need you. I need your bite. Come claim me. I want you." Her sobs racked her body.

Lethia's hands loosened on Savanah's hair. She released the donor and stood from her seat. She walked across the room to stand in front of Alima. She reached out and cupped her face. Alima leaned into it, calming down.

"Why all of a sudden have you decided you want to mate with me when you have resisted me for so long?" Lethia breathed. Just hearing the words flowing out of Alima's mouth erased all of the rage and anger she had held on to since Alima had rejected her.

"You were right. The bond has its hold on me. I can sense your feelings, you are always on my mind, and I can't fight it anymore. Take from me. Let me heal you." She bent her head to the side, exposing her neck.

Lethia licked the column of Alima's throat. Her mate's pulse was racing. She lifted her head and stared down into Alima's eyes.

"I've been waiting for so long for you to accept me and the bond," Lethia whispered.

She glanced over at Savanah who was standing near them. Her gaze roamed Alima's body.

"She's very pretty." Savanah's gaze lingered on Alima's breasts. "The three of us can have fun together. No extra charge." She grinned.

"You will not touch my mate," Lethia growled. She pointed to the door. "Get your clothes and leave."

Savanah's eyes widened. She must have seen the threat in Lethia's eyes. She snagged her dress from the floor. She threw it on and headed toward the door. Lethia waited until the door closed before she reached over and punched in a few buttons on the panel on the wall. The cuffs around Alima's wrists dropped away from her.

"Are you sure? The bond is forever," Lethia said.

Alima stepped to her, closing the gap between them.

"I'm sure. I couldn't stand that woman being near you. I want to be the one who gives you everything you need," Alima breathed. She trailed her finger down Lethia's sternum and continued on down her stomach and came to a stop at her mons. She pressed a kiss to Lethia's neck. She slipped her finger into Lethia's slit and connected with her clit.

Lethia exploded. There was no time to take her mate to the claiming room in her castle. They could go there later. She gripped Alima by her waist and turned her around and walked her backward to the bed. This would be the first time she and her mate would lie together in it. Alima hefted herself up on the large bed and scooted back until she was in the center. Lethia crawled over to her, forcing her to lie on her back.

"Fate has willed the two of us together," Lethia whispered. She would be forever grateful that the fates had brought Alima into her life. She lowered her head and dropped a kiss on her lips. She sat up and straddled Alima. She slipped her robe off and tossed it onto the floor. She brought her wrist up to her mouth and nicked it, causing it to bleed. She took a drop of the blood and placed it on Alima's forehead.

"We shall thank the fates for the bond that has formed between us." Lethia's heart raced. She had never thought she would ever perform this ritual.

Alima trembled underneath Lethia. Her wide eyes were locked on her.

"We shall forever be joined together." Lethia took another drop of blood and coated Alima's lips with it. The sight of it on Alima's mouth was erotic, and her arousal grew. "Through our bond, you shall live throughout time standing by my side."

She held her bleeding wrist out, allowing the blood to drop over Alima's chest. She reached down and smeared it all over Alima's skin. She covered her breasts and abdomen with it.

Alima's back arched off the bed, a moan slipping from her lips. Her breaths came in pants. Lethia's focus was locked on Alima's neck. She helped her mate up into a seated position while she was still straddling her.

Alima's hooded eyes watched her.

"I vow to protect you. To honor you." She gripped Alima's braids and pulled on them, forcing her to tilt her head back to expose her neck. She ran her tongue along it. "I vow to please you."

"Yes," Alima hissed. Her eyes fluttered shut. "Please, Lethia. Take me."

Lethia nuzzled her neck before she lifted and sank her fangs into Alima's throat. Alima gasped, her muscles going tense. Lethia hungrily drank in Alima's sweet blood. It was as if her body had been starving.

Immediately, a wave of heat washed through her. All of her senses enhanced; her skin on her stomach appeared to start repairing itself. She raised her head, remembering she shouldn't take so much during the first time. She panted, welcoming the flood of power that hit her from drinking from her mate.

She drew her wrist to her and nicked it, allowing blood to flow freely again.

"Drink, *miere*," Lethia whispered.

Alima opened her mouth and covered the wound. She drank from Lethia without hesitation. Her big brown eyes were locked on Lethia. Her audible swallows were music to Lethia's ears. Knowing that her mate was officially drinking from her had moisture collecting between her thighs.

"That's enough, *miere*. You can have more later." Lethia grinned. She pushed her mate back down onto the bed. She smeared more of her blood onto her. It turned her on that her human had her blood on her skin and now inside her.

She opened Alima's legs and moved her hand to her pussy. Alima's core was slippery and wet. She pushed two fingers deep inside her. Her warmth wrapped around her fingers. She pumped them in and out of the tight channel.

"Lethia," Alima moaned.

Lethia massaged the one breast still in her hand. She teased the nipple with the palm of her hand before she squeezed the bud. She pinched it hard, tugging on it.

"More."

Lethia's own core was slick with need. She withdrew her fingers from her, tasting her honey on her fingers. She pressed Alima's legs wide while she straddled her, bringing their centers together. Alima groaned, throwing her head back, and she undulated her hips against Lethia.

She held Alima's leg to her chest while they slid against each other. Lethia ground down on Alima, sending a wave of pleasure through her. Alima's hands gripped the blanket underneath her as she thrust in rhythm with Lethia.

Their pace quickened. Lethia's body was overheating. She leaned down and covered Alima's mouth with hers. Their movements became frantic. Lethia tore her mouth from Alima and forced her head to the side. She sank her fangs into her neck again.

Alima's body shuddered, her breaths coming in pants.

Lethia drank from her, welcoming the tasty essence of her blood. Lethia rocked her hips hard, applying pressure between them. Alima wrapped her arms around Lethia's neck, bringing their bodies completely together. She released a scream, falling into her climax. Her body trembled uncontrollably.

Lethia lifted her head, the waves of her orgasm slamming into her. She threw her head back and roared. Their bodies jerked and swayed, and they rode the waves of their release together.

Alima sobbed and shook. Her nails dug into Lethia's back, and she writhed on the bed. Her body grew hot, and Lethia recognized what was happening. Her body was going through the change. She wasn't going to be a vampire, but she would age like one. She would now walk this earth by Lethia's side.

Lethia moved to her side on the bed and held her. She reached up and bit her wrist again that had sealed itself. She brought her wrist to Alima's mouth.

"Drink, *miere*. You need more." Lethia coaxed Alima to open her mouth.

She latched on to Lethia's wrist and drank. Lethia pulled Alima into her arms while the tremors shook her body.

"It's the change."

After what seemed like hours, Alima flopped down on the bed, spent. Sweat coated her forehead. She released Lethia's wrist, blood spilling out the side of her mouth. Alima's eyes flicked to hers before fluttering closed.

Lethia smiled and bent down, pressing a kiss to Alima's forehead.

She was officially mated.

CHAPTER TWENTY-SIX

Alima woke to Lethia licking her neck. She sighed and tilted it to the side to give her better access. She moaned, leaning into Lethia. They were still naked and underneath the blankets on the bed. At some point, Lethia must have closed the drapes. They were basked in darkness. Alima couldn't see at all, but she knew her mate could see just fine in the dark.

Her mate.

She never thought she would ever be saying that term. Now, she was mated to the warden of the east, a fierce vampire warrior.

She pressed on Lethia's shoulder to make her rise.

"How is your wound?" she asked.

"It's completely healed," Lethia murmured. She cupped Alima's face and covered her mouth with hers.

Alima parted her lips to allow Lethia's tongue to sweep inside. Their bodies were tangled together. She broke the kiss but quickly kissed Alima's lips.

"I'm back to myself, thanks to you. How do you feel?"

"Weak like a newborn baby," Alima admitted.

"That is normal. It should last for a few days. Your body is getting used to the new aging process, and it took a lot of energy from you." Lethia turned Alima around in her arms to where her back was to her chest. She wrapped her arm over her waist. Her breasts were firmly against Alima's back. She dropped a kiss on her shoulder. "But I will take care of you until you are back to normal."

"And how will you do that?" Alima whispered. She blinked, wishing she would be able to see in the darkened area. It was intimate and cozy. She felt as if they were the only two people in the world.

Lethia's hand slipped beneath the blanket and

pushed its way between her thighs. Her fingers parted her folds and connected with her clit.

Alima widened her legs and rested her head back on Lethia's shoulder. Her mate strummed her clit, sending waves of pleasure through her.

"I'll make sure my mate is well pleased, just as I vowed," Lethia breathed.

"What about food? Unlike you, I need to eat," Alima's breathing was ragged.

Lethia's finger slipped into her slit and gathered some of her arousal and brought it back to her clit. Her finger expertly flicked her swollen bud.

"I'll give you whatever you want." Lethia nipped at her shoulder.

Alima's body warmed up and became intolerable. She pushed the blanket off her and rolled onto her back. Lethia took advantage of the move and withdrew her fingers. She slid down Alima's body, replacing her fingers with her mouth. Alima's back arched off the bed, a moan slipping from her mouth. She reached out and held on to the back of Lethia's head while she rode her face.

Her mate's talented tongue was working her over. Alima thrust against her face, feeling her muscles tense. Lethia slipped two fingers inside her slick channel and pumped them in and out of her.

"Lethia," she cried out.

Her body arched off the bed again when her climax hit her. She screamed, trembling as the waves of her release washed over her. She yelped at the sensation of her mate's fangs sinking into the flesh of her thigh. Lethia's bite was right in the fold of her mons and thigh. Her fingers were still lodge deep inside her while she drank from Alima. Minutes later, she licked the puncture wound closed. She withdrew her fingers and then took her time licking Alima clean before she crawled over her.

She settled down in the valley of Alima's thighs. Their breasts were crushed between them, but Alima didn't care. She loved the feeling of Lethia on top of her. They lay there, sharing soft kisses and caresses.

Lethia rolled to her side and brought Alima into her arms.

"You said you'd give me anything I wanted," Alima murmured. She ran her fingers along Lethia's hip.

"I did." Lethia pressed a kiss to her forehead. "What is it you want?"

"I want to see Javari and for you to set him free."

Lethia was quiet. The only sound coming from her was her breathing. "And that will make you happy?"

"Yes, very much so. Javari is my brother. We may not share blood, but we are as close as a brother and sister can be."

"Very well then. I'll take you." Lethia's hand skated along her bottom. "Anything else?" There was a teasing tone in her voice.

"I'm not sure how long he's been here, but I'm sure since he was locked up, he has lost his job. Do you think there is something he could do here at the castle?"

"I'm sure there is something for him, but shouldn't you ask him if he'd want to work here?" Lethia chuckled.

"I'll talk him into it. Can we go today?"

"Today? I had planned for us to not leave this room at all," Lethia admitted.

"Don't you have some princess or warden stuff to do?" Alima asked.

"Well, I had notified my mother and Aubrey that we had officially mated." She pinched Alima's bottom. "Fine. If you want to go see your friend, then let's shower and then we'll go."

"Shower and no hanky-panky?" Alima arched her eyebrow.

"That I can't promise right now."

* * *

ALIMA HAD ASKED for her to meet with Javari alone first. She would have to smooth it over about his capture and her mating.

"I'll be right here," Lethia murmured.

She hadn't liked to let Alima go alone, but Alima had assured her that Javari would never harm her. There was a guard posted at the end of the hall, but it wasn't good enough for her. Lethia stood by the door. Alima stood up on her tiptoes and pressed a kiss to her lips before turning away.

She walked down the hall, anxious to see her friend. She arrived at the cell he was in and stepped forward, wrapping her hands around the bars. Javari sat on the floor in the corner of the small room. It was designed identical to the one she had been in. His head was down, almost as if he was sleeping.

"Javari," she called out softly.

His head flew up, and he squinted, looking in her direction.

"I must be hallucinating," he said. He pushed up from the floor and ran a hand along his face. He hesitated in taking a step forward, then paused. "Alima? Is that really you?"

"Yes, it's me." She hiccupped a sob.

He rushed to the bars, his gaze scanning her.

"What are you doing here?" he asked. He covered her hands with his. He didn't look harmed and even appeared to have gained weight. "I thought you were—"

He stopped whatever he was about to say, a pained expression crossing his face.

"Thought what?" she asked.

"Nothing, just don't worry. You appear fine. How are you here?" He leaned his head against the rails.

"Well, as you see, I never made it to my destination." A nervous chuckle escaped her.

He glanced over at Lethia who hadn't budged from where she was standing. Alima sighed, feeling full of all the new emotions that filled her. She didn't know how, but Lethia had crawled into her heart. Who would have thought that the fate crap was real? She had not believed in it. Humans decided their destiny, not some made-up belief. Boy, had she been wrong.

The power of fate was real. She now couldn't even begin to think of how she would survive without Lethia.

She turned back to Javari and gave him a small smile. "My vampire captured me and brought me here."

"You have been here this whole time?" he asked in disbelief.

"Yes." She shared with him the story of the night she had been captured.

He didn't say a word while she spoke, but listened intently.

"I've been here and now I'm mated to my vampire."

He stared at her without saying a word. He backed away from the bars and gaped at her. She grew worried. Was he going to turn on her because she had mated a person she had once considered an enemy? She hoped she wouldn't have to choose between him and Lethia. She needed both of them in her life.

"Did they force you? Who is this vampire?"

"The princess, Lethia Riskel."

"Are you shitting me? You matched with the princess?" His eyes grew wide. He paced the cell.

"She's the one who imprisoned me. I don't even know why unless she discovered—"

He stopped walking and turned his back toward her.

"Discovered what?" she asked. He wasn't making sense.

He stared at her again and came back to the bars. "After you left, I discovered some shit that was jacked up. I thought I had lost you forever."

"The point of the relocation was so no one would know where I was. So in a way you would have."

"That's not what I meant," he replied softly. He visibly shuddered. He closed his eyes briefly before opening them. There was a tortured look that she had not seen in his eyes since his parents had died.

"What is it? You're scaring me," she said. She reached out and rested her hand on his. "I'm safe here. The only time I haven't been is when I ran away and the lycans found me."

"Lycans? You know?" he asked. He swallowed hard. "I swear I didn't know what he was doing until after you disappeared."

That sense of dread she experienced before filled her. She shook her head, not wanting to believe it. When she'd escaped, there was only one person who knew exactly where she would be, and that push had sent her to the corner.

"No," she whispered. She shook her head, not wanting to believe the man she had worked for, the man she believed was doing good for their people would be the one who was betraying them.

"Reed was selling us out," Javari spat. He ran a hand over his face. "He had been lying to us all. None of us questioned that we would never hear of the humans who were relocated. It made sense that if we escaped to avoid the vampires, then we shouldn't contact our friends and family so they wouldn't know anything. But no, he was giving our people to the lycans." He slammed a hand to the bars in anger.

"Oh my God," she gasped. "So many people. I drove people to the meeting points. What have I done?" Tears swelled up in her eyes. He heart broke to think that she had been convinced she had been helping people get a new start in life, but instead she had been a part of an evil scheme. She felt sick. "How did you find out?"

"I overheard Reed and Nolan talking about how they needed more people to disappear. I thought it was weird since everyone who didn't want to be matched with a vampire came to us. He spoke about meeting the monthly quota. Not sure what they were talking about, I followed them. They didn't know I was in the warehouse after our most recent rally. They joked and laughed, saying the lycans would pay for more humans. As soon as I heard that I, put two and two together and ran home. That's when the vampires got me. I've been here ever since."

Alima couldn't even process what he'd just told her. She was in shock. Men she had believed in were committing the ultimate form of betrayal to human kind.

But she knew how she could help her people. It may not fix the past and help the ones who had been handed over to the lycans, but they could put a stop to it.

Lethia.

This was the answer they were looking for when it came to the lycans and how they were growing their numbers. Lethia would know what to do.

"I'm going to take care of this," she began. "First, I came here to free you."

"How? I'm sure the princess thought I had a hand in giving humans to the lycans. There had been rumors of humans disappearing. Everyone had been talking about it."

Alima shook her head, a small smile gracing her lips. She wiped the trails of tears from her face. “You really want to know why the vampire princess had you imprisoned? She thought you were my lover,” she admitted.

Javari made a weird sound in the back of his throat.

“She wanted to take out her competition for my heart.”

“And does she have it?” He studied her closely.

“Yes, she does,” she said honestly. She glanced toward the door where her mate stood.

“I never thought I’d see the day where you would be in love with a vampire.”

She knew what he was hinting at. He had been by her side through it all. Earlier, she had shared with Lethia the story of her sister’s death. Matter of fact, the entire half of the day had been spent talking about their families.

“People change. That thing called fate they believe in is real,” she whispered.

“I haven’t seen you look like this in a long time.” He motioned to her. A small smile came onto his lips. “But if you’re happy and safe, that’s all that matters.”

“I am.” She beckoned for Lethia to come to

her. She turned back to her friend. "Don't worry, we are going to take care of you."

Lethia arrived at her side. She put a possessive arm around Alima and dropped a kiss on her temple. Alima held back an eye roll. She was going to have to get used to having someone who was so protective of her. Alima leaned into her embrace and rested her hand on Lethia's abdomen.

"Is everything okay, *miere*?" Lethia asked.

"As soon as you get my friend out of this cell it will be," she replied haughtily.

Lethia punished her slightly with a hard squeeze on her bottom.

"I had already agreed before we even came down here, *miere*," Lethia said. She waved for the guard to join them.

"Good, because you need to hear what Javari just told me."

CHAPTER TWENTY-SEVEN

"This human is trustworthy?" the king asked.

Lethia and her mother sat in her office on a hologram call with her father and sisters. After listening to Javari give a recount of what he had learned, she had immediately requested a meeting with her family.

This issue was a matter of national emergency for not only vampires but humans also. Her mate was certainly shaken up over the news.

Lethia was pissed.

According to her mate, the night she was

captured by Lethia's guards, she was on her way to be relocated. She would have been handed over to the lycans and she would have been lost to Lethia forever. She had suspected that someone had led those lycans to her mate when she had escaped the castle. It had been a little bit too convenient that the wolves would just happen to stumble upon Alima.

"Yes, I believe him. He and my mate are shaken up by this. He had feared he had sent Alima unknowingly to the wolves. They grew up together and are as close as a brother and sister can be." Lethia at first was wary of Javari around her mate. But after seeing the two of them together, she knew she didn't have anything to worry about. They reminded her of the relationship she had with Lane.

"What are we going to do about this human leader, Reed?" Hegna asked.

"Don't worry, sister, we are going to take care of him," Lethia promised. "He will definitely get what is due to him."

Lethia had Kane go and meet with Javari and Alima. They both had agreed to share everything about the Rebel organization. With the amount of humans they suspected had been turned, it wasn't just the branch here in Crystal Cove who was supplying humans to the lycans. This was nationwide.

It also explained why Azura was willing to sacrifice some of her lycans.

Alima had been insistent on Javari getting settled in his new suite in the castle. He had agreed to stay with them. There was plenty of space. He'd even agreed to see if there was a job he would be interested in. If not, then Lethia vowed to assist him in obtaining a new one somewhere else.

Lethia could already tell Alima was twisting her around her finger, but she didn't mind. She would be willing to give her mate whatever she wanted.

"And the alpha?" Velika growled. The hologram of her younger sister paced back and forth.

"I had sent Dru and her men back to the den while your sister was recovering," Mira chimed in. "All of the lycans from that den are either dead or have scattered, I'm assuming with their alpha." She slid a sly look over to Lethia. While Lethia and Alima were locked in her room completing then bonding, the queen had stepped in.

The queen was so excited about her second

daughter mating her matched human that she had already sent the notice out to Lethia's coven and the entire kingdom of the mating. Word spread extremely fast. Lethia was already getting requests from the council for their official meeting with their new princess, and other dignitaries had sent their congratulations and well-wishes.

There would be a celebration soon.

Vampires loved to party, and Aubrey had volunteered to help the council coordinate the event.

"The alpha was nowhere to be found," the queen continued. She came to stand by Lethia and rested a hand on her shoulder. "I have placed a bounty on her head. Dead or alive, I want that lycan captured and brought to me."

"Preferably dead," the king growled. He stood from the chair and stopped in front of Lethia's desk. He eyed his wife with a fangy grin. "You know how I love when you get vicious."

The Riskel sisters groaned simultaneously. Their parents laughed at them. It didn't matter how old she got, that she was a commander of an army, Lethia didn't want to see her parents eying each other as if they were ready to devour each other.

"What I want us all to start doing is putting our

ears to the ground. Azura said her wolves were all over the country. We need to find them quickly," Lethia said.

"I will have my people begin immediately. There are a few places here I know that will give up information for the right price," Hegna said.

"Same here," Velika murmured.

"We need to start pinpointing them. Azura wants her war. If she survived, she will present herself soon. I have a feeling that this den here was for her disposable wolves. The one we had captured said that it was an honor to sacrifice himself for the greater good, or something along those lines," Lethia said.

"If she can afford to lose a hundred wolves, then their numbers must be higher than we expect," Niall said. He shook his head, a fierce scowl on his face. "And this may be just here. Who knows what is going on around the world. I will reach out to the other kings and call a summit. They need to be aware of what is going on here so they may take actions in their own kingdoms." King Niall was one of the seven vampire kings who ruled on this earth.

Velika turned away to speak with someone,

while Hegna's hologram came and sat in the chair in front of Lethia's desk.

"Well, since you are officially mated, I'm going to head your way. I want to meet my new sister-in-law before everyone else." Hegna grinned. "And we can continue planning how we will defeat this bitch of an alpha. This will be fun. Almost like when we were kids."

"You are more than welcome to come here anytime." Lethia returned her sister's smile.

"Hold that thought, sisters," Velika said, turning back to them. For the first time ever, she appeared afraid. Her hand visibly shook as she tucked her hair behind her ear. "They just sent word that Quinn's water broke."

"I'm on my way," Mira gasped. The queen smiled and jumped in place with excitement. "Fate is shining down on us this week. A new daughter-in-law and the first of the new generation of the Riskel family is arriving."

"I'll meet you there, my dear." The king blew his wife a kiss. He then turned to Lethia. "I take it you can handle this from here."

"Of course. You all go to Velika and Quinn. I'll send Lane with Mother. As soon as I can, I will gather my mate and we will join you."

"See you all soon," Hegna announced before she disconnected from the call.

Velika and Niall also disconnected.

"I'm so proud of you girls. Now if only fate will hurry up and reveal Hegna's mate to her." Her mother bent down and kissed Lethia on the forehead.

The eldest Riskel sister was not wanting a mate. Lethia was surprised her sister had not found a way to pull her name from the draft. If and when she was ever matched, Lethia pitied the poor soul already.

"Don't take too long," her mother said. "Bring Alima and come meet your niece or nephew. We have so much to celebrate." The queen was all smiles. This was exactly what she had been hoping for when she had submitted her daughters' names into the draft. Their immediate family was finally growing.

"Yes, Mother." Lethia smiled watching her mother scurry away.

She flew through the door and was gone in a blink of an eye.

Lethia sat back in her chair, truly feeling happy for her sister. Velika and Quinn would make great parents. She felt that little thing called envy, thinking of how her sister's life was about to change.

Lethia paused.

She knew she wanted children, but did Alima?

They had a lot to learn about each other, but first it was a matter of tying up loose ends.

LETHIA WALKED down the hallway with Enoch at her side. She bit back a smile at the look on Lane's face when she'd shared with him that his sister was in labor. His eyes had widened, he'd visibly swallowed a couple of times, and he'd even appeared as if he was going to pass out. He'd taken off running when she'd told him to go and take as much time as he needed.

"The Riskel family sure is blessed," Enoch said. "Congratulations, Your Grace."

"Thank you, Enoch. I can't wait to meet the baby." The new generation of the Riskel family being born was news that would reach around the world.

They arrived at the moon room where her mate would be meeting with Kane and Dru.

She opened the door and stepped in. Javari

looked like a new man with a fresh shower and clean clothes. Alima sat next to him on the couch as she was in the midst of speaking. The conversation paused as Lethia strolled across the room. Enoch shut the door and stood in front of it.

"Is everything all right?" Alima stood from the couch and walked to Lethia.

It pleased Lethia that her mate was seeking her out. It wasn't too long ago that Alima was telling her to fuck off. Lethia sat on oversized chair with Alima settling down on her lap.

"Yes. We are going to have to make a plan, then Alima and I will need to fly out to Velika's," she announced.

"The baby?" Dru arched an eyebrow.

"Yes, Quinn's water broke. Our hologram conference was cut short due to the news," Lethia said. "But I can assure you that my mother has issued a bounty on the alpha's head. There won't anywhere Azura can hide."

There were plenty of bounty hunters that wanted to cash in on the payday that the royal family could offer. And for it to be the alpha of the lycans, not only would a hunter want the cash but the fame that went along with catching her.

"I've never flown before." Alima's eyes widened.

"Don't worry, *miere*. We will use my private plane." Lethia rubbed her mate's back. Flying would be the safest way to get to Washington. She didn't want her to have any anxiety about it. She would be right there with her. "But first it is the matter of catching this Reed character."

"And Nolan. He's the second in charge. He was in on all of this, too," Javari said.

"Even better for the plan I have in mind." Lethia ran a gentle hand down Alima's back. There was nothing she wouldn't do for her. It may have taken her human a while to realize what she felt for her, but Lethia had known all along from the moment she'd first seen the photograph of Alima.

The second the two men of the Rebel organization had targeted her mate, they'd become an enemy of hers, and no one wanted to be on her bad side.

"What do you have in mind? I can see the wheels turning in your head." Dru zeroed in on Lethia.

"I want Reed and Nolan captured and thrown into our dungeons. They will be our bait for drawing out the lycans."

"What?" Alima gasped and twisted around to

look at Lethia. "You're going to give them to the lycans?"

"We are going to take them all down. Even when the alpha is captured and killed, someone may try to rise to take her place. We will not tolerate that. Once we find another pack, then we will draw them out. Reed and Nolan will get a taste of their own medicine." Lethia paused and stared at her. For once, she couldn't read her expression. "Do you object to this plan, mate?"

"Hell no. Can I help catch them?" There was a special glint that appeared in Alima's eyes.

Lethia smiled. Alima was as bloodthirsty as any vampire warrior she knew. Fate certainly had paired her with the right woman. She brought Alima's face down and pressed a hard kiss to it.

"Of course, *miere*. We need to act right away. Once we have them in custody, then we will go meet the newest member of the family."

"I can call Terry. He will know how to get a hold of Reed," Alima said. She looked at Javari. "When I escaped and went back to the compound, I called the number they give out and Terry was the one who answered."

Lethia didn't want to think of her mate leaving.

It was just a reminder of how she'd almost lost her again, had the lycans got their paws on her.

"Let's get the woman a phone," Dru said. She motioned for Enoch.

He slipped from the room.

"I hope Terry wasn't involved. We don't know who was involved," Alima said.

Lethia wrapped arms around her mate and brought her back against her.

"For what I have in mind, we'll only need Reed and Nolan. We well make an example of them," Lethia announced.

The door opened, Enoch returning with a phone. He brought it over and handed it to Alima.

"The phone is clean and untraceable," he said, returning to his post by the door.

Lethia gave him a nod

"Thank you," Alima said.

Lethia assisted Alima to sit next to her on the small couch.

"I want you to sound desperate when you speak with them. Let them know you have information about the vampires you need to share and it can only be told in person. You will then set the meeting place, and this time we will be ready for his lycan welcoming party."

"It's been a while since I had to act, but I'm sure I can be convincing." Alima grinned.

"Won't he be shocked to hear from her." Javari chuckled.

"That's exactly what I'm counting on," Lethia growled.

CHAPTER TWENTY-EIGHT

Alima and Javari stood together hidden amongst a few trees. There was a playground located near them. Lethia had coached Alima on what to say to Reed. He'd sounded relieved to hear her on the phone. According to him, when the vehicle that was supposed to pick her up arrived at the meeting place, she was nowhere to be seen.

She didn't know who was the better actor between them. He had agreed to meet the following day which had been perfect, giving them plenty of time to prepare.

Lethia and her warriors were not that far away

and would capture Reed and Nolan. She felt safe knowing her vampire was close by. Lethia would protect her at all costs. Having someone focused just on her pleasure and well-being was something she would have to get used to. She felt cherished when she was around Lethia and didn't ever want that feeling to go away.

"Who would have thought we would be on the side of the vampires," Javari murmured.

"Honestly, we are doing this for our people. I still can't believe what Reed is doing. I believed in him. This hurts, knowing I probably played a hand in someone being forcibly turned into a lycan."

"It's not your fault. None of us knew," Javari said.

Alima wrapped her arms around herself. She was going to be plagued with guilt for a long time. All of the faces of the people she had helped flashed before her. Had they suffered? Had some of them been killed for resisting?

"I want to expose them. Let the world know what Reed and Nolan did. Then we can tear down the entire organization," she said.

"Would that be wise? Many people depended on the Rebels."

"Who would trust them after this comes out?" Alima shook her head.

What they needed was an organization that promoted peace between vampires and humans. That was what they needed. She and Lethia had spent all of their waking time together since they'd mated. They were really getting to know each other, and she would have to agree that fate had got their match right

"You're right. What do you have in mind, Princess?" Javari dodged her punch she sent his way. He laughed and pushed her out of his reach. "What did I say? You are a princess now." He laughed.

"Well, my first line of duty, as a human princess mated to a vampire, will be to hold events geared toward bringing vampires and humans together. I want you to help me." She turned to her friend.

"I'd be happy to. We could even expand it with programs for both humans and vampires."

Alima's smile faded at the sound of an approaching vehicle. They would have to finish this conversation later. The SUV crept down the road and pulled into a parking lot.

It was a little after midnight, and the large

moon hung overhead. Alima breathed in the fresh air and took in the scenery. She wanted to remember this night forever. When Lethia had revealed her plan for Reed and Nolan, Alima was immediately on board. Yes, they needed to put a stop to the lycans, but it would only be fair if Reed and Nolan got to experience what they'd committed others to.

The air grew still. The driver and passenger doors opened. The figures emerged from the vehicle, shutting the doors. They met by the side of the SUV and paused.

"Showtime," Javari murmured.

He rested his hand on the small of her back and guided her over in their direction. She slumped her shoulders and walked closer to Javari as if needing his support. Nolan leaned on the truck while Reed stood tall. He folded his arms in front of his chest, studying the two of them approaching. Alima tried to look at him as she once had when she'd respected him. Now he was lower than scum, and she hoped her face didn't give away her true feelings.

"Alima. Javari. I thought both of you were lost to us," Reed said. He glanced over his shoulder at

Nolan before turning back to them. He flashed his infamous smile that drew people to him.

Now all Alima saw was the smile of an evil, sick man who didn't care about his people but selling them out for big bucks. She hoped he'd had fun with all the money he'd pocketed.

"You know I'm a little stubborn." Alima smiled.

"And, Javari, we thought you were dead, too, when you didn't show up for the rally and we heard you hadn't reported to work." Reed waited for Javari to expound on his absence, but her friend remained elusive.

"Some things came up." Javari shrugged nonchalantly. "Nothing you need to worry about."

"Please do tell us why we had to meet you in the middle of the night that was so urgent?" Nolan yawned, interrupting.

"I'm curious as well, we could have met first thing in the morning after breakfast." Reed leveled them with a hard glare. He had never raised his voice or been mean to anyone before. He had always presented himself as fierce, dedicated, and a fighter for human rights, and everyone loved him. Now he looked at them as if they were bugs on the bottoms of his shoes. "You said you had some important information on the vampires that would help our cause. I'm not sure what someone like you would have or would know what we don't already know. So go ahead and tell us. This better not be a waste one time."

Alima had to swallow the explosive retort on her tongue. How dare he speak to them like that? Someone like her? She had to breathe to keep from yelling out for Lethia. Her mate would be at her side in seconds.

"There are rumors that the vampires have a new enemy. Someone that we need to fear. As members of the Rebels, we have a duty to our people to protect them," Alima began.

"You don't need to lecture me on the duties of our commitment." Reed sighed. "Get on with it. Who is this new enemy that we need to know about?"

"The lycans."

Reed and Nolan glanced at each other then burst out laughing. What was so funny? Alima flicked her gaze to Javari, who arched an eyebrow at her. Had these two gone nuts?

"Are you going to tell them?" Nolan asked, wiping his face.

"We might as well, because they won't be repeating anything they hear." Reed's smile disappeared and was replaced with a sneer. "We've been known about the wolf shifter people. There is a war coming, and humans will have to pick a side, and I chose the wolves."

"But why?" Alima cried out. She just had to know if it was truly all about the money the lycans were paying him. These were people. Good people who wanted to just make it in the world.

She hoped Lethia would give them another minute or two. Alima had wanted to hear it from his mouth that they were indeed selling humans to the lycans, and he didn't disappoint.

"Why? I'll tell you fucking why. The lycans didn't come and destroy our world as we knew it. For a small sacrifice, they were willing to let humans live in peace. There would be no draft," he snarled, taking a step toward her.

Reed had transformed into someone she didn't recognize.

Javari stepped in front of her with his hands raised.

"You might want to keep your distance, my man," Javari warned.

"Do you know who you're talking to?" Reed demanded.

"And you think that they will be satisfied with the people you've given them? You've betrayed the same people who followed you. Believed that you were truly helping them when in reality you were throwing them to the wolves." She shook her head and took a step back away from him. She just couldn't look at him anymore. He was truly insane if he thought the lycans would stop there. Now a war was on the horizon against lycans and vampires.

There would be no reasoning with him.

Lethia had the right idea.

"I am helping them. In this day and age, we have to learn how to survive, and if surviving means sacrificing some so the rest may live and prosper, so be it."

"Well, I'm actually glad you said that," Alima whispered. She moved to stand beside Javari, unafraid of Reed. She could feel the pulse of her mate's heart as she drew closer. This connection between her and Lethia was something she was still having to get used to.

But she wouldn't trade it for anything in the world.

He paused his ranting and stared at her. He took a step away from her.

"Wait a minute. You were matched," he began. He took another step back, shaking his head.

Nolan heard what he'd said and must have come to the same conclusion as Reed. He pushed off the vehicle and made his way to the driver's door.

"Let's go, Reed," Nolan snapped.

"Who were you matched to?" Reed demanded.

Alima had never been more prouder of this moment than to utter the words that spilled to her mouth.

"Princess Lethia Riskel."

The color drained from his face. He shook his head, mouth flopping open, but no sound came out.

In a blink of an eye, the scene around them burst into chaos. Reed ran back to his car, but a blonde-haired figure moving at extreme speeds crashed into him before he could take one step. The two of them tumbled down on the ground. Nolan was snatched back, away from the truck, and thrown completely away from the SUV.

Alima leaned against Javari's arm while she

watched her mate and her warriors surround the two males. Lethia stood from the ground and lifted Reed up with one hand. She was dressed in her black fighting leathers and looked every bit the badass warrior princess. Her long blonde hair had been plaited into two braids, matching Alima's hairstyle.

"You sent those lycans after my mate," Lethia growled.

Her vampiric powers were on full display, and Alima couldn't look away.

"Why do you care what happens to humans?" Reed gasped. He struggled to breathe and fought against her hold, but she didn't even budge.

"I care, because you are arming my enemy with soldiers, and that I will not stand for." She brought him closer to her face.

Alima's heart pounded. Would Lethia lose control and tear his throat out?

"And as I said, you sent lycans after my mate. For that I should kill you right now, but instead, I will return the favor of what you've done."

Lethia threw him into the waiting arms of one of her warriors. Alima breathed a sigh of relief. Even though in the back of her mind she wanted him to suffer, she knew putting him in the hands of the lycans would be the best payback.

"He set everything up. He worked with the lycan alpha. Take him. He made me do it," Nolan shouted.

The large vampire holding him dragged him away. Nolan's scream filled the air. He continued to thrash and kick.

"Shut him up," Lethia shouted.

The vampire didn't hesitate in hitting Nolan on the back of his head. He crumpled to the ground. The warrior leaned down and hefted Nolan's still form over his shoulder and kept walking to their vehicles that were hidden.

Alima couldn't stand being away from her mate any longer. She ran to Lethia who caught her with one arm. Lethia wrapped her arm around Alima's waist and held her tight. Alima leaned her head on Lethia's chest and met Reed's hate-filled eyes.

"And you insinuated that I was a traitor. Look at you whoring yourself out to the vampires. What do you think she will do with you when she's done? Drain you dry and toss you aside," he spat.

"I'd watch what you say to my mate if I were you," Lethia growled. She tightened her hold on Alima. "I might just drain you dry myself."

* * *

ALIMA STOOD on the veranda located off the side of the moon room. She stared at the sky, taking in the beautiful stars painted on the black backdrop. No longer was she under lock and key in the castle. Her guards were back on the job and trailing her everywhere, but it wasn't to keep her from leaving, but to protect her. Zetta was healthy and doing well. Alima had gone to visit the small vampire that morning with guilt in her heart, but Zetta didn't blame her for the lycan attack. She was actually happy Alima had gotten away without injury.

She was about to enter her new life and was ready to see what it would hold for her. She was mated to the woman of her dreams who was crazy over her, and Alima couldn't ask for anything more.

"Are you almost ready, *miere*?" Lethia's warm arms wrapped around her from behind.

Alima smiled and leaned back against her. Her mate nuzzled her neck and kissed her claiming mark.

"I am. I'm a little nervous about it." She was actually embarrassed that she had never flown before, but then again, after the war, flying was a luxury. She wouldn't have been able to afford it even if she wanted to. Now she was going to be flying on Lethia's royal jet.

"There is no need to be nervous. Flying is quite safe." She pressed another kiss to Alima's neck before lifting her head.

Alima spun around and leaned into Lethia.

"So, have you heard word from your sister and her mate?" Alima asked. The other reason she was nervous about flying was that she would be meeting the rest of Lethia's family. She'd already met her mother, the queen, and it wasn't the best first impression. Her face warmed remembering the queen coming in and finding her chained to her daughter's wall in nothing but a blanket.

"Yes, the baby is here. It would look like the prince has made his appearance." Lethia's face relaxed at the mention of her nephew.

"Oh, a boy! Congratulations." Alima hugged her. She leaned up and pressed a hard kiss to her mate's lips. The birth of a child was a wonderful occasion. "I'm so happy for you."

Lethia ran her fingers along Alima's temple. Her icy-blue eyes filled with love and wonder.

"I'm happy, too," Lethia murmured. "I'm an aunt and I've mated the woman the fates had lined up for me. There is nothing else I need in my life. Now come, we must head to the airport."

"Will you hold my hand during the takeoff?" Alima asked.

Lethia tightened her arms around her and brought her in for a soft, gentle kiss.

"Anytime you need me, *miere*, I will be there."

EPILOGUE

"Are you sure I have to do this?" Alima whispered fiercely. Her grip on Lethia's arm tightened immensely.

Lethia turned and glanced down at her beautiful mate. She was still in awe at how beautiful she was.

Tonight was their official mating celebration.

With the birth of Velika and Quinn's son, she had respectfully put everything on hold. Her nephew had been named Prince Blayze Heath Riskel. From his name alone, Lethia knew her nephew was going to be a strong dhampir. He would have all the strengths of humans and vampires. He should even be able to withstand sunlight. He was the first of his kind, and Lethia saw a bright future for him. He would be a strong warrior and future warden.

"I'm sure, *miere*. The coven needs to meet you." Lethia glanced again at Alima's dress and almost changed her mind.

Her mate was breathtaking in a red form-fitting dress that put all of her curves on display. It was low-cut in the front, showcasing her ample cleavage. The back of the dress dipped down almost to her bottom. Her makeup was light, but what attracted Lethia the most aside from her shapely ass, was her ruby-red lips. She had even styled her hair to wear it down. It was full and stopped mid-back.

Lethia was blown away.

She lifted Alima's hand and brought it to her lips.

"You are beautiful," she said.

Alima's lips curved up into a wide smile.

"You are, too." Alima's warm gaze slid along Lethia's body that was draped in a black dress. It was short and low-cut. Lethia had left her blonde hair down, falling around her shoulders.

"Now, come on and stop procrastinating." Lethia entwined their fingers and pulled her away from their bedroom door.

They walked down the hall, meeting Lane who was posted at the ledge. He was dressed in his formal uniform and since returning from visiting with his sister and Velika had an almost permanent smile on his face. Unclehood fit him well.

"My princesses." He bowed to them and turned. He descended the stairs in front of them.

The castle was alive with their guests who were coming to celebrate their union. Aubrey had gone above and beyond herself. She did love planning parties, and Lethia already knew when it came to vampires, this party would be very interesting for Alima. They arrived at the first level of the castle. Security was high with as many people who were present for the party. It was a formal event, where everyone would be dressed in their finest.

Lethia paused and held up a hand to Lane. She pulled Alima close to her. The music from the party was floating down the hall. In a few minutes, her coven would finally meet their new princess.

"I need to warn you about something," Lethia said. She reached up and brushed a few strands of hair from Alima's face. There were going to be things that she may see that Lethia wanted to prepare her for.

"What is it?" she asked.

"There are going to be some things that may be going on at the party that you may find weird and strange." For vampires, this was all normal. Vampires were very sexual in nature, and it was expressed at any of their gatherings. "I don't want you to be afraid by anything you see."

"Like what? Feedings?"

"Yes, but all of the donors will be volunteers. No one is forced to do anything," Lethia started. She always made sure of that. There were plenty of humans who wanted the thrill of the bite. They didn't need to attack humans openly. That was against vampire laws. Rogue vampires gave them a bad reputation when they violated these rules. "All I'm asking is for you to keep an open mind."

"Of course I will. This is my new life, and I want to see everything." Her eyes glistened up slightly, and Lethia went on alert.

"What is it, *miere*?"

"I just wished my sister was here. Want to know something crazy?" she asked, blotting the corners of her eyes with the backs of her fingers. She sighed, a wistful smile appearing on her lips.

"When Joslin and I were little girls, we used to play dress-up like little girls do. We would stare up at this castle and dream about what it would feel like to be a real life princess. My sister called me Princess and even made me a crown." Her eyes grew bright as more tears collected. She blew out a deep breath.

Lane stepped over to them and handed her a handkerchief from his uniform.

"Here you go," he murmured.

Alima smiled her thanks and blotted her eyes again, trying to not mess up her makeup.

"It's like she knew," Alima said. She leaned into Lethia with love shining in her eyes. "It's as if my little sister predicted that one day I would be a princess living in this castle."

If Lethia wasn't convinced before, she was now. Alima was made for her. She had fallen into her role as the mate of the warden as if she were born for it. She and Javari had been working day and night getting her ideas off the ground. Lethia would support all of her initiatives of uniting humans and lycans.

"That, *miere*, was a beautiful story. I'm sure your sister is smiling down from the heavens." Lethia bent down and pressed a chaste kiss to her lips. "Now, come, mate. Let's go meet our coven."

"Okay, I think I'm ready." She offered up a big smile and wrapped her arm through Lethia's.

They strolled down the hall toward the welcoming room where the council and other dignitaries were waiting. They would stop there before they made their rounds.

Alima paused and turned to Lethia. "So about these parties. If I see something I want to try…" She wagged her eyebrows at Lethia.

"Just say the word."

FROM THE AUTHOR

Dear Reader,

Thank you for reading Iced Heart! I hope you enjoyed Lethia and Alima's story. The Immortal Reign series is turning into one of my favorite series I've written. There is something about vampires that I love.

We will be diving into Hegna's story next in Royal Bite! The stubborn, heir to the throne will soon meet her match!

If you would like for me to continue this series, please let me know when you leave a review!

Happy reading,
Ariel Marie

ABOUT THE AUTHOR

Ariel Marie is an author who loves the paranormal, action and hot steamy romance. She combines all three in each and every one of her stories. For as long as she can remember, she has loved vampires, shifters and every creature you can think of. This even rolls over into her favorite movies. She loves a good action packed thriller! Throw a touch of the supernatural world in it and she's hooked!

She grew up in Cleveland, Ohio where she currently resides with her husband and three beautiful children.

For more information:

www.thearielmarie.com

The Nightstar Shifters

A FF WOLF SHIFTER ROMANCE SERIES

No wolf can resist the call to mate.

Strong female wolves are in search of their mate. The desire is strong for these women who long to find the one person meant for them.

They are fierce and determined, putting their trust in fate.

If you love lesbian wolf shifter romance filled with action and adventure, then you will love the Nightstar Shifters series.

Start the series today!

ALSO BY ARIEL MARIE

Blackclaw Alphas (Reverse Harem Series)

Fate of Four

Bearing Her Fate (TBD)

The Midnight Coven Brand

Forever Desired

Wicked Shadows

Paranormal Erotic Box Sets

Vampire Destiny (An Erotic Vampire Box Set)

Moon Valley Shifters Box Set (F/F Shifters)

The Dragon Curse Series (Ménage MFF Erotic Series)

The Dark Shadows Series

Princess

Toma

Phaelyn

Teague

Adrian

Nicu

Sassy Ever After World

Her Warrior Dragon

Her Fierce Dragon

Her Guardian Dragon (TBD)

Stand Alone Books

Dani's Return

A Faery's Kiss

Tiger Haven

Searching For His Mate

A Tiger's Gift

Stone Heart (The Gargoyle Protectors)

Saving Penny

A Beary Christmas

Howl for Me

Birthright

Return to Darkness

Red and the Alpha

Printed in Great Britain
by Amazon